The Last Notch

ARNOLD HANO

Introduction by David Laurence Wilson

Black Gat Books • Eureka California

THE LAST NOTCH

Published by Black Gat Books
A division of Stark House Press
1315 H Street
Eureka, CA 95501, USA
griffinskye3@sbcglobal.net
www.starkhousepress.com

ISBN-13: 978-1-944520-31-1

Book design by Mark Shepard, SHEPGRAPHICS.COM

First Stark House Press Edition: August 2017

FIRST EDITION

"For about six and a half years Hano
  wrote westerns with a unique perspective.
  He looked for untouched subjects and
  unusual formats. He was challenging,
  subversive, and he didn't repeat himself."
    —David Laurence Wilson,
    "Citizen Hano"

"Brilliant chronicler of the blazing West."
    —*Male Magazine*

"Fast-paced with strong characters in
  troubled waters."
    —*Midwest Book Review*

FLINT

"Arnold Hano's Flint is a classic story of
  lust, murder, and bleak desperation and is
  one of the best Western noir novels I've
  ever read."   —James Reasoner

"Flint is a brooding, dark, ultra-noir
  western, unpredictable and riveting, and
  easily one of the finest westerns I've
  read."   —Kristofer Upjohn,
    Noir Journal

ARNOLD HANO BIBLIOGRAPHY

Fiction

Western Roundup
(editor; 1948)

Western Triggers
(editor; 1948)

The Big Out (1951)

The Executive (1964)

Marriage Italian Style
(movie tie-in; 1965)

Bandolero
(movie tie-in; 1967)

Running Wild
(movie tie-in; 1973)

Sports

A Day in the Bleachers
(1955; reprinted in new
editions in 1982, 2004
with new forward by Ray
Robinson & new
afterword by the author,
and 2006)

Sandy Koufax: Strikeout
King (1964)

Willie Mays: The Say-Hey
Kid (1966)

The Greatest Giants of
Them All (1967)

Roberto Clemente: Batting
King (1968)

Willie Mays: Mr. Baseball
Himself (1970)

Kareem! Basketball Great
(1975)

Muhammad Ali, the
Champion (1977)

As Gil Dodge

Flint (1957)

As Matthew Gant

Valley of Angry Men
(1953)

The Manhunter (1957)

The Last Notch (1958)

The Raven and
the Sword (1960)

Queen Street (1963)

As Ad Gordon

The Flesh Painter (1955)

Slade (1956)

As Mike Heller

So I'm a Heel (1957)

As Ghostwriter

Why Me? An
Autobiography by
William Gargan (1969)

CITIZEN HANO: An Unlikely Western Storyteller

By David Laurence Wilson

When I said I lived in Laguna Beach he asked me if I knew his friend Arnold Hano.

Sure, I knew Hano. Hano was not a native but a Californian by choice, a transplant from New York City; Bonnie, his wife, was from Sioux City, Iowa.

Since the age of seventeen, nearly three quarters of my life, I'd known Hano, who was born in 1922, thirty years before me. Though we had many friends and acquaintances in common it was mostly the public Hano I knew. He was an adult, a full-grown and successful journalist. And I wrote for *Teen-Page*.

Laguna was a beautiful Hollywood by the sea. When you stood on the beach, facing the ocean, this was the far west, the wide open spaces, an ocean with a new color and temperament every day. Painters craved these colors and in 1932 they established a summer art pageant that still has a big economic heft in the town.

The same issues that were discussed by the city council, and on the front page of The Laguna Beach *News-Post* were also discussed on the paper's "Teen Page." The paper's usual policy was staunchly opposed to most of Hano's agenda, including things like civil rights, freedom of speech and environmental regulation. At *Teen Page* we had a little more latitude—and a substantial following.

Years later, an old movie hand described Laguna to me as sort of a *Day of the Locust* place, and of course, he was right. There was always a trace of the mystic and the depraved in Laguna.

In both silent and sound film the coast was staged as a perennial island. Sennett featured his "Bathing Beauties" in its south Orange County waters. Its Hollywood pedigree included the actors Bette Davis, Fredric March, Sterling Holloway, Ozzie and Harriet Nelson and director Edward H. Griffith, no relation to D. W. ... Slim Summerville's home had been turned into a bar and restaurant. The town's writers included Richard Halliburton, Dudley Dean McGaughy, Richard Prather, Peter Rabe and Skip and Gloria Fickling, godparents of *Honey West*. Cartoonists, particularly, seemed to grow—and drink—in Laguna.

In July of 1955, the Hanos, their dog and baby daughter left New York City looking for a home. They paused in Taos, visiting a friend, but New Mexico didn't seem like the right nest. They drove as far west as they could without getting wet and then came south along the coast to Laguna Beach, a town they found by chance.

And there they stayed. For the first time the Hanos would live in a house, instead of an apartment. They traded Wall Street's concrete canyons of concrete for California chaparral and surf. From that moment on Hano would devote himself to this strip of California coast. He learned to appreciate salt water and became a swimmer. By 1961 he was receiving an Orange County Press Club award for his weekly column in the *Laguna Post*, a precursor of the *Laguna Beach News-Post* and its' *Teen Page* feature.

"I would try to do — knew I had to do ten pages but I would try to do 20," Hano said. "I would work in the morning from let's say, eight until one, and I would have my 20 pages. Then I would go to South Laguna with Bonnie and we'd swim the rest of the day. I was fast, as you probably know. I was probably as fast a writer as there existed back then. One of the things is that I could type 120 words a minute. That does not hurt, if you can do that."

Hano promptly joined the Orange Coast Democratic Club. Later he became the chairman of the Laguna Beach Interracial Citizen's Committee.

Hano's letters to the various local papers were as frequent as sports scores. From time to time he'd have a niche as a featured columnist, often under the pen name, *Woody Cove*. When I arrived in Laguna for my senior year of High School, Hano became my neighbor in the broad, beach city sense. We marched together. We attended meetings at city hall and both wrote for *The Village Sun*, Laguna's version of the alternative press. I attended the University of California, Irvine, and Hano taught there in the extension program.

In 1975 I wrote a story for the *Los Angeles Free Press* on the arrest of the owner and the temporary shut-down of a Laguna Beach book shop, Fahrenheit 451, for selling Zap comics. I quoted Hano when he called Laguna: *"a unique community with six times the county average for bookstores. We read just about everything, and we like it like that!"*

In 1976 Hano ran for the city council and lost by about 150 votes out of 10,000 votes cast. It was a polarizing and galvanizing time; contrary ideas were freely and vigorously exchanged. It was a contentious little town and if you didn't wear beads and sandals you might be considered part of the establishment. Dr. Timothy Leary was the city's best-known part-time resident.

Though he was clearly over 30, crew cut and conventionally dressed, Arnold Hano was no defender of the status quo or the "powers that be." This alone was enough to make him attractive to the teen-agers of our community. He was above all things ethical, reasonable, logical. There are flakes of all ages. Arnold wasn't a flake but he could use the word "square" and have it mean four or five different things. He was a liberal with a fiscal conscience; he considered self-government a dynamic responsibility. And he deeply respected the past and its traditions.

If you go to Laguna Beach, you can see Hano's profile. He materially affected the size and shape of this town. He wanted it to survive into the twenty-first century with its height limitations intact.

Gary Phillips and I were trading books, a Whittington collection for a new edition of his 1999 novel *The Jook*. Gary hefted the Stark House collection and murmured, in his casual, deep-voiced way, that it would be a great thing if a publisher began reprinting some of Arnold's novels.

"Sports Stories?" I asked. A lot of pulp writers had started out writing sports. Hano's first novel was sports fiction: *The Big Out* (1951), often incorrectly described as a book for young readers. Michelle Nolan, author of *Ball Tales: A Study of Baseball, Basketball and Football Fiction* (2010), described a moment in *The Big Out* as "*one of the most erotic statements ever written into a baseball novel.*"

Hano's first nonfiction book, *A Day at the Bleachers* (1955), was a sports story for adults, a long moment — about 24 hours — caught in time. The day was September 29, 1954, the first game of the 1954 World's Series. After that day, from the eighth inning on, Hano would have a symbiotic relationship with the Giants' great center-fielder, Willie Mays. Later Hano published two book-length studies on Mays, *Willie Mays: The Say-Hey Kid* in 1966 and *Willie Mays, Mr. Baseball Himself* in 1970. They would always have "The Catch."

At the right times, and in the right places, *A Day in the Bleachers* was revered. Hano argued convincingly that the game was meant to be seen from the cheapest, most distant, bleacher seats at New York City's Polo Grounds.

According to Robert Cromie, reviewing *Bleachers* for the *Chicago Tribune*: "*Hano's day in the bleachers, ... is touched with some special magic when he puts it on paper. ... Willie Mays' now famous catch of Vic Wertz's long smash to center ... is more than just a catch. It becomes a work of art, ranking with the baffling tricks of the late Houdini.*"

A sports story is like a telegram—it is all but stamped with an expiration date. The survival of *A Day in the Bleachers* is an achievement, a mix of folk-tale, statistics and a thrilling, baseball moment.

Phillips corrected me, diverting my reverie. Hano had written a lot of things, he said, a little bit of everything: crime fiction, westerns, and now he was working on an autobiography he called, *Hack.*

Hano was low-balling himself. From what I knew of his sports writing he was at the top of the heap. His stories were published in *The New York Times, The Los Angeles Times, TV Guide* and you name it, there was a lot of Hano out there. It wasn't quite the Golden Age of sports but it was close. Hano wrote all over the place, mostly sports, but also profiles on other notables, stories on technology and opinion pieces. Hano rubbed shoulders with the shakers and bakers of sports and entertainment.

He wrote scores of articles, "Sport Specials" for *Sport* magazine, giving the magazine close-up looks at American athletes. *Sport* was a home for "new journalism," which was really also basic "old-fashioned" sports writing, since sports writers had always tried to put their readers in a spectator's seat. It was all P.O.V., that "new journalism."

Hano received the Magazine Sportswriter of the Year

Award for 1963 from the National Sportscasters and Sportswriters Association.

He also continued writing full-length sports biographies: *Sandy Koufax: Strikeout King* (1964); *The Greatest Giants of Them All* (1967); *Roberto Clemente: Batting King* (1968).

Mr. Hano liked baseball. And he really, really liked the New York Giants.

The sports stories came naturally. But crime fiction? And westerns?

There are good reasons for the disconnect. The first is the use of pseudonyms. Hano wrote plenty of books but most of his fiction he shared with other names: *Matthew Gant*, *Ad Gordon*, *Gil Dodge* and *Mike Heller*. All these other fellows confused and muddied Hano's eclectic accomplishments. He seemed to reserve his own name for the sports stories.

I had a couple Gant books and an Ad Gordon novel but I'd never connected them with Hano. If you add up all the pseudonyms it totals 11 novels written between 1951 and 1964. Not bad.

In the early sixties, when the market for adult fiction tightened up, sports writing beckoned. Hano became stereotyped as a writer of nonfiction sports. His fictional pieces became rare acts of opportunity. He began writing a crime novel, still unfinished.

Had success, home runs and the roar of the crowd (sporting and political) seduced Hano away from fiction? Perhaps. But there was also an unwillingness on Hano's part to repeat himself. Sports was a first love he never left. He wrote sports before suspense or western fiction and he may have been better at describing action than plotting it. All in all, he had a damn good job and a life of travel and service.

As a nonagenarian Hano was watching—with some discomfort— the Laguna's city council deliberations intended to honor him, the naming of some civic edifice. It could be the Arnold Hano Bridge, if there was a bridge. Even better would be no plaque—but a better sense of history. An open, meditative, recreational space would fit Hano best. He had spent years fighting for open space in an urban area. The Hanos didn't want to clutter up the town now, to see a memorial or hear about one. Their very real reluctance only made them more endearing to the new establishment.

It was intended as a joke but Arnold seemed to have made a concession when he suggested that the podium at city hall might one day bear his name. That would be appropriate, too. Along with their letter writing Arnold and Bonnie Hano were constant, steady observers of the council and the local scene.

A conversation, let alone an interview with Hano, was both a pleasure and a task. His comments were honed by discipline and innate skill — the moving around of words. Nearly 90 years of books, articles, letters and public comments—that was Hano's exercise. He revered the battle of words and ideas; he tried to preserve its process. He was bashed in print. He seemed to believe that the best ideas, with the help of the best words, might survive. He believed in social responsibility.

Hano's head, his eyes and voice sat forward on his shoulders. The outcome of a war injury, this gave him the posture of a listener or interviewer. Memory had become his function, he had become a source of knowledge for baseball and books and the writers who wrote them. His was an age of reason. He was more thoughtful these days, perhaps, than enthusiastic. He was not yet cynical.

He was always quick and trim. He became smaller but not slack as he aged. His glasses became bigger until he became legally blind. This did not lessen his engagements, though it made them more difficult. Hesitation was not in his makeup. He still gave the impression of a man with a full schedule.

As a sportswriter he gave voice to the taciturn, the whimsical and the wandering of thought. He would pull or prod, as necessary. You had to be on task, focused, in an interview with Arnold Hano. He talked like a man who doesn't need much copy editing. He seemed to both answer and edit the questions.

Arnold and Bonnie lived in a quiet, shaded neighborhood in Laguna Beach. We were sitting in an informal, easy-access area near his kitchen, a table garnished with two shelves of Lion paperbacks. Some of the Lions had wandered off.

Arnold was operating in the rarefied air of 93 years of age.

Hano had begun Lion Books after leaving Bantam in 1949, hiring on with Martin Goodman, owner of Magazine Management, taking over the offices and numbering of Goodman's "Red Circle" books. We were talking about the beginnings of Lion paperbacks and I asked if he recalled the first Lion Book.

"Why would you care?" Hano asked.

"Because I'm a scholar."

He laughed but accepted the premise that their might well be an interest in his slice of literary history. At least I hadn't suggested naming a park after him.

While Arnold could be an orator, a skill refined during hundreds of hours before the Laguna Beach City Council, Bonnie was a hidden gem. Her husband said, without the waste of a single adverb: "She writes the best letters to the editor because they are precise, exact and brief."

She had fewer words but they were carefully selected. On the day of our interview she was serene in white, a retired marriage and family counselor.

Hano met many legends during his career, but his hero

was his brother Alfred, three and a half years older. When Arnold was eight his brother was publishing *The Montgomery Avenue News*, a weekly mimeographed newspaper he sold door to door for a nickel. Arnold began writing a serial, what he later called "his first novel," the adventures of a New York policeman nicknamed "Sitting Bull" ("Also my first pun," Arnold noted.)

Ink ran in the brothers' veins. Their uncle, their mother's brother, was the screenwriter Bertram Millhauser, who entered the movies in 1911. Circumstances allowed him an eclectic career that included screenplays and scenarios for *The Perils of Pauline*, *Ebb Tide* (1937), *The Lone Ranger* and *Sherlock Holmes*.

At Long Island University in Brooklyn, Hano found his life's calling. He began working for the student newspaper, first as sports editor, then as editor in chief. He graduated with a degree in English, and began working as a copyboy for the *New York Daily News*.

Then came World War II. Hano served as a Corporal in the U. S. Army, 7th Infantry Division, 1942-1946, in the Aleutian Islands Campaign and the Battle of Kwajalein Atoll. His brother, who was in the Air Force, went missing in action in a mission over Germany. Even in death, Alfred remained Arnold's hero, often in the pages of his books. Arnold used his brother as a physical model for some of his characters.

"See, if you look at the cover of *The Big Out*, that's my brother," Hano said. "I used my brother a lot, my dead brother, who was killed in World War II. I didn't tell anybody it was him—I didn't give them a photo—but I had enough of a description of the guy that it was translated to the artist, and he gave me back my brother, and I liked that."

Along with Salvatore Lombino, better known as "Evan Hunter" and "Ed McBain", Hano began reading and writing reports on manuscripts submitted to the Scott Meredith Literary agency. Donald Fine and Jim Bryant were the other readers operating out of the office. Hano also used Meredith as an agent for his own short story sales.

"Yes, he was a shyster but he was keen, very smart, and he liked me," Hano said of Meredith. Meredith sold three of Hano's short stories to *Street and Smith's Sport Story Magazine*. None of them were baseball stories.

In 1947 Hano learned about a job opening at Bantam books, though the terms of the position were vague. After three interviews, he was hired to produce western anthologies for the young company, established in 1945. Hano estimated that he read ten short stories for each story selected.

"I was in over my head to begin with," he said.

"I read every western I could get my hands on. I wanted to see if I could find something similar from one to the next. I discovered that yes, a good western had a western theme, like rustling, or land grabs, hired guns, these were the things that were generic and endemic to the western.

Western Triggers and *Western Roundup* were released in February and September of 1948. Four of Hano's favorite writers appeared in both volumes, the brothers Luke Short and Peter Dawson, H. A. DeRusso and Henry Wallace Phillips. Other writers included Stewart Edward White and Bret Harte, Charles Russell, O.Henry, Alan LeMay, Max Brand, Bennett Foster and Ernest Haycock. A short story by Mark Twain, *Aurelia's Unfortunate Young Man*, received the most attention from critics.

There was another accomplishment at Bantam. Arnold met Bonnie Abraham, who was working in the business department. Both were married to others at the time, and Arnold had a son and daughter. In June, 1951, Arnold and Bonnie were wed.

"We got involved because of our interest in politics,"

Bonnie said. "We used to sit in Madison Square Garden singing, 'Wallace is my leader. We shall not be moved.' Henry Wallace, do you remember him?" (Wallace was F. D. R.'s Vice President, 1941-1945, and the 1948 Presidential nominee of the Progressive Party, winning 2.4% of the popular vote.)

Some days Hano would take a box to the park near their apartment so he could stand on it and speak for civil rights.

Through attrition Hano became Bantam's managing editor. It was a short tenure. In 1949 he was fired for trying to unionize the company.

He soon landed a job as editor in chief of Lion Books, a subsidiary of Martin Goodman's "Magazine Management." a low budget publishing empire headquartered in the Empire State Building. Along with Lion, and Timely Comics (later to become "Marvel"), Goodman was also the wizard behind the curtains for *Stag* and Humorama Publications, managed by relative Abe Goodman, an array of digest-sized magazines with sexy cartoons and titles like *Jest* and *Joker*. Hano edited the pocket-sized picture magazine *Focus* for several issues.

For about a year Bonnie Hano worked as a reader for Lion. Later she was a personal assistant for Editor Stan Lee and Production Manager of the comics division. She recalled Stan as a man who was creative but somewhat shy: "Who ever knew that Stan Lee was going to become the big famous deal that he is today?"

Bonnie wrote several of the short, 2-page text stories that appeared in the comics as a sop to postal regulations. In 1951 Arnold wrote his only story for the comics, "The Voice of Death", illustrated by Russ Heath in *Journey Into Unknown Worlds*, #6.

"We all helped out," Arnold said. "At the end of the day Goodman would wander around the offices. He'd have a drink with the editors, and I kept a bottle of Scotch in my desk. He'd want to play scrabble and he'd beat me every time."

There was a visceral quality in the paperbacks and comics that came out of Magazine Management. Lion hummed with the dissolute energy of the streets.

To some, it might have seemed like downward mobility. Hano had exchanged prestige and money for creative control. As the editor of Lion, he believed he was able to follow through on his social beliefs, so he pushed the envelope, allowing the publisher to become a home for "outsiders," writers like Jim Thompson, David Goodis and David Karp, but also proletariat and left-wing writers: Sam Ross, A. I. Bezzerides, Pietro Di Donato and Benjamin Appel.

"I thought a lot of good left-wing novelists were being disregarded," Hano said. "At Bantam, I said, "Why don't we do *All Quiet on the Western Front?*" They said, 'Oh no, we can't because it's a pacifist novel, a communist novel!' Well, I thought they were stretching it a bit but I couldn't get it past them."

Lion began with reprints but became one of the earliest publishers of original paperback fiction. Hano published first novels by Karp, Richard Matheson, and Fletcher Flora, and early novels by the prolific pulp writers Robert Bloch, Day Keene and Howard Browne.

Hano tried to publish two westerns every month. He published two original westerns by H. A. DeRosso, *.44* (1953) and *The Gun Trail* (1953), and reprinted two Peter Dawson novels from Dodd Mead. Other western writers included James Warner Bellah, Lee Floren, Bennett Foster and Steve Frazee.

Hano was not included among Ed Gorman and Lee Server's 1998 list of 100 noir authors. Perhaps this was because of the camouflage. Nevertheless, he belonged near the top of the list of editors associated with the genre.

"I wanted to publish good, atmospheric suspense novels," Hano said. "I never used the word 'noir' but that's what we were doing."

From Hano's point of view, Lion's greatest achievement was to discover Jim Thompson, an unsuccessful, alcoholic journalist and sometime novelist who became perhaps the most important of all post-war crime writers. In this, Hano was certainly correct. As editor, Hano generated short synopses of the kind of stories he would like to purchase, and he distributed them to his writers. The complete text of these suggestions were about two hundred words. Thompson used two of the synopses to create *The Killer Inside Me* and *Cropper's Cabin*.

"With *The Killer Inside Me* Jim picked a story about a New York City cop," Hano recalled. "He turned him into a Texas deputy sheriff and turned our trite melodrama into art."

Reviving and nurturing Thompson's career —handing him the fortune-cookie of an idea that became *The Killer Inside Me* would be a great success for any editor. Coming up with eleven more novels for Lion Books was even better. Lion gave a spine to Thompson's career. Without Lion Thompson may well have remained an obscure, disappointing novelist.

I asked Hano what it was about Thompson's writing that so impressed him: "I liked his stuff immediately," he said. "He was a bright human being dealing with a savage world. He was very up-close. He presented dreadful things, but you were so up close, that you were almost part of those characters. He wanted you to feel that they were universal. These terrible things this guy is doing are all what we dream of doing, or want to do. He made that work. It was the up-closeness of it that I found so fascinating."

Hidden among Hano's credits were the westerns.

He certainly didn't seem to have any trouble writing or

selling a western novel. Between 1953 and 1960 Hano wrote five of them and one historical novel set in the west. Despite the use of three different names, and four different publishers this was the greater part of Hano's fiction writing.

Other than growing up on the west side of Manhattan, Hano had no particular reason to become a western writer. Before his stint at Bantam he had read one western, Zane Grey's *Riders of the Purple Sage* (1912), and he had not enjoyed it.

"The reason I started writing westerns," Hano said, "is that Bonnie was slow getting dressed one night. We were going to somebody's house for a supper party and she was in the bathroom. I put a piece of paper in the typewriter and I wrote, "'*The year 1876 was the meanest year I can remember yet I think well of it.*' It demanded a second sentence to explain what I was talking about. By the time she was ready to go I had written six pages.

"I did forty pages on Saturday, 40 pages on Sunday. Then Monday, Tuesday, Wednesday Thursday, Friday I got out of bed an hour early, and I wrote for an hour. I finished it on Saturday. Eight days, fifty thousand words. That was how I got involved in writing westerns. I had never written one before.

Hano was reluctant to publish his own novels at Lion. He elected to use a pseudonym, Matthew Gant, and submitted the novel to Knox Berger and Donald Fine, editors at Dell. They passed on the manuscript but Gold Medal was eager to take it. They paid on print: 400,000 copies printed and, an advance of $4,000. "I got four thousand dollars for the equivalent of 24 hours of work," Hano said.

Hano's western characters are outsiders—par for the course— but in these westerns, the characters sometimes have twentieth century attitudes and solutions. In Hano's westerns what would commonly be a gunfight can become an act of passive resistance. Forget the macho and the adrenaline, these were thinking men.

In *Valley of the Angry Men* Hano's hero, *Brandy Little*, is a tough guy who recognizes there's a good chance that gunplay would be to his disadvantage. Consequently he tries to minimize the use of a gun. It's a post-Ghandi, also a post *Destry Rides Again* western.

"I certainly care about gun violence," Hano said. "I make my voice heard. I'm still that same person, obviously, but I didn't realize that it was part of my fictional life too.'

He describes a gunman: "*He slumped to the floor, all of him but that long, graceful left arm, and that hand holding the gun more perfectly than any man ever held one.*" It is like a baseball game, with managers and their strategies for a team. The conflict is told through the spirit of sport, with mutual goals. Even the cover, a lone gunman on a cow-town street, looks like nothing so much as a pitcher on his mound.

All through the years with Bantam and Lion Hano also free-lanced, his stories appearing in *Esquire*, *Argosy* and *Ellery Queen's Mystery Magazine*. In 1954, when Goodman announced an across the board editorial pay cut during a recession, it seemed like a cue. Hano quit. Fortunately it was an amicable parting and he continued to publish with Lion and Magazine Management.

Hano also continued his personal and professional relationship with Jim Thompson. Dell Books hired him as editor for Jim Thompson's novel, *The Nothing Man* (1954) and he arranged for Popular Library to publish *After Dark, My Sweet* (1955).

One of his Hano's assignments was to write profiles of legendary philanderers, including Casanova, and Gauguin for Goodman's Men's magazines. They were collected In Lion Library's anthology *Rogues and Lovers* (1956).

Goodman's wife Jean read the Gauguin story and suggested Hano expand it to novel-length. He considered the result, *The Flesh Painter* (1955), published by Lion Library, to be his best novel. For this Hano received yet another pseudonym, "Ad Gordon," a name he also used for two short stories in Goodman's short-lived 1955 crime fiction digest, *Justice*: "Justice Is Blind" and "Two Little Bullets."

Slade, (1956) a second Ad Gordon novel, received a cover blurb from *Male* magazine, yet another Martin Goodman publication: "*Tough, Tense, Fast... Gordon is a brilliant chronicler of the blazing West.*" *Slade* was written during the Hanos' migration west, during a month-long stopover at Bonnie's mother's home in Sioux City, Iowa.

Slade is a discomforting read, stark and harsh, amplifying the darker moments of *Valley of Savage Men*. There is an uncomfortable distance between the characters, and treachery. It seems like the old west a la Ingmar Bergman. There's an awful sense that these characters are not going to make it.

In *Manhunter* (1957) Hano returned to a story of a hesitant and cerebral, reluctant gunman, conscious of the negative power of a gun. It resulted in one of the most unusual fast-draw demonstrations in any western: "*His hand flashed, under an iron control that whispered: speed, damn it, speed.*

"*Ross had the element of surprise working on his side. All about him he heard breath being sucked in, while his hand kept streaking, drawing, clearing leather—and then dropping the big gun to the grass, in front of Caesar. ...*

"*He had gone for his gun, not to use it, not to fire it, because Ross knew that suicide lay that way, firing it. He had to get rid of it, get it from as far from him as possible. He had to reduce himself to a defenseless, helpless human being. That way he would—might—live.*"

Flint, adapted from Jim Thompson's contemporary

novel, *Savage Night*, featured an undependable narrator and both a first and third person perspective. The 2012 Stark House reprint restored a dedication and thank you to Thompson that was left out of the original printing.

Hano was working within the thematic conventions of the western form but even in these violent, patriarchal novels, he tried to stretch the boundaries. In *The Last Notch*, published in hardback by Dodd Mead & Company, Ben Slattery is another kind of athlete, a high-paid man-for-hire who appears to be more political assassin than simple "hired gun." He likes the Governor's offer of amnesty but can't abandon his gun. It's a dark, P.T.S.D. flavored story. Slattery has gone way past gunslinger to serial killer. This is a post-Jim Thompson novel, all the way to post-existentialist.

"In that first scene, I was writing as if I were writing about The Mafia," Hano explained. I used modern language, and values that were more sensible to day's audience than to the eighteen seventies. It's just having a gang of guys hanging out in a safe haven. I didn't know if anything like that existed."

Hano's protagonist has a characteristic that is unusual in the westerns of the day: he is a former slave. "I wanted to find out a reason why he might be such a nasty human being as to go around killing people," Hano said. "I decided, 'Well, I'll make him black. I'll make him a slave."

If his race is a stigma, it is all internalized. No one else seems to notice.

Slattery is the only one who knows the details of his parentage: "*Next to the dresser a cracked mirror was nailed to the wall. Slattery turned his head slowly until he faced himself in the mirror. He stared at his image. He ran a hand over his face. Thick black crisp hair. Skin like faded walnut, worked over by the sun. Big heavy nose, splayed nostrils slightly flaring. Heavy sensual lips.*

"*'Nigger,' he said to himself.*"

This is just a piece of the psychological burden Slattery feels.

Dodd Mead told Hano they had a problem with his protagonist because there weren't any African Americans in the American west. According to Hano, "I said, 'Well with this book there's going to be one.' So they caved in."

In 1965 this same publisher, Dodd Mead, published *The Negro Cowboys*, by Philip Durham and Everett L. Jones, explaining that there were many African-American cowboys, including former slaves, who had moved west. As many as twenty-five percent of the men who were raising and moving cattle were black.

Bill Pickett, the child of slaves, was the most famous of the black cowboys. He became a featured star with the Miller Brothers 101 Ranch Real Wild West Show and was the star of the silent films *The Bull-Dogger* (1921) and *The Crimson Skull* (1922). In 1971 he was the first black cowboy inducted into the Pro Rodeo Hall of Fame.

Black cowboys had appeared in American films for both African-Americans and in the wider marketplace. Herb Jeffries was a mixed race singer in actor who used makeup to darken his skin when he starred as a singing cowboy in *Harlem on the Prairie* (1937) and *Two-Gun Man From Harlem* (1938). The fine actor Woody Strode, who later was one of the first black football players in the NFL, appeared in westerns films as early as in *Stagecoach* (1939). He recalled shoe polish being used to darken his skin. In the 1960s he became a star in western films.

Despite these successes, African Americans only infrequently appeared in popular western fiction and were sometimes relegated to comic relief. A contrast to this was *The Homesteader* (1917), a novel written by the African American writer and filmmaker Oscar Micheaux while he lived in Sioux City. This was not quite a western but an ambitious, autobiographical novel that featured a turn-of-the-century African-American farmer in South

Dakota. Between 1917-1919, Micheaux filmed his own novel, producing the first feature-length film made with a black cast and crew, for a black audience.

By 1950 African-Americans had begun to appear more often in the westerns. *The Last Notch* was certainly a part of this trend.

To today's reader Hano's African-American character is perhaps less surprising than his most direct confrontation with gun violence. Hano's anti-hero Ben Slattery has a face off with a professional associate: Billy the Kid. In a dramatic sense, an existential sense, at least, Slattery wins.

"That's what I was hoping," Hano said. "I was hoping for some sense of that. But at the same time, at some point, killers have to pay." Sixty years later Hano said that if he were to write it again, his character would be deeply black, unable to pass unnoticed. It would then be a completely different novel without the same psychological feelings generated by a bi-racial parentage of a slave mother and slave-owning father.

The Last Notch could have been the basis for a fine film for the right actor. For a brief euphoric time Hano was lead to believe that film rights for the novel had been purchased by the singer and actor Harry Belafonte for $12,500. Hano was already spending the money when he learned the deal was only wishful thinking on the part of an agent. Later Belafonte appeared with Sidney Poitier and Ruby Dee in the western film *Buck and the Preacher* (1972)

One last western was *Bandolero*, (1967) a novelization of the 1968 motion picture starring James Stewart, Dean Martin and Raquel Welch. Then came *Running Wild* (1977) a novelization of a film about the Olympic Gold Medal-winning native-American runner Billy Mills. This was the end of Hano's fiction career.

In 1988 Hano had heart bypass surgery.

In 1991 Arnold, at 69, and Bonnie, 65, volunteered for the Peace Corps. They sold their car, rented out their home and were assigned to Costa Rica. They arrived on June 27, just three days before their 40th wedding anniversary. They lived in Costa Rica for five years.

Dennis McLellan, of the *Los Angeles Times*, interviewed the couple shortly before they left California.

"I do wonder what we will do next," Arnold told him.

Fate had offered the Hanos a dramatic life of many acts. Upon their return to Laguna, in 1996, these skeins came together. Part of Arnold's task, it seems, was simply to receive accolades with grace. He continued to work on the autobiography he had begun in Costa Rica.

He made big contributions to two biographies of Jim Thompson: *Jim Thompson — Sleep With the Devil* (1991), by Michael J. McCauley and *Savage Art* (1995), by Robert Polito.

In 2006 Arion Press produced a 426-copy edition of *A Day at the Bleachers*, illustrated by the New Yorker cover artist Mark Ulriksen. The cover of the pricey collector's book is revisionist, showing both Arnold and Bonnie in the bleacher seats on a day that Bonnie had elected to stay home.

In 2011 and 2013 Hano spoke before the Laguna Beach Historical Society. Both events were posted on *Youtube*.

In 2010 he wrote an introduction for Arion's new edition of Jim Thompson's autobiographical novel *South of Heaven*, a lavish, 400-print run, $700 per copy with 44 illustrations by the artist Raymond Pettibone.

Gary Phillips followed through in his reprinting suggestion and in 2012 Stark House published *Three Steps to Hell*, a representative collection of Arnold Hano's little-known fiction: *The Big Out, Flint,* and *So I'm A Heel.* It included an introduction by Phillips and gave a surprising boost to Hano's long-distant fiction career.

In 2013, for Laguna's Patriot's Day Parade, Laguna

Beach Arnold and Bonnie rode down Park Avenue from the High School to City Hall as co-Citizen's of the Year.

In 2013 Hano put aside his initial skepticism and agreed to go forward with a documentary based on *A Day in the Bleachers*. The documentary's optimistic title, *A Century in the Bleachers*, was in counterpoint to Hano's own sense of mortality. He ruefully accepted the fact that he could no longer throw a baseball with the same precision of seventy or eighty years earlier. Still, he could demonstrate the screwball.

Work on the film began in November of 2013 and was completed it in October, 2015. Its premier was in Laguna Beach.

Hano consented to many interview requests: for books, magazines and newspapers, the internet sites and documentaries. The subjects were inevitably baseball and Jim Thompson.

So what makes a man and his career? How much can a fellow point his own direction? Part of it is opportunity and magic. If Willie Mayes had not caught the "Catch" in that World Series game would Hano have remained "Matthew Gant", a western writer? Maybe he could have stayed in Taos, adopted a bolo tie and embroidered shirt and written two or three westerns every year.

Probably not. That would have been a different life.

I've met a lot of good western writers and Arnold didn't fit the mold; he never took on the accouterments of a successful writer of westerns, never joined The Western Writers of America and was much more interested in the present than the past. He simply didn't seem to perceive himself as a western writer.

But for about six and a half years Hano wrote westerns with a unique perspective.

He looked for untouched subjects and unusual formats. He was challenging, subversive, and he didn't want to repeat himself. Then the market turned towards continuing characters and more predictable plotting. Hano had run out of west.

Nearly sixty years after his last original western novel, in his tenth decade, Arnold could still write like an angel. He'd probably tell you that he could do it fast, if his eyesight permitted.

He'd say: "I'm a writer. I'm always going to be on the writer's side."

—May 2017
Portland, OR

The Last Notch

ARNOLD HANO

1

The saloon door banged open, and The Kid stood there, yellow oil light spilling on his face and the Territory night like a black frame around him.

Slattery shivered, wishing it was the cold black night that chilled him, knowing it wasn't. It was The Kid. Slattery sat at his table nursing a shot of rye whisky, a hand of solitaire in front of him, his eyes on the boy at the door. There was sullen hate in his heart for The Kid, grudging admiration in his brain.

"I'm back," The Kid said to the room, and then he walked in, sweeping his hat from his head, yellow hair falling over the unlined brow. The door banged shut and all one could hear was wind-whipped sand blasting against the windows, the night alive and howling. Slattery watched him swagger to the bar, a boy of eighteen in this room where men like Slattery spent so much time, a saloon outside abandoned Fort Heck on the west bank of the Pecos sixty miles west of the Texas border and forty miles from nowhere, a saloon that was refuge to Slattery when he needed it, Slattery and the rest, a room for fugitives, for boys learning the trade, for skilled craftsmen like himself—Ben Slattery, hired killer. And for The Kid, too. Just as skilled, and maybe more so.

"You're back," Slattery said, the burr of the South in his speech, the words slow and liquid. "You're back all right," he said, knowing he would be, even though he'd heard that The Kid had been killed, in Colorado this time. Last time they said he had gone under in Jackson County, in the cattle rustling war that split the Territory in half. The time before it had been a lucky shot that got him in a sheep town in Mexico. But Slattery never believed the word about The Kid. The Kid would live forever.

The Kid said, "Don't sound so happy about it, Wolf."

He turned to the bartender and said, "Kee-rist, she's a twister out there. That wind'll curl your hair for you." Then he leaned against the bar and downed a shot of whisky and shoved the glass at One-Eye McCall behind the bar, and the one-time highwayman who had lost his right eye to a bullwhip in a stage holdup that back-washed, took the bottle of whisky and shoved it toward The Kid. "Pour 'em yourself," McCall said.

There it was, Slattery knew. Nobody in the trade liked The Kid. Nobody ever would. And someday, somewhere, in some fetid alley probably, a man would wait and The Kid would ride by on his big gray mare, because little men usually liked to ride big mares, Slattery knew, and the man in the alley would wait until he was sure, until he saw The Kid's blond hair like a spilled banner over his brow, until he heard the high giggle in the throat, and then his finger would squeeze and the last noise The Kid would ever hear, his back muscles suddenly tight as a clenched fist, would be a firing pin, falling. There'd be a hole in his back then, and The Kid would go down even before the blast of the ambush gun stopped its rolling waves of noise.

But the thought nagged at Slattery. Even so, The Kid would live forever. He didn't know what he meant by the thought, and it irritated him. Slattery cursed to himself and sat up sharply. Daydreams. What did it matter? They came and went. The Kid and the others. It was himself to watch and worry over. Not The Kid. The Kid was good. Let The Kid worry about himself. Slattery ran a tanned hand through crisp black hair and let his eyes steal to the front door of the saloon.

The Kid, his back to Slattery, looked into the saloon mirror and caught the fleeting eye. He said, "Wolf, you waiting for somebody?"

Slattery flushed. He didn't like being called Wolf. It meant lone wolf. His name was Ben Slattery but the men in the trade had been calling him Wolf ever since The Kid wandered into the Territory, his gun for hire. All right, he worked by himself. So did most of the others. Only The Kid had a gang. *Had* had a gang, Slattery corrected himself. Now the gang was shot up, dispersed or dying or dead. Still, The Kid liked to talk it up, involve as many people as possible in his schemes before he went out into the dark night to do as he had been bid.

Wolf Slattery carried his thoughts tight inside, a man who walked quietly and rode even more so, a big man yet unprepossessing. An old man, as these things went, a man of thirty-seven, the oldest man in the room except for One-Eye McCall. McCall had quit the business twelve years before after a gutty stage driver dropped his guns and, when McCall relaxed, snapped his whip in McCall's face. The eye had whished out without the slightest flicker of pain, but more than that went with it. McCall's courage had fled. He was through. He scrabbled over a near shale hill, blood streaming down his cheek, a whimpering frenzied man with but one eye and no heart. Now he served drinks in this saloon on the Pecos, inhabited mostly by men on the dark side of the law, giving them a lying-up place, a breathing spell after the run against the posse or before the next job. And for doing this, One-Eye McCall was protected by men who would never talk.

Slattery said to The Kid, "That's right, Kid. I'm waiting for somebody."

They'd know, sooner or later. It wasn't secret that Slattery worked at his trade. The men in the room surely knew. McCall. The Kid. The three men at the round card table, playing that dreariest of all games, three-hand draw poker, they knew: Tompkins, who had killed a crooked deputy in Tombstone because the governor wanted the town cleaned up and that was the only way it could be done, the governor paying Tompkins a thousand dollars, the most money any of them had ever received up till then; Vulka, on Tompkins' right, round-faced, pink-cheeked, looking younger than his twenty-three years, a veteran of four years at the trade, eight kills; Wilson, tossing in his cards now, a hawk-nosed man with bitter black eyes, and Slattery sometimes found himself nodding his head, sure, the man ought to be bitter. Wilson had had a wife and two kids, and a shaky claim in a mining field in Colorado. One night some drunken miners came down and raped the wife and shot the screaming kids, and stole Wilson's gold that lay in three fat bags under his sleeping roll. Wilson was in town that night, having a drink, just easing some of the sweat and dust down his throat.

He'd gone crazy, Wilson had, for a little while. Then he declared war. And when he started to cause trouble, they chiseled him out of his gold claim. That was ten years ago. Now he was thirty-five years old, the fires burned down low, but still simmering, and in a way he was most like The Kid because he seemed to enjoy doing his work, killing for hire. Then Slattery thought grimly: No, Wilson was more like himself. Wilson took the money, but it was still in payment for what had happened in that Colorado gold camp. Wilson was still getting even. *And so am I*, Slattery thought swiftly, and as swiftly wiped the thought from him.

They knew, all of them, that Slattery did his business right here in McCall's saloon.

The Kid giggled now, at the bar, and he turned around and faced Slattery full on. He said, "Guess what the number's now, Wolf?"

Slattery shrugged. "No idea," he said. "A hundred and one?" His face was an innocent mask, trying to rub The Kid.

The Kid swore softly. "Yeah," he said. "It'll be a hundred and one some day. It's nineteen, that's what it is."

Tompkins looked up from his hand. "Still counting that Chink in Copper City, Kid?"

The Kid spun. "Why not?" he snarled. "He's dead, ain't he? Just as dead as that rheumatic old deputy you shot in the back in the Tomb, Tommy." It was The Kid's pride that every man he killed he faced.

Tompkins shook his head. "Haven't shot a man in the back yet, Kid. And I stopped counting my kills five years ago."

"Sure," The Kid said. "I bet you have. Why, there ain't a man in this room who doesn't know how many men he's killed."

Tompkins said, "Nineteen, eh? That's pretty good. You must be only ten behind Slattery then."

The Kid giggled again and stepped from the bar, swaggering over to Slattery's table. He took the cards that lay face up and without concern shoved them into a loose pile and then glanced up at Slattery's face to see how the big man was taking it.

Slattery said, "Sit down, Kid. Have a drink." He said it easily, because by now he had himself under fair control. He didn't like The Kid and he hadn't liked The Kid seeing his eye stray to the door, waiting for his contract to walk in. But not liking these things wasn't important.

These men in this room were in a way his life insurance. Slattery knew it. Each man in the room knew it of one another. They weren't a gang. Nothing like that. But in a way, they were. That's why they had their contracts walk in here, where others would see the contract, stow away the face and the name, and then in case Slattery didn't come back or word reached them that the contract had welshed, that Slattery had been done dirt (or any of them, it didn't matter who), then each man had a tacit bargain with Slattery (or the man done dirt) to even it up. That's how they stayed strong, each man with his own police force behind him in a Territory where law was suddenly, startlingly beginning to take root.

Why, Slattery thought, two years ago he could have waited in any bar or hotel in the Territory, even up in the open plaza of the governors, in the capital itself, his name known to every man there, and he could have done his business with anybody who wanted his gun. Nobody would have interfered. Not that he would have operated so openly. It wasn't his way. But he could have; any of them could have. Now it wasn't so. There were places where Slattery didn't dare show. The capital, for one. Nor did he go into Jackson County ever since The Kid had started his ugly war down there and got everybody involved, one way or the other. Hell, in Jackson a man's life wasn't worth dirt, just walking the center of any main drag in the county.

Still, Slattery didn't blame The Kid. He had done what he thought had to be done in Jackson, hiring himself out to protect a rancher from some wildcat rustlers. The rest mushroomed beyond him, beyond anybody. It wasn't The Kid's fault any more than it was his, Slattery's, or Vulka's or Wilson's or Tompkins', or any other man who pursued this calling.

The man who now kept Slattery out of the capital and out of other parts of the Territory was the governor, the new man in the plaza, a long-maned Union general with a smooth tongue and a new word: amnesty.

Amnesty. Slattery chewed on the word. A pardon. Full, complete pardon for any man who was willing to lay down his gun and side with the governor in his fight to stamp out lawlessness. Amnesty. At first nobody knew what it meant. Now the whole Territory did. The Territory was alive with the word.

They had argued it out, Slattery and the rest, in McCall's saloon six months ago when the word and its meaning swept down that far. It had been an ugly night.

Slattery had said, "What's wrong with it, Kid? What's wrong with the notion?"

The Kid had stalked up to him then. "You're getting soft, Slattery. That's what's wrong. Amnesty!" He spat on the floor, two inches from Slattery's boots.

Vulka, from the never-ending poker table, said, "I dunno, Kid. If Slattery thinks the governor can be trusted—"

The Kid's eyes flashed. "Trusted! Sure he can be trusted! With a bullet in his tongue, that's how I'll trust him. How do I know he won't drop a noose on me once I've turned my gun over to him?"

Tompkins laid down his cards. He grumbled for a moment to himself and then he said, "From what I hear, he hasn't gone back on his word yet. There's lots of men taken advantage of it, so far."

Wilson nodded, his eyes brooding and black. "You can't tell about men, Kid. Sometimes an honest one, by mistake, gets into the governor's chair. This one may be honest."

The Kid strode the room on the balls of his feet, angry clear through. He said to the far wall, "Kee-rist, how dumb can you get? Sure he's pardoned some craps who've dropped their guns. But who? Who were they? Tinhorn rustlers. Two-bit cardsharps. Some man who slapped his wife. Has he come down here and said. 'Kid, you're free. Give me your gun and I'll see to it no man harms you'? Has he? Can he?"

Slattery nodded grudgingly. That was the crux. Not that

the governor might or might not be honest. But could he actually give a man protection? Suppose The Kid, for one, walked into the capital and gave up his six-gun. What was to stop some joker from Jackson County, his cattle rustled from him during all the shooting, from following The Kid up there, a hideaway gun in his sleeve, and, when The Kid walked out of the governor's plaza unarmed, what was to stop the Jackson rancher from putting a hole in The Kid's heart? What kind of guarantee did any of them have? None.

Still, Slattery thought, it was worth looking into. He said, that night six months back when the word and idea were new, "I may just wander up there, myself. To check on it."

The Kid had stopped walking the room then. He stepped over to Slattery's table in the rear shadows of the saloon and leaned over the table, his face like a shining wet blade. He said, "Slattery, don't do it. I'm telling you, Slattery, don't go on up there."

Slattery said mildly, "Don't tell me what not to do, Kid. I do as I please."

"And so do I," The Kid said, the words like a knife thrust. "So do I, Wolf. You go on up there and play ball with the governor, you answer to me. You understand?"

Slattery understood. A man who sided with the governor sided with the law, and therefore sided against The Kid and anybody else outside the law. "I understand," Slattery said. "I still may go up there."

That's where it had ended, six months ago. But from then on Slattery felt The Kid's hate and suspicion directed like the barrel of his six-gun.

And now, when The Kid walked over and finally sat, Slattery said casually, just to keep The Kid from bothering him, "What's new in the wide wide world, Kid?"

"Aw," The Kid said. "Nothing. Not a goddam thing. Amnesty, that's all you hear." He stared at Slattery, measuring the man. "Amnesty, Wolf, amnesty. That's all the chowderheads are talking about. Men walking in and dropping their guns and getting a kiss on the butt. What do you think of that, Slats?"

"I don't give it much thought, Kid."

"No," The Kid said. "I bet you don't. Why, you think about it all the time. Here you've got business coming in and you're thinking about it. You're thinking how you'd like to go on up to the governor and say, 'Pardon me, Gov, Please, please pardon me. I didn't mean it. I'll be a good boy. Those thirty or forty critters I killed, they don't really count. So pardon me, pardon me.'" He swore bitterly, foully.

Slattery sat silent. He didn't say anything because there was nothing to say. The Kid had said it for him. Up till now, he didn't know it, but it was exactly like The Kid said. He wanted out. At long last, he wanted out. Why, with a few dollars in his jeans he could buy himself a little piece of land, raise crops or run some cows. One more job—like the one on tap—and he'd have the money. He hadn't pulled off a job in nearly half a year, what with the heat on and only The Kid nervy enough to bust out where the chips lay, the rest of them just waiting, lying low and waiting for something to happen. Slattery knew that was no out, waiting. Nothing was going to happen. The law was getting bigger and tougher, stronger every day. Colorado, up north, had just become a state. Texas, to the south, had been a state for years now. The Territory knew that only in statehood did progress lie, and only with law and order did the Territory stand a chance of becoming a state.

The Kid said finally, "Forget it, Slats." He grinned at Slattery, wet-lipped, and the giggle started rising up. Slattery couldn't stand it but he didn't do anything, couldn't say anything. The Kid had him paralyzed tonight. He didn't know why.

Then The Kid said, "All right, how big is it?"

Slattery frowned. "How big is what, Kid?"

The Kid shook his head. "Don't con me, Slats. You know what I mean. How big is the job you're pulling off? Big business? Real big?"

"So-so," Slattery said. He shrugged his shoulders and let his weight sprawl deeper into his chair. He was tired and he didn't want to talk about his job. He never did, but this time he felt even stronger about it. And again, he didn't know why.

The Kid squinted. "What's the matter, Wolf? Afraid to jinx yourself?"

"Maybe," Slattery said agreeably. The Kid was shrewd. He was always on top of you guessing, digging at your thoughts.

"You're just getting old," The Kid said flatly.

Surprise washed through Slattery. That was exactly it. That's what he'd been thinking, that he was getting old. The Kid had hit it on the nose. Then Slattery grinned to himself, in the dim yellow gloom of the saloon and he wiped his mouth with the back of a large hairy hand, almost an automatic reflex when he grinned, as if to wipe it away and keep his thoughts even more his own. He knew what the grin meant, though. It meant, hell, no, you're not *getting* old. You *are* old. You've lived past the line they draw for men like you.

"Must be real big business," The Kid persisted. "When Wolf Slattery can't keep from grinning about it, it must be big. How big, Slats?"

Slattery stared at the boy. "Five years ago, Kid," he said, "I'd have pulled you across the table for calling me that, or anything except my name. I don't like it, Kid."

The Kid giggled. "Five years ago I would have been thirteen years old. That's why you would have done it— five years ago. Now you'd be too scared to do anything foolish like that."

Slattery looked at the cruel-cutting mouth, the sharply curled sneer. There were times this boy made Slattery feel like a novice. Five years ago he'd have slapped anyone silly for making him feel like that. Today, Slattery took it.

"Kid," he said, "I'm not scared of you. Don't ever think I am."

The Kid waved his hand in disdain. "How big, Slattery, how big?"

Slattery said, rare anger heating him, "Quite big, Kid, very big. The kind of money you'll get some day, too, if you keep your mouth shut long enough to live."

The Kid tilted back, enjoying himself. "My," he said. "Must be very big money. How much?" He let his chair rock forward, his own face up close, egging the big man. "How much, Slats? Fifty dollars? A hundred? Two hundred?" The upper lip lifted and the two large front teeth stuck out. Then he started to laugh, the terrible high giggle that was The Kid's trademark, and it went on and on, The Kid's head thrown back, tears streaming down his cheeks.

Slattery said quietly, cutting through the laughter, "Five thousand dollars." The room was silent. Slattery wanted to laugh, suddenly, and say heartily, "Sure, five grand. Or was it five hundred grand?" Anything, just to make them not believe him. But they would anyway, because they knew it was the truth. It was. Five thousand dollars. Four more than Tompkins had got for his Tombstone job. Three more than Vulka got last year for wiping out a railroad surveyor in El Paso, money paid because the surveyor could not be persuaded to change his survey and shoot a trunk line through a piece of New Mexico Territory that a big cattle rancher controlled. So the rancher had found Vulka and given him two grand to kill the surveyor, hoping the next man might listen to reason.

Five thousand dollars. Twenty-five hundred more than The Kid had been paid just last month. Twice as much.

The Kid stared at Slattery, and Slattery found he was enjoying this scene, suddenly. The Kid was hit and hurt. He said, "Five? Why, the goddam fool. Who'd pay you five, Slattery?" He was calling him Slattery now and that made it even better.

"Wait and see," Slattery said.

"I will," The Kid said. "Kee-rist, I will. Must be some halfwit who doesn't know any better."

Slattery was silent. No, not a halfwit. A man who wanted his work done, done well, done quickly, done quietly, done with the least possible notice directed to the deed. When you added up those requirements you went to only one man if you knew the trade that well. This man had. He had come to Slattery through a middle man. Now the man himself, the contract as they called him, would be in the saloon, to cinch the deal and get it started.

Slattery picked up his drink and took a sip. Not too much, not when the contract was coming.

The Kid said, "What kind of deal is it, Slattery?"

"Shut up," Slattery said mildly.

"Come on, Ben. Let's hear about it. Don't you want your pals to know so we can get that kind of money too?"

"No," Slattery said.

"Wolf," The Kid said bitterly. "Lone-wolf bastard. Go-it-yourself. Big shot."

"That's right," Slattery said, "Keep it up. You're doing fine."

"Afraid," The Kid said, his mouth twisted. "That's what it must be. Afraid we'll start stealing his business. Afraid we'll grab off one of those mushheaded contracts of his and show 'em how to really do a job up. No wonder he doesn't talk."

"That's right," Slattery said. "You couldn't be righter."

The Kid got up then and looked at Slattery, The Kid's yellow hair falling across his face, the two front buck teeth showing, a boy who looked like a rodent, and he said, "Kee-rist, Slattery, sometimes I wish you were a guy I'd been asked to put under. Sometimes I wish a contract would walk up to me and say, 'I want Ben Slattery dead, and pay you six thousand dollars for it.' You know what I'd say, Slattery?"

Slattery looked at the boy. "No. What would you say?"

"I'd say keep your goddam money. I'll do it for pleasure."

Slattery nodded slowly. He picked up the cards and began to riffle them. He started to deal out a hand, and then he stopped, because he knew The Kid would wait there all night for an answer. He put the cards down again.

"Kid," he said. "The pleasure would be mine. Nothing would be more fun than knowing you were gunning for me." Slattery picked up the cards and continued the solitaire deal. He heard The Kid walking away, the noise in the room suddenly loud, forced noise, as though noise now could cover what had just been heard.

It couldn't, Slattery knew, because The Kid wouldn't let it. Slattery didn't hold for men challenging others. It wasn't the business he was in, and maybe there was a word of honor to be said for a man calling out to another man that he'd like to gun-duel him but, honor or not, it wasn't Slattery's job.

He'd lived as long as he had—not just now, but before, in the old days he never tried to remember but couldn't really ever forget—because he'd learned to take abuse. He had to then. Now, he no longer really had to, but the habit was grained in. Only once had he not kept it in. The first time he'd killed, a man's hand pointed out, accusingly, calling Slattery something he wasn't and Slattery had wiped the hand away, and the accusation, with a pistol shot.

But that was then, Slattery thought fiercely. Now he didn't leap to the first ugly word that whiplashed him. He had learned to let ugly words pass him by unnoticed,

Still, The Kid had laid it on the line and he, Slattery, hadn't backed away.

So there it lay, shining as new gold and just as eager to be picked up. Some day, he felt he'd have to face down The Kid. He hoped it wouldn't be soon. He expected it would be. The Kid wasn't the type to let bygones be. What had been a surly relationship was now open dislike. The Kid was a hired killer like the rest of them. But he was more than that, worse than that. He killed for the fun of it sometimes. He killed when he disliked somebody.

Well, Slattery thought, that was for the future to work out. The Kid—and some of the others too—dwelled on past kills. They counted them, they remembered them. Despite memory that plagued him, raw as a man's flayed skin, Slattery tried to forget them as quickly as he could. It wasn't the past he lived on, nor was it the future. It was the here and now, the job given him to be done now, this job, not that past job or the next one. That's how a man lived, Slattery felt, from job to job, doing this one and forgetting the last one, not worrying about the next one. Tompkins had said The Kid's nineteen kills were still ten short of his, Slattery's. It had surprised Slattery. Not because it was so many—but just because anybody had counted.

The minutes dragged. Slattery kept sipping at his drink, but slow as he was, the drink disappeared. One-Eye Mc-Call hurried over and poured Slattery a shot. The Kid sneered, "Mama's boy."

Tompkins got up from the poker table and stretched, tall, clean-cut, neat small hands. He said to no one, "Getting near bedtime for this old coot." Wilson's eyes flashed like live coals. He said, "Who can sleep?" Vulka said, half surprised, "Why, I can. Any time. Just show me the bedroll and lay me down." Wilson swore bitterly, and

Slattery knew it was one of those nights that would be hard for Wilson, a night he would be remembering things. Slattery knew how that was. Past ties could rip up a man's life. You had to forget them. You had to bury your past. But more than that, you had to play a lone hand. He was a loner. The Kid was right. Wolf Slattery. All right, he'd be Wolf Slattery.

Tompkins started to walk out then but halfway to the door he stopped and strode over to Slattery's table. "Good night," he said pleasantly. "Good luck to you, Slattery."

Slattery smiled. "Thanks, Tommy."

"When you figure on getting back?" Tompkins said.

Slattery stared at his fresh drink. "It ought to take three or four weeks. Leastways, that's what I usually figure. I'm going into this one blind, so far. He hasn't told me a thing."

Tompkins grinned. "Don't worry. He'll tell you. For five thousand, he'll tell you plenty."

"Well," Slattery said, "whatever it is, give me two months on the outside."

"You'll be back," Tompkins said warmly, and he walked out.

Above the wailing wind, Slattery heard Tompkins beating it into the night to wherever it was he had his cabin or his tent, or perhaps just a roll under the dark glowering sky, a scrub-oak fire over smoldering greasewood, his horse tethered in a patch of cottonwoods near the Pecos. Slattery didn't bother keeping track of things like that either. He never inquired of a man's life; in return he expected no man to inquire of his. That was his code. He used the saloon, himself, as seldom as possible. Just to make his contract and to hole up after a job. If it meant waiting around more than a day, he'd sleep upstairs. He paid McCall a dollar a night for the use of an upstairs room. There were men, lots of them, small operators mostly on the fringe of the trade, who had never seen

Slattery, men who swore he didn't exist, was only a ghost. Slattery grinned thinly. Let them think he was a ghost. He'd live.

Vulka left too, youthful and foolish-looking, a tubby young man with soft fat hands that could put five bullets in a playing card at a dozen feet and not one bullet hole touching any of the others. He stopped at Slattery's table and said, "See you, Ben." Slattery smiled at the youngster. From the bar, The Kid said, "Sure you'll see him. Him and me, we've got a date. Haven't we, Slattery?"

Vulka put a hand on Slattery's shoulder, and Slattery was surprised that he had been halfway out of his chair. Vulka said, "Lay off the man. He's got business to do. Nobody bothers you when you've got business."

The Kid snorted. "Nobody could. I'm not an old man, sweating blood over every little job."

"Little is right," Vulka chuckled. "Five thousand." He shook his head admiringly. "Good for you, Slattery. Someday I'd like to watch you work. They say you're the best. You must be." He walked out and at the bar, The Kid snorted again.

Wilson stayed the longest of the card players, brooding over his drinks, getting sloppy-eyed and finally staggering to his feet, a big man, sharply featured, strong hands. He said to himself, "Got to go home, you stupid digger. Got to go home and dig me some gold." He smiled crookedly at Slattery, winked and said, "Give 'em hell, Slattery." Then he lurched past and out into the night.

Slattery and The Kid were alone except for McCall, making quiet noises behind the bar, polishing glasses and keeping his eye open, a wary man now that he had lost his bravery, hoping nothing would happen because if it did happen, here in his saloon, he wouldn't know what to do or where to go. He thought nervously: There won't be need to go any place if The Kid guns down Slattery. McCall knew the way The Kid operated. He'd gun down

Slattery and then look around to see who had seen him do it. McCall would have seen him. The giggle would pierce the room. And The Kid would lift his heavy gun and put a hole in McCall's good eye.

The Kid said, "Quit your damn' shuffling around, Blinky. Slattery and I have some talking to do.'

McCall said, "Sure, Kid."

The Kid sat quietly at the bar now, his back to Slattery, his voice low, but he was talking to Slattery. "I've been thinking, Slattery," he began.

"That so, Kid?" Slattery said, fingering his glass but not drinking.

"Yeah, thinking. Thinking hard. And you know what I finally decided?"

"No," Slattery said. "What'd you decide?"

"I decided you figure on making this your last pay day, this five-thousand-dollar deal. You said you'd be back inside of two months. Well, I don't think you intend to."

Slattery hefted his glass. He knew The Kid. Now Slattery was supposed to say, "Are you calling me a liar?" or words to that effect, and The Kid would answer, "Yeah, I'm calling you a liar, Slattery. You're a no-good liar. That's what I'm calling you." And then Slattery would be expected to do something, say something, draw his gun or pull back his fist or call The Kid an equally provocative name.

Well, Slattery thought, that's how The Kid worked. But it wasn't the way he worked. He said, "That's an interesting theory, Kid. Mighty interesting." He drank from his glass.

The Kid shook his head and swore. He drained his own drink and tilted the empty glass at McCall who hastily refilled it. It wasn't like the first drink, The Kid just trying to shove weight. Now it was ugly. They were all walking on a hair. McCall knew what he ought to do, right now. He ought to finish his work and go upstairs, just in case

The Kid chose to make this night the night. Not that Mc-Call thought The Kid would get away with it. No matter what, there was something about Slattery, sitting there, big and composed, a softeyed man with a furrowed forehead and deep lines running from his wide-spreading nostrils to the corners of his heavy mouth, an easygoing quiet man who knew how to take care of himself. Like the way he refused to come up to that punk bait The Kid was dangling in front of him. Still, tonight Slattery had talked more than usual and McCall could see that it worried Slattery.

But The Kid wasn't quitting. He drank a half-inch of whisky and looked into the bar mirror. He said, "You know why you won't be back? You figure on getting amnesty from the governor when this last big deal is over. That's what you figure, Slattery. You're going on up there to the plaza, Slattery, and you're going to hand over your guns and you're going to work for the law."

Slattery said nothing. He took a small sip of his drink and let it lie on his tongue before swallowing it.

McCall wanted to walk upstairs and leave the two men alone, but it wasn't right. He had no guts, McCall knew, because if he did have guts he wouldn't even have thought of walking out and leaving the two men alone. It wasn't guts. It just wasn't right, pulling out. So he stayed, trying to be quiet as he worried his glasses, watching The Kid drink steadily and quickly, and Slattery steadily and slowly.

The Kid said, "And when you're working for the law, you'll be working against me. You get that, Slattery? Against me. You and me, we'll be through then, Slattery. What do you say about that?"

Slattery looked up into the bar mirror, into The Kid's eyes. He could rise up now, Slattery knew, his gun in his hand, and have the drop on The Kid. The Kid would come around, sure as hell, reaching, But Slattery would have the drop on The Kid, and it would be over. *Provided.*

Provided it went just that way. He had to draw clean, stand free of the edge of the table and he had to shoot clean, straight to the mark. Because if he didn't—

If he didn't, he'd be dead, and suddenly, for the first time in years, Slattery didn't want to be dead. Slattery wanted to live, and now he knew why he had walked so cautiously all these years and why he had walked even more so tonight, and why he was so excited and worried about pulling off this job. He wanted to live through it and get his amnesty. Just because he wanted to live.

And why not? he thought excitedly. *Why the hell not?* Why doesn't a man have the right to live? He'd done wrong. Okay. He'd do right. If the governor was willing to forgive him, willing to forget the kills, the wars, the duels, why, then, it would be like a new life, like a new man. Like a snake, he'd peel off his skin. That's what he'd be. A new man. To hell with Ben Slattery. To hell with Wolf Slattery. He'd be a new man.

And that's why he didn't want to talk about this job. He wanted it to go right and smooth and be over, and he wanted to do the next thing: see the governor and get his amnesty. Never before had he worried about the next step, only *this* step. Well, now the governor was going to ask him if he was over his past and Slattery would have to dwell on his past and say, "Yes, I'm over it. Thank God." Then he could face the future. Because he wanted to live, and suddenly, for the first time in years—he didn't know how many, but many, many—there was a chance he could live and live normally, live decently.

And that's why The Kid had him paralyzed tonight. He had to be paralyzed. He had to keep the gorge down where he could control it. Otherwise, he and The Kid would be swapping bullets and, though he thought he could beat The Kid, he didn't know for sure—you never know until it's over, one way or the other.

The Kid said, "What do you say, Slattery? Me against

you, that's how it will have to be. Do you get that, Slattery?"

The saloon door banged open and wind howled into the room. McCall felt his breath whoosh out of his heavy chest as though he had not breathed once in the twenty minutes the two men had been at it on the other side of the bar.

Slattery looked up at the door from his table in the rear of the saloon. He watched the man—his contract, he knew—case the room. The man saw The Kid straight ahead, turned around to watch, and took a half step toward The Kid. Then the contract stopped, as though he knew it wasn't The Kid he was supposed to deal with. He looked around and there, to the side of the door, he found Slattery.

Slattery said, "I'm Slattery," gathering up the cards again, and the man walked over, uncertain.

"Sit down," Slattery said. "You're Frick?"

The contract nodded and then he frowned, taking in the saloon, realizing he had been identified in front of the youngster at the bar and the bartender too. He didn't like it, Slattery could see. They never did. They wanted to do the whole thing under cover, never caring how much the hired man had to expose himself. Well, with the saloon set up as it was, the boys had been able to get around it. There was invariably some man, and always McCall in addition, to see the contract. It was part of the life insurance.

Frick sat down heavily, a sweating man in an old-fashioned sourdough jacket. He took off his hat and Slattery noticed the graying hair. He had a body going to fat, but not sloppy yet. There was power in all that weight. A cattleman, Slattery thought, a big cattleman. A man who used to ride a lot, but didn't any more, but who still ran his show. Slattery kept measuring his man. He had never heard of Frick, or of a cow spread run by a man named

Frick. That wasn't surprising. Always there were big cattle ranchers sweeping the range into their fists, men coming in from Texas or down from Colorado, Easterners and even Englishmen, big-moneyed men who wanted to own a fat parcel of land and twenty thousand head of beef because that had suddenly become the mark to measure a man in this primitive half of the nation. And from there they went into banking, into railroading, into the governor's chair. Slattery knew of them, men who aimed first to own all the land they could see and, when they did, had to own things they didn't see—farmers' mortgages, steaders' deeds, rail workers' pay checks, votes.

Slattery knew he could be wrong. He knew he was letting himself be swayed by the offer of five thousand dollars. But even without the deal—the biggest any of them had ever heard of—Frick looked like a big man, bucking to be bigger.

"How do I know you're Slattery?" Frick said, finally.

"How do I know you're Frick?" Slattery grinned easily. "How do I know you'll pay me five thousand dollars?"

"Turn over your left wrist," Frick said.

Ice-cold shock jolted Slattery. The middle man had been good—too good. Slattery had never noticed him looking. What else had the man seen? Slattery slowly turned over his left wrist, the skin pale under the far-off overhanging yellow lantern. A patch of dead tissue about an inch long and a quarter-inch wide puffed slightly on the underside of the wrist. Slattery stared at his wrist, remembering. He said tautly, "Satisfied?"

Frick nodded.

Slattery took a deep breath. "Now it's my turn, bucko. How do I know you'll pay me the money?"

"Simple," Frick said crisply. "A postdated check will be deposited to your account at any bank you choose, or handed over to you or to an intermediary you select. If you pull off the job, the money is yours."

"Check?" Slattery had always received cash. But sometimes after the job it had been a problem to meet his contract to collect. The check idea might be better.

"That's right. A check." Frick laughed shortly. "Don't worry about my end of it. It can't be traced back to me. I'm not dumb."

"What's to keep you from stopping the check the day I pull off the job?"

Frick smiled. "You're a killer," he said quietly. "That's what would stop me."

Slattery sat staring at his dark blunt-fingered hands, lying on the rough unfinished wood table. That was so. That was it. Always, he'd been paid. They knew he was a killer, so they paid. But now it was different. Frick didn't know it, but it was different this time. This would be the last kill. After this, amnesty. Still, if Frick reneged, Slattery would have just cause for doing him in. He took a heavy breath. Even when it looks all finished, sometimes it isn't. There's no sure end.

Slattery said, finally, "Well, who is the man? Do I know him by name?"

"It's all settled then? You'll do the job?"

"As best I can. Who's the man? Do I know him?"

Frick smiled slowly, a different smile, a bright dawning smile. "You ought to," he said. "By God, you ought to. Every man jack in the Territory ought to by now."

"Who?" Slattery said, his heavy dark fingers drumming the table. He eyed The Kid, sitting at the bar, drinking, watching—but not hearing. Slattery knew. He didn't want The Kid to know. It was his job—his last job, Slattery thought fiercely, because Frick wouldn't renege, he wasn't the kind—and he wanted to get it going so he could get it over. He was bursting inside. The last one. The last time he'd put his gun out for grabs. The last notch. They could all stop counting, after this one. "Who?" he said again.

Frick leaned forward, hunching his back and turtling

his head into his heavy sloping shoulders, so that neither the blond boy at the bar nor the one-eyed bartender could hear, so that only Slattery could hear, and he said it so low that Slattery didn't really hear. "The governor."

Slattery said dully, stupidly, crossly, "Who? Don't drag it out, man. Just tell me. Who?"

And Frick said it again:

"The governor."

2

A big circle. You begin one place and you ride like hell, beating your horse until blood and foam come out of its mouth, you ride all night and you ride all year, clods of dirt kicking up all around, and then you get there, and where are you? Right where you began. Because all the time you're buried in a mountain of your own dung. No end and no beginning. Just a middle as thick as the night, and as long as a whore's dream, or eternity.

They stood at the stable, Frick saddling up, the horse nuzzling a feed bag. Frick said. "That's all you want to know? You sure? Damn it, Slattery, I want to help as much as I can."

"That's all," Slattery said. His head was clear, his body never felt stronger, keener. He was letting it all sluice off, the past and the future, the kills that had given him his past name and the amnesty that would have given him his new one. They were all forgotten, all dead. It was the present. The job. "No need for anything else," Slattery said.

"You don't even want to know why we want the governor de—"

"No," Slattery said sharply. "No, I don't want to know why. To hell with why. I don't want you talking out here either." It was a dark night, the stableman inside and warm but close by, and even though the May night still howled with wind, a desert wind that whipped handfuls of sand into the men's faces, there were times the wind stopped dead and voices would have been like thunder in that hollow silence.

"You're right," Frick said. "'Well, then, it's so long until—"

"So long," Slattery said. "I'll be up to do the job first chance."

"Not too long, now," Frick said. "We've got to have it done before the roundup in the fall. That's why—"

Slattery said quietly, "I'll be up first chance. I'm not bursting into the capital with a firecracker on my tail. I've got to go in quietly. That's a hot place for a man like me."

"I know," Frick said quickly. "I appreciate that. But we've got to have it done."

"It'll be done," Slattery said.

Slattery was getting tired now, tired of Frick, and he wanted to sleep so he could start out fresh the next day, thinking how he could enter the capital, a hundred law-dogs carrying guns and just looking for men like him, law-dogs who yesterday were outlaws but now had turned in their guns and got them back again, to protect law and order. Amnesty gave a man license to carry his gun. That was the governor's latest sweetmeat offered to the outlaws. Amnesty. Slattery thought a moment, frowning in the dark night, nodding his head slowly. Amnesty. Why not? He could do it under the cloak of amnesty. It made the job of getting into the capital so simple. He had no problem of hiding and lurking, trying to steal a look at the governor, at the plaza. With amnesty, he could bring the governor into full view, and himself too. He nodded decisively, squelching the annoyance that rebelled against the deceit. Why the hell not? It was a topsy-turvy world, Slattery thought, where the governor pardoned killers and made them deputies. It was funny, in a way, Slattery thought, a killer one day and a deputy the next; you could hardly tell the difference between the two. It should have been—Slattery thought with a cruel smile—the difference between black and white. It wasn't. Well, that's how he had felt all along, about men who carried guns. It didn't matter why you carried them, just carrying them gave you the mark.

"Good," Frick said. "If you want me, I'll be up there too."

"If I want you," Slattery said dryly, "I'll find you. Don't worry about that."

Frick forced a short laugh, then he climbed up and put out his right hand. "So long, Slattery. You're a hell of a white man."

Slattery looked at Frick's hand and then shook it, and inside he felt himself crawl. "So long," he said. The horse started off, and night swallowed them.

Slattery watched the blackness for a long minute, and then he turned heavily and walked back into the saloon. He let the door swing shut, surprised at first to see The Kid still there. He said, "McCall, is there a blanket upstairs?"

"Sure, Slattery," McCall said. "And more in the shed outside if you need them."

"What's the matter," The Kid said, "no job? Chicken out of it, Slattery?"

"No," he said. "It's a job."

"A tough one?" The Kid said.

Slattery shrugged. "They're all alike."

"That Frick," The Kid said. "Who is he? What's his trade?"

"I don't know," Slattery said. "I never asked. Cattleman, I think. Why?"

"No reason," The Kid said. "Just curious."

"He'll pay me," Slattery said flatly. "The whole contract's worth. He'll pay."

"And when he does," The Kid said wickedly, "then you'll go on up to the capital and get yourself pardoned?"

Slattery looked at the boy. "No," he said heavily.

"And when you're pardoned, you'll come down here, looking for me, a gun on your hip and handcuffs hanging from your cartridge belt, a warrant in your pocket? Is that the way it'll go?"

"No," Slattery said.

"And if I don't want to walk back to the capital with you, so they can put me in jail and hang me, you'll have to drag iron to make me? Is that it?"

"No," Slattery said.

"You better not," The Kid said through tight teeth. "Kee-rist you'd better not. You want to live, you better not."

"I won't, Kid," Slattery said.

"You're all over that amnesty crap, is that it? You've decided it's not worth getting me on your tail?"

"I'm all over it," Slattery said.

The Kid grunted. "Scared," he said decisively. "Scared of me. I never thought I'd see the day Wolf Slattery gave in to anybody, even to me. Scared out of his boots."

Slattery said, "Wait here, Kid. I'll be right back."

He went swiftly outside and walked to the stable. He called, "Watson, come out here, boy." *Boy*, he thought quickly, shame streaking him. The way a man talked to a Negro. *Boy!*

The Negro stableman came out. He squinted into the darkness and Slattery thought a sly smile appeared to work its way across his mouth. Watson said, "Yassir, Mister Slattery?" Softly he stressed the *mister.*

Slattery said, "You've got a beam inside, an old two-by-four, maybe ten feet long. Can I have it?"

"Beam?" Watson said.

Slattery said quietly, controlling himself, "Yes, damn it, a beam. A length of wood. I saw it before when we got

Mr. Frick's horse for him. Do you need it? Can I have it?"

Watson said slowly, "He'p yo'se'f, Mister Slattery." He went inside and Slattery followed him, the red lantern lighting the neat horse-smelling stable. Slattery went to the rear of the stable where he had seen the beam and he tugged at it, getting it to his shoulder. Watson watched him come forward, the beam on Slattery's shoulder, a big sweating man, his face like blood in the red light of the room, and the stableman began to hum softly:

> *"Oh Canaan, sweet Canaan,*
> *Ah'm boun' fo' the lan' o' Canaan. . ."*

Slattery swept past the man and into the night, but the words hung in the air, swept with him:

> *"Ah thought Ah heer'd them say*
> *They was lions in the way*
> *I don' expec' to stay*
> *Much longah heah. . . ."*

With a great curse, Slattery pushed the door open with the beam and went stalking through the bar. He laid the beam on the bar counter, propped so it stood four inches high, ten feet long.

The Kid said, "What the hell, Slattery? What are you doing? Building a new bar for McCall?"

"Just watch," Slattery snapped. "Mac, give me seven glasses, tumblers if you've got that many."

McCall reached under the counter and dragged out the glasses. Slattery stood them up, one next to the other, each glass two inches away from the next. He lined them up in front of the two-by-four. He said to McCall, "I'll pay for any I break. The wood's just to make sure I don't shoot up your back shelves."

Then he walked away from the bar a half-dozen steps, nearly twenty feet. He said to The Kid, "You can sit there if you like. You won't get hurt."

The Kid was five feet away from the row of glasses. He turned and stared first at Slattery, and then at the glasses. "You aim to break all those glasses?" The Kid said.

"No," Slattery breathed. "I aim *not* to break them." His hand flew to his hip, and automatically he said to himself, his lips unmoving, but the words shrieking inside the way they always did, *white man, white man, white man, whitemanwhitemanwhiteman.* He heard two gasps, first The Kid's because the speed of the move had surprised him, the blur of Slattery's hand down and then halfway up, pointed and then the other gasp from McCall when he realized what Slattery was going to do.

Slattery fired six rounds, and the separate cracks of his .45 merged into one booming inside the high old saloon. The rounds followed one another, one on top of the other, and all one could see for a moment was a spiral of white smoke curling gently and gracefully to the ceiling.

The Kid jerked his head to the bar. The two-by-four had leaped back a foot. The glasses were untouched. He said, "Good God, man!" Then he got down from the bar chair and walked over to the counter, leaned forward and examined the two-by-four. There were six holes in it, each one separated from the next by approximately the width of one of McCall's tumblers.

McCall began to laugh quietly, his face ashen. "You put each round between two glasses. You did, I swear you did, and I'll swear it to anybody who ever asks."

The Kid kept staring at the wood and then at the glasses. He pulled the length of timber up to the glasses. Each bullet hole was exactly in between two glasses. Slattery had fired through six two-inch slits.

Slattery said quietly, "Now. Do you believe me? I'm not scared of you, Kid. I'm not scared of anybody. Now. Do you believe me?"

The Kid shook his head. "I don't know, Slattery. I just don't know. That's a hell of an act you got there. But how does it stand up when you put a man in front of the bar instead of glasses? You know, those glasses can't shoot back."

Slattery said grimly, "You just won't believe me, will you?"

"It's not that. I'm willing to believe you," The Kid said earnestly. "In fact, I'd rather believe you. This way, if you're right, I just know we'll tangle. You won't pull out of it if you're not scared."

Slattery walked to the bar. He felt let down, drained. He started to pull the lumber over the edge of the counter.

"No," McCall said, "leave it right there. I'm keeping that piece of wood. That's a souvenir. Let them talk about shooting, *I* know. I don't care what they say, *I* know." He looked at The Kid. "Don't ever tackle him, Kid. I'm telling you for your own good. Don't ever tackle him. The man is murder."

The Kid waved a hand. "Aw, to hell with that act. I still want to know how he does with a man in front of him, a real man. Face to face."

McCall shook his head. "If I were you, Kid, I wouldn't try to find out. That's my best advice. Keep out of the man's way. That man is murder. I'm telling you."

Slattery walked to the rear stairs of the saloon. "Good night," he said to McCall. "Good night, Kid."

He walked up the stairs and pushed open the door. Through the dark he walked to the dresser and lighted the oil lamp. Next to the dresser a cracked mirror was nailed to the wall. Slattery turned his head slowly until he faced himself in the mirror. He stared at his image. He ran his hand over his face. Thick black crisp hair. Skin like faded walnut, worked over by the sun. Big heavy nose, splayed nostrils slightly flaring. Heavy sensual lips.

"Nigger," he said to himself.

3

"Next!"

The fat man with the gold watch chain across a black vest was stationed in front of the closed heavy oak door, the governor's door, and before him, lining the 100-foot-long dobe-walled corridor, stood a milling mass of men and women. *The whole goddam Territory*, the fat man snorted to himself. "Next!" he bellowed. "Who the hell is next?"

A Pueblo pushed forward, thin wrinkled arms holding a heavy paper-wrapped package. "Me," he said, quavery-voiced. "I next."

"What's your bitch?" the fat man said.

The Pueblo blinked. He said, "Meester Chiz—the wells. Why do the American soldiers poison our wells? I want to ask the governor—"

The fat man swore. "Chisholm," he said venomously. Chisholm's the name. I don't want to hear you calling me Chiz." He turned and stared at the patient-moving mass, extending to the great tree-pillared portico that marked the entrance to the governor's palace at the north edge of the square. "You all hear me? I don't want to hear one of you call me anything but Mr. Chisholm. You get me?" There was a shuffling noise that might have been a sibilant sound of assent, or merely Indian skirts, rustling.

"All right," he said, mollified. He turned back to the Pueblo. "Nobody's poisoning your wells." The stupid, ignorant bastards, he thought. Now the Army and the government were poisoning their wells. What would they think of next? Chisholm mopped the sweat from his brow. It was going to be another scorcher. The place was crying for rain. No wonder they were bitching about their water supply, he thought. "What's that you got in the package?"

The Indian clutched it tight to his grease-spattered buck-skin. "No," he said. "I show it to Governor Fallon."

"You show it to me."

"No," the Pueblo squealed.

Chisholm reached roughly for the package. They struggled briefly, dark eyes glowering on them from the waiting petitioners. Then the package spilled open.

The carcass of a scabby dog fell at Chisholm's feet. "What the hell is this?" he roared.

The Pueblo said, "My dog! He dead! You poison the wells. You and they—" He pointed outside to the plaza where Americans with guns strapped to their hips marched indolently in the sun of the open square, lean-faced, feral-featured men, the sheen of violence on their hard tanned faces. "They! They poison our water! They dry up our land! They drive us from our land!"

"Shut up!" Chisholm bellowed. His heavy arm reached out and grabbed the Indian by his skinny shoulders. He shook the old man until his head lolled about like a broken rag doll's. The crowd stopped moving. They stood, eyes burning black, emitting their message of hate for the *bruto Americano*.

The door opened. A man stood there, slightly below medium height, slender as a ramrod, straight as a mountain pine, a man whose sharply chiseled features were modulated by a soft drooping mustache and by a mane of silver hair, and then hardened by eyes the color of a spark coming off rock, flint-blue eyes that fastened on Chisholm and the shaken frightened Pueblo.

"Cut it," he said quietly, yet the words whipped down the corridor. He was Stewart Victor Fallon, General, United States Army (retired), Governor of the Territory. "Chiz, keep your hands off these people."

The crowd surged forward, then, chattering, arms out. "*Gobernador* Fal-*yon*, *Gobernador* Fal-*yon*," they cried.

Fallon ignored them. He said to Chisholm, "What's this man's problem?"

Chisholm's foot reached for the carcass. He toed it. "There," he panted. "He says we're poisoning his wells. His dog's dead and he blames us."

Fallon looked down. Dead dogs now, he thought. Dear God, where would it end? He stared through the corridor to the flag atop the mission. It lay limply, unmoving. The very ground seemed to be panting. Then he snapped, "Tell the man to bury his dog. Tell him to bury him deep. If he wants or needs lime, he should check at the commissary. But he's got to be buried and damn' fast." Then he looked at the Pueblo. He had a nagging thought. "And don't bury him in the well. Do you understand?"

The Pueblo's eyes fell before the governor's cold stare. "Yes," he hissed.

The governor grunted. "You better understand." No wonder they were complaining about the water. A dog died from some cause or other—he looked at the sick matted fur of the poor beast—and they blamed the well water, and then they threw the carcass in the well and kept drinking from it. He grimaced. "Anything else?" he said to the man.

The Pueblo shook his head. He started off.

Chisholm roared, "Hey! Your dog!" But the man was gone, in the mass of humanity that packed the outer hall.

Fallon grinned wearily. "Get one of the sentries to bury the dog," he said. He turned and went back to his desk, where a pile of papers lay. He picked up the top one. Amnesty request. He looked at the second. Amnesty request. Nearly all of them the same. By God, if nothing else was working, amnesty was! Seven hundred already and they were starting to pour in, men who wanted to swap their guns for a pardon, a clean slate, a new start. He nodded his head, picking up his pen, and he began to scratch his initials to the requests.

Then, four or five papers down into the pile, was the sheet that had disturbed him most when he had seen it. It was a letter from the Jackson Cattlemen's Association, president, Wesley L. Frick—he'd have to ask Chiz about Frick, he'd never heard of the man—asking for another postponement of the Territorial order that had demanded all cows be branded by November 1 so an official count and check could be made. It was the second time Frick had written him. Before Frick, Fallon had other letters from other ranchers, Jackson County ranchers.

He set the sheet aside.

The door opened. A Mexican laborer came in, timidly. Chisholm called into the room, "He's okay now. Wants a health permit."

Fallon motioned the man forward, thinking: governor means lawyer, doctor, general, and, yes, even dog burier. He said, "What's your name?"

"Mendoro. Miguel Mendoro." He gulped, a waxy-faced man, holding a report from the Territorial clinic. Fallon had established the clinic four months ago, just two months after he'd taken office.

Fallon extended his hand, snapping his fingers. Mendoro gave him the report. Fallon read it quickly.

"Syphilis," he said, nostrils twitching. God, how he loathed these people. No, he thought, that wasn't fair. He didn't loathe them. He loathed the things they did. Mostly he was sorry for them. "You're a lucky man, Mendoro, getting cured so fast." He wondered how cured the man was. A smear of mercury ointment and a finger waved in his face. That was the cure. "Watch yourself." He took a blank health permit and filled in the man's name and initialed and dated it. He said, "Here."

Mendoro took it, face lighting. Now he could work again. He could tell Rosa he worked again. Then he thought: *Fools*. A man is not allowed to work because his *cojones* itch.

Fallon said, "All right, now, get out. Don't forget to check in to the clinic in a month. You understand?"

"*Sí*," the man said bland-faced.

Fallon shook his head. He doubted they'd ever see him again. "Get out," he said again, and he made a quick note on a paper of the man's name. He'd have to follow it through himself. The man shuffled to the door and was gone.

The door stayed open and Chisholm came a step inside. "Here," he said roughly, holding an American by the arm. "Another one come crying, Governor."

Fallon's head shot up. Amnesty, he thought. *Good!* He got to his feet, looking like an icicle, straight, hard, frigid, silver. He said, "Thank you, Mr. Chisholm," his voice grave, weighted, and Chisholm went out, wondering whether the governor was acting or was really dedicated to this amnesty business. Amnesty, Chisholm thought, what a crock!

The man walked inside, long swinging strides. He looked at Fallon indifferently, then went to the window and looked out, seeing the American sentries before the palace, walking the dusty cobbles, guns at their hips.

"Your name?" Fallon said.

The man turned, his lazy eyes half open, yellow-flecked. He measured Fallon, and then he said, "Savage. Charlie Savage."

Fallon didn't let his face change expression. They had named the man well, a cruel-faced man, hard-eyed, thin-lipped, a man with a natural cat-quick grace. By God, he was a bag, this one. The worst—and therefore the best—Fallon had seen thus far. "Savage," he said, "what do you want?"

The tall man shrugged. "Amnesty, I guess. That's what it's called, ain't it?"

Fallon nodded. "That's what it's called. What would you call it?"

The man stared at Fallon, a thin smile at his mouth, his eyes untouched. "What's the difference what I'd call it? You handing out pardons or ain't you?"

Fallon stiffened. "That depends," he barked. "What have you done?"

"I was down in Jackson, with The Kid," Savage said.

Fallon didn't dare breathe. One of The Kid's gang. "Kill? Rustle? What did you do?"

"Both," Savage said, eyes narrowing, watching Fallon, measuring the governor to see how much the man would take before anger showed through that icy face. "Both and maybe more. Whatever The Kid asked me to do."

"And why are you here?"

The man took a half-step forward. "I told you, Governor. Amnesty. That's what."

"But why now?" Fallon asked. The two men stood four feet apart. "Why have you come in *now?* Why not two months ago when the Jackson wars ended? Why now?"

The man looked away. He was silent. Savage didn't know whether he could tell Fallon the truth, that he had laid up for two months, waiting for The Kid to make a move, to organize the gang again, but apparently The Kid was on his own now. The gang was dead. Bill Dellinger was dead, Savage knew. That he knew for sure. He'd seen Dellinger killed. And Matty Vance was dead, so everybody said. Kling was hit and hurt bad, his spine broken by a deputy's bullet. Maybe he was dead too. Savage didn't know. They all were dead or hurt bad. All except The Kid, and The Kid was at Fort Heck, they said, lying low, picking his shots. That's why he was here. There was nothing left for Savage to do except try to cash in on this pardon racket.

Savage said finally, "I don't know. I waited, I guess, to see what would happen. And when nothing happened, I figured I was through."

"You sorry for what you've done?" Fallon said harshly.

This was the worst part, asking them whether they repented, knowing damn' well they hadn't. Well, maybe repentance would come later when they saw what a clean way this way was.

"Sorry?" Savage said, his lip curling. "Sorry? I'm only sorry I didn't get that deputy who shot Kling in the back. I'm only sorry I didn't get the man who got Dellinger." He leaned forward. "And that man you've got out there—that's Chisholm, ain't it?—I'm only sorry I didn't catch that bastard running off cows. I'd have stopped him."

There it was again. Fallon had heard it a dozen times. How Chisholm had rustled cows under cover of the Jackson County wars, claiming abandoned herds from burned-out spreads right and left, until his own herd numbered close to 20,000 head, maybe more. No wonder Chisholm was pushing Fallon to enforce the November 1 deadline for branding cows and keeping what you branded. By November 1, Chisholm would be cleared. Amnesty for rustlers. That's what the November 1 order meant. And no wonder men like Frick and his Jackson Cattlemen's Association didn't like it. They represented cattle owners who were suddenly short of cows, and now the Territory was readying up an order to all cattlemen to brand their cows by November 1. The cows you had branded by November 1 were your cows, no matter how you got them. To some owners it could mean a final wiping-out, complete bankruptcy. Until the order was signed and put into force, these cattlemen were hoping against hope they could somehow prove whose cows were whose and get their rightful herds back.

Fallon said stiffly, "We're not discussing Mr. Chisholm. We're discussing you."

The tall outlaw moved his lips, and Fallon knew he was swearing to himself. Savage walked back to the window. He pointed. "Out there," he said. "Those men. They've cashed in on amnesty, haven't they?"

"That's right."

"And they're carrying their guns again?"

"That's right. They've been deputized."

Savage smiled thinly, wickedly. "Could I be deputized?"

"Does a gun mean that much to you?"

He shook his head, the grin breaking over his face, making him more youthful, more human. "You're damn' right it does, General." He shook his head. "A gun's the only thing that counts in this place. Without a gun, a man's dead. That's for sure."

"Not if no man had guns."

The man laughed and hit his thigh with a heavy palm. The noise was like a shot in the room. "That's for sure, General." Fallon knew Savage had started to call him General now that they were talking about guns. It happened automatically, every time. Fallon said, "I mean it. Suppose nobody carried guns?"

Savage shook his head again. "General, you're sure some fooler. Who's going to know who's got a gun on him, who's got a gun in his pocket or under his armpit? Why, when I was down in Jackson jail for a spell, they brought in The Kid once"—he raised his hand to stop the governor—"yes, they did, General, but nobody's talking about it. They don't want to lose their jobs. They had The Kid once."

"What happened?" Fallon was frowning, not sure he believed this man. Stories of The Kid were legends now. But Savage had said he was there, had seen it.

"They threw The Kid in a cell, and a guard stripped him down naked and went over him with a comb. Then the guard must have relaxed a minute—I ain't snitching who it was, it don't matter anyhow—and The Kid reached up his own you-know-what and pulled out a shiv four inches long and buried it in the guard's throat. Then he took the guard's gun and keys, put on his clothes and got us all out of there."

Fallon swallowed. "So?"

"So, General, you take away all the guns from everybody you can and The Kid wanders in here naked as a jaybird at the hip and everybody relaxes, and the next thing you know he's got a little old derringer from some place or other and we're all dead on the cobbles down there. No, you can't take away guns from us. Just so long as one man carries one out there"—he waved his hand to the south—"we all have to carry them. If amnesty depends on giving up my gun for good, I'm not buying it."

"The Kid's got you scared?"

Savage's mouth stiffened. "Not exactly scared. But—I was one of his boys and he won't like hearing I've turned in my gun to you. I just don't want him coming up on me unless I got a gun too."

"Suppose we had The Kid? Then how'd you feel about this business of guns?"

Savage shook his head. "No sirree. No different at all. Why, The Kid's plenty bad but he's not the only one. There's Vulka and Wilson and the Cotton brothers and Butcher Baker. There's Tompkins and Colman and—and there's Slattery. Hell, yes, there's Slattery."

"He the worst?"

"I dunno, General. I don't want to know. I saw him down in Jackson once. Without a gun on me, I'll stay clear of Ben Slattery, thank you."

Fallon moved back to his desk and reached for a cigar. He lighted it, watching Savage through the pall of blue smoke. "Suppose," he said slowly, "we cleaned up Fort Heck? Suppose I got federal troops to come and hit Heck and run those men into the ground. How'd you feel then?"

Savage straightened. "Now you're talking," he said, and Fallon winced, the man's loyalty so easily bought, hoping now that the men he'd stood with were run down and trampled under. And yet wasn't that what Fallon wanted? He wondered how clean amnesty was. Savage nodded eagerly. "That's the idea. Send an army in there. Fill them full of holes. If they come easy, hang them from the nearest trees. That'll do it brown."

Fallon kept his eyes on Savage. He was just one man, but you could multiply Savage and have the Territory mind. Bring in the Army. Always bring in the Army. Fight a war to end a war. Dear Lord, didn't they know there had to be better ways? The memories of the Civil War swept him, sitting there in the governor's chair, his cigar pleasant, the room warm and stuffy. Blake's Woods, Tennessee Junction, the whole Shenandoah campaign, getting the everlasting crap kicked out of him by Stonewall Jackson's foot soldiers. Then the time you had to send fine young boys into Chickamauga, counting the dead two days later, realizing it would be easier to count the living, there were so many less of them to count. And men thought it was a way to solve things. It was a way to solve only one thing: a man's lifespan. It solved that pretty damn' fast.

Then he thought swiftly: no, there was more to it than that. The war had freed black men. Still, where were they now? President Hayes had pulled the federal troops out of the South, and freedmen were right where they started from, shackled, except this time you couldn't see the chains. So what had the war solved? Nothing, not a blessed thing.

"Thanks, Savage," the governor said, keeping his voice calm. He picked up a blank amnesty sheet and scrawled in Savage's name, the date, and initialed the amnesty. Then he said, "Show this to Chisholm on the way out. He'll see to it you're deputized. That means you'll be working for us, for law and order. You'll be on call whenever we need you. To stand guard or do whatever we want. We pay you ten dollars a month. It's not enough to live on, but it's all we can afford." Fallon knew they might have been able to pay better than that, but it was another weapon to force the men away from their guns. They'd have to find work to live, cowpunching, laying rails, working in the stores that sprinkled through the mushrooming towns. Work might wean them from the gun. "You get all that?"

Savage nodded. "Fine, Governor," he said, lapsing back to the other term. "Whenever you need that army to go to Fort Heck you can count on me."

"Thanks, Savage," Fallon said again, quietly. "Good day." He didn't look up and soon Savage walked to the door and through. Amnesty, Fallon thought. He wanted to smash his fist against the gypsum-coated dobe wall, he wanted to scream. Instead, quietly, he puffed his cigar, turning over the sheets of paper, initialing swiftly with one scratch of the pen, converting outlaws into respectable citizens.

He was a tired man at sundown, pausing for a moment, raising the scratching pen while from the east edge of the plaza the evening Angelus was spelled and all noise hushed. He waited for the last tolling to cease, for the movement to begin again, and then he put down his pen and walked to the door. He opened it and said, "Chiz, I'd like to talk with you." The corridor was empty now, the flotsam of the Territory life all taken care of until the morning when they would fill the corridor again, crying, complaining, cursing, each man filled only with the knowledge that each new governor and each new law was somehow directed only against himself.

Chisholm said, "Now, Governor?"

Fallon nodded. Then he stopped and said, "No, not here. Let's get out of here."

"All right," Chisholm said. "I'll tell one of the sentries out there to accompany us." Chisholm was under the impression that one of the complaining peons or Pueblos or one of the pardoned outlaws was going to put a hole in

Fallon's back, for no reason other than ill will. Then Fallon had a sudden thought. Maybe it was Chisholm's back he was worried about. He chuckled softly. "No, don't," he said. "We can trust them." Sometimes Fallon had half a notion to go on down to Fort Heck himself, alone, unarmed, just to talk to those men. He doubted they'd do him harm. And maybe he could show them, tell them. Then he smiled wistfully. He hadn't been able to show or tell Savage anything: How far would he get with Slattery or The Kid?

Chisholm shrugged his beefy shoulders and said, "It's your funeral, Governor." They walked down the corridor past lounging sentries, through the portico and into the cobbled plaza. Above them, on the low roofs crouched old cannons, three three-pounders, dragged up there after the Indian massacre of the old governor and his family. Fallon looked at the cannons, black and foolishly out of date, too rusty to swing open their breeches but at least looking like guns. He sighed. That was all they were supposed to do, he guessed.

They walked through the square, pushing past the harsh squall of men and wagons and animals, the rise and fall of dispute and discussion, the din of life. Fallon looked back, once, and his eyes strayed over the square, over the palace, past the black futile cannons to the timberlands that rose 10,000 feet toward a swiftly darkening sky, mountains that even now were so vividly crimson they were called the Sangre de Cristo. Blood of Christ.

"Here," Fallon said, turning into one of the bumpy hard roads that led like spokes from the center hub of the capital, from the square plaza of the governors to the outreaches of the town. They walked past dobe houses that squatted like brick kilns until they reached the edge of the town where the range suddenly rushed at them and enveloped them, grama grass hip-deep (but not chest-deep, Fallon noted sharply, not chest-deep now that it had been overgrazed by greedy ranchers) and before them was a faint lowing, the sound of cattle.

Fallon picked up a dry blade of grass and stared at it before his fingers crumbled it. The land was going to burn up soon if they didn't have rain. "Whose cattle are those?" he asked quietly.

Chisholm shifted, a big man with splayed legs. "You know damn' well whose cattle they are, Governor. They're mine."

Fallon nodded. "Yes," he said. "I know. But whose were they a year ago?"

Chisholm was glad night fell so swiftly. He felt his cheeks redden. "Who the hell knows any more? They're mine now."

"Chiz," Fallon said. "If they had been my cows a year ago and I knew now where they were, I'd want them back. That make sense to you?"

Chisholm was silent.

"Well," Fallon went on, "it makes sense to me. Not that I'd strap on guns for them. That's not my way of doing things. But I'd want them."

"Sure," Chisholm said. "And I'd want my cows. Somebody swiped plenty of my beef during the Jackson wars. The Lord knows where they are now. I say it doesn't matter. If you're willing to let killers go scot-free—and, yes, even carry their guns—then you ought to be willing to let ranchers who lost and found herds during the wars keep what they've got now."

Fallon nodded again. "That makes sense too," he said pleasantly. "The only thing I wonder about is outfits like the Cattlemen's Association down there, that man Frick and his group, how can I tell them to keep what they've got and you to keep what you've got when they feel you've got their cows. Can I do that in full and fair conscience?"

"Governor," Chisholm growled, "those men are just trying to steal my cows. That's all it amounts to. They're pressuring you because they think you're a soft man and because I'm working with you."

Fallon cut in swiftly, his arm on Chisholm's. "And don't think I don't appreciate it, Chiz. I do. Why, I don't know where I'd have started from unless I had a man like you who knew the Territory and who knew in particular all the events of Jackson, both sides of the story." Inside, Fallon cursed himself for the hypocrite he was. When a man—like Chisholm—boasts how he knows both sides of a war, then there's something intensely wrong. One side or the other, or none at all, but not both—unless you're playing one against the other. There was something even more dishonorable about such a man—if Chisholm was such a man—cutting beef from under one man's nose and then going around and cutting it out from the same man's sworn enemy.

Chisholm said, "That's another reason. They're sure I'm filling your ears just because I do know the lay of the land down there."

"Who is this man Frick?" Fallon asked.

Chisholm said bitterly, "Frick! Who the hell knows? He doesn't belong, that I know. Somebody with a slick way about him, selling those cattlemen into joining up with him just so he can steal my cows."

"He's not a Jackson rancher?'

"Hell, no!"

Fallon shook his head. Frick didn't ring right. It added up like Chisholm said, a man stirring up trouble. He said, "Chiz, spell out your idea for the cattle situation, again."

Chisholm said, "Governor, you know it backward and forward."

The governor plucked up another blade of grass and set it between his teeth. It was dry, but sweet. "No, I don't, Chiz. Not out here I don't. Out here it's different. This is where I ought to hear it, not in that stuffy room full of papers. It means more out here."

"Herds changed so fast in Jackson County that today no man can rightfully say whose cows are whose," Chisholm said. "It's a mess."

Fallon nodded. "It sure is. Go on, Chiz."

The man took a deep breath. "So we just set a date, some time after the fall roundup—November 1, let's say—to give every man a chance to get his brand on the cows on his grass. By November 1, we send men around to count heads, to make an official report on how many cows each man owns. And that's that."

Fallon sucked on the grass. He turned around and faced the town, lights on now, evening noises springing up. It hadn't sounded any better, or worse, out here than it had back in his office. Amnesty for cattle rustlers.

He said, "The Association—Frick's boys—suggest we make a check now, before any new branding is done, and then if there's any disputed heads, call in some impartial group to decide who owns which cows. They think it's a better idea. They don't want to wait around and see what they consider their rightful cows claimed by some man who happens—right now—to be sitting on them. That's why they want me to hold up on that November 1 order. Check first, they say, and then brand only the cows nobody disputes ownership on."

Chisholm snorted. "A better idea! War, that's what it would be. All over again. Why, nobody knows any more whose cows are whose. That's the only thing anybody knows. So write it all off—the past wars and rustlings and changed brands. Write it all off and begin with a clean slate. Just like your killers. Amnesty for cows." He grinned, trying to push it through fast.

Fallon started back toward town. "Amnesty for cow thieves, you mean, Chiz," he said dryly.

"Call it what you like," Chisholm hurried alongside.

Fallon shook his head. "I don't know, Chiz. I can't see what harm a check would make. A man grazes longhorns for ten years, nothing but long stuff, it's pretty obvious there's something rotten when a herd of white-faced Herefords shows up on his spread."

"Sure," Chisholm said. "That's pretty obvious. But what happens when a longhorn man who used to have eight thousand head now has six or ten. All longhorn. Nothing but. Then what? Do you figure, well, maybe he's lost a couple of thousand through disease and stampede and burned-out grass, or maybe he's kept the bulls working hard, moved his herd to safer quarters and picked up a thousand more or bought some? What do you do? Who answers questions like that?"

Fallon fell silent again. It was a problem. One of many. But it could be solved. Chisholm was wrong. Nobody would start a fresh war over the order, one way or the other. Men would make money—maybe great piles of money, hundreds of thousands if many thousand head of cattle were involved—but that was all. All? Fallon thought ruefully. Men today seemed to live and die over money. Still, no war would start. A man might be sore, but that was all. The cattle wars were over. Amnesty for cattle thieves wouldn't start it up again. But was it fair? That was the crux. Always, was it fair?

"I don't know," Fallon murmured into the night.

"Eh?" Chisholm said.

"Nothing," Fallon said. "Not a blessed thing." He thought: tomorrow's another day. The Mexicans sure had a great philosophy.

4

Slattery woke at dawn, shivering. Then he remembered. He got up and dressed and went quietly downstairs to the well. He pulled up water, and shaved, his skin tightening under the icy lather.

He had sixty miles to go. His horse could do it all in a day, pushing. There was no need to push like that except the need to get up there, do the job and get out. Frick had come to Slattery for just that, speed and care and skill. Well, he'd give him all three. No man could give Frick any better. The thought, instead of bracing Slattery, riled him.

He walked back into the saloon. McCall was behind the bar. McCall roused easy. Like most of them, he sometimes found himself rolling to the edge of his bunk at the first unexpected sound, hand clawing for support, thinking: *they've come for me.* But nobody ever came for McCall any more. All that was behind him. Still, the wariness persisted.

Slattery said, "That was a damn' fool trick last night."

McCall swung out from behind the bar, with two cups of piping coffee. He rubbed his one eye. "I ain't so sure," he said. "It'll make The Kid think twice."

Slattery shook his head. "Nothing makes The Kid think twice. If anything, it'll push him."

McCall drank from his coffee. He was a nervous man who knew enough not to take sides, but he couldn't help it. A man like Slattery was worth a dozen of The Kid, "Just watch yourself. That's all."

Slattery said, "The Kid ride off finally?"

"Yeah." Slattery was still asking more questions, saying more than he usually did. It wasn't like him. "Took off about an hour or two after you went upstairs. Had a real nasty load on him."

Slattery stared down at his big hands for a brief moment. They were steady. He was trying to let last night wash away from him. "Tell the boys I'll be back quicker than I figured. Two weeks or so. Maybe less."

"I'll tell 'em."

"Mac," he said, "you know something? I'm scared. You know that?"

McCall drank from his coffee and didn't say anything.

"That's the first time I can remember being scared, real scared."

"The Kid?"

Slattery shook his head. "No."

"Tricky job?"

"I've seen trickier." That might not have been true, but somehow the job always seemed easier in the doing than in the planning. Amnesty was going to get him into the capital. The rest would follow. So it wasn't the job. He didn't know what it was. "Damned if I know," he said.

"Maybe you're rushing it," McCall said.

"Maybe," Slattery said, with a crooked grin.

McCall studied the gun fighter. Then he said, "You need a woman."

Slattery shook his head in surprise. He said shortly, "I don't need anybody," and swung down from the bar stool. He laid a silver dollar on the counter. "Do I owe you for the coffee, Mac?"

McCall snorted and said, "Don't be a fool."

Slattery waved his hand. "So long," he said. "See you." He walked out of the saloon and into the morning, the first rays of sunshine slanting in and stirring the mist. The wind had gentled. It would be hot by midday and stay hot until evening. Sixty miles was a hell of a push.

He got his horse from Watson. The Negro stableman looked once at Slattery and clamped his mouth shut. Slattery saddled the sorrel gelding. He said to Watson, "You think he can do sixty miles today?"

Watson walked around the horse. He looked at the shoes, holding the horse's tail so he wouldn't kick. "Ah'd trade him halfway theah," he said. "Or else do it in two shif's."

Slattery nodded. "My account straight, Watson?"

"Couldn't be straighter, Mister Slattery." He wasn't hitting the mister this morning. There was something about Slattery.

"Thanks, Watson," he said. He started to reach for a silver dollar, and then stopped. His money was running low. The job would come in handy. Too many weeks, sitting idle, his hands in his lap or else holding a shot glass. That wasn't the way out, Slattery knew. A gun fighter was a gun fighter, not an idler and not a drunk. When he was either, he was soon dead. The Kid knew this better than any of them. He kept moving. He wouldn't go stale. Still, Slattery never felt sharper. That act last night with the two-by-four. He doubted he ever drew cleaner than that. His hand patted his gun butt.

Watson watched the man, standing in the early morning light, pale and drawn. He said, 'Yo' wan' a leg up, Mister Slattery?"

Slattery shook his head quickly and mounted. He turned once and saw the stableman, leaning against the fence of his tight sweet-smelling corral, a piece of straw between his teeth. Slattery tightened the checkreins. He said, "Watson—"

"Yassir, Mister Slattery?"

"I'll be back in a few weeks." Now, what the hell. What did that mean?

Watson said dryly, "Thas fine, Mister Slattery. Ah don' aim to tell nobody.

Slattery felt the blood heat up his throat and climb to his cheeks. He let the reins fall loose and forward, and he kicked the gelding hard.

He rode into the morning, the sun behind him but climbing his back. Far ahead, like a smoky smudge against the deepening blue sky, loomed the indistinct peaks of the Sangre de Cristo. He headed for the hills, a single horseman kicking a faint spiral of dust toward the immense empty sky. He let the horse have its head, sitting deep in the saddle, a big bronzed man of shambling gracelessness. The capital lay sixty miles away. Slattery kept the twisting Pecos to his right. Far off to the left was the beginning of the desert, stretching out to no place. Slattery glanced briefly toward the dried brush that led to the undulating brown dunes. His tongue licked his lips to keep them from cracking. One jerk of the left rein and he'd be headed for the desert. A man could ride the desert at night, a man who knew the desert, ride it carefully, hitting the small water holes and horse-trading posts. In a week's time, a man could get through to the border. A man could lose himself in the squalid little sheep towns that crawled over the high plains of Sonora. A man could bury himself down there or, if he wanted to, a man could find a job shagging cows or chasing sheep, shape up a small stake and then head back into the States, into California.

There were places a man could yet go and be hidden, safe.

Sure, thought Slattery, like in a grave.

He pushed his horse toward the smudge on the horizon, and behind him the sun burned a hole in his back.

Slattery was a careful man. Had he known how carelessly he was riding, he'd have caught himself up short like a lassoed steer. He thought he rode alone, but he never bothered checking. Not that he'd have seen anything. The Kid was too shrewd for that. He'd moved his large gray mare under cover to a rocky mesa where three-ton boulders had tottered off balance for centuries, without falling, and from behind the boulders he watched the big man ahead of him, moving steadily to the northwest.

The Kid finally smiled and swore into the clear piñon-scented air. His hand twitched, each finger like a separate live snake.

The gelding started to play out a little before noon. It had been steady going, uphill nearly all the way. The capital lay at the base of the mountains, but even so the tableland was some six or seven thousand feet high. Piñon and aspen climbed the foothills. Small mud villages dotted the meadowland, washed by the dribbling creeks that crawled down the hills and merged into the Pecos to the east or the Rio Grande to the west. Sheep bent their heads in placid gray clusters, feeding quietly. Beyond the hills and out of sight, grama grass grew thick and sweetly in the protected bowl-like valleys. That was cattle graze, cow country where the American ranchers had driven off the Spanish sheepherders, defending the brazen theft with the words: manifest destiny. Now the sheep were out in the open broken shale slopes, wending their way through the hamlet-pocked fields.

Slattery studied the slumped neck of the horse. He turned the animal reluctantly toward the river. He watered the sorrel, fed him grains of corn that he kept inside a slicker in his bedroll, pegging the slicker to the ground so that the corn lay in it as in a cup. Slattery gave the horse a long-roped breather while he sat on thin grass, watching the horse. Then he got back up and moved toward the nearest dobe sheep village.

He forded Pintada Creek and followed the creek upland, passing from old gnarled cottonwoods that threw blue-black shadows over the pink river sand to new lilacs, nearly as thick as grass and seemingly growing out of black volcanic limestone. A tiny patina of smoke stained the sky ahead and two meadowlarks flew straight up to the sky when they heard Slattery's ambling horse. He saw seven adobe huts, a handful of chickens. A naked brown child, maybe seven or eight years old, suddenly leaped from behind a house and leveled a small stiff finger at Slattery. The boy yelled, "Poof! You dead," and melted back into the brush, laughing like crazy. Slattery grinned and followed the boy along the creek.

A woman crouched at a bank of near-brown water, washing clothes. A lone salt cedar tree threw cool shade over her dark sweating yet sweetly impassive face. She looked up at Slattery and her eyes narrowed.

Slattery said, "I want to swap my horse."

The woman stood and quickly touched her *rebozo*, patting her iron-gray hair beneath. She eyed the gelding with a practiced detachment. She said, "He not worth much." Slattery said, "You got a horse to swap?" The woman said, "No. He not worth much. Ten year old." Slattery said, "Seven," lying by a year. The woman said, "No matter. He in bad shape." Slattery waited patiently. The woman walked around the horse. She said, "My husband, he take your horse and ten dollars for a much better one."

"Swap. Not sell," Slattery said.

The woman bent back to her washing. Slattery turned the sorrel and started off. The woman called, "Hey. Wait a minute. Five dollars."

Slattery continued to walk his horse. "Swap," he said. "Not sell."

The woman said, "All right."

Slattery turned and followed her. She led him to a hut near a sagging fifteen-foot square corral. Three horses, swaybacked, munched on brown sun-dry grass. Slattery looked at their legs, at the joints. The knuckles were badly spavined. Slattery grinned at the woman. "You give me ten dollars and one of those nags for mine," he said.

The woman said, "Wait here." She ducked into the near hut, the *jacal*. Presently a man came out, sleepy-eyed, buttoning a faded yellow shirt that he wore outside of his blue jeans that smelled of yellow soap. He looked quickly at Slattery's horse and said, "Your horse is worn out. Not live much longer."

Slattery said evenly, "Not more than ten years or so."

The man said, "My horses all very young."

Suddenly Slattery was tired of the small haggling. He needed a horse, a fresh horse. Not one of these. He'd be better off keeping his own and sleeping out tonight, doing the trek in two shifts, the way Watson had suggested. But somehow he wanted to make the capital by dusk, where he stood some fair chance of moving under cover. He didn't want to hit the capital by daylight. He knew he could move in, easily, with amnesty as his stated aim, but in a corner of his brain he was fighting off amnesty, he was trying to see if it could be done without the brazen deceit of amnesty. Without amnesty, it would have to be dusk or night. Of course, he could sleep out and wait until it got darker, tomorrow. But that meant another day. Slattery wanted to get this one job over quickly. It was a new thought, and a disturbing one. But it was there, and it would have been more disturbing to have tried walking away from it.

He said, "Get me a decent horse."

The woman waved her hand. "This one here—" she said, but Slattery shook his head quickly. The man said, "Shut the mouth, Lola, this man knows horses. He is no fool." He walked away and around the *jacal* to the back. Slattery heard the man whistle and a horse nicker softly. Then a handsome bay gelding moved out of a patch of trees at the edge of the village clearing.

The man said, "My best."

Slattery nodded.

"Ten dollars and your horse."

Slattery shook his head. The bay was worth it, but he couldn't afford ten dollars.

The man studied Slattery, looked at the gun at his hip. He said quietly, "You *fugitivo?*"

"Yes."

The woman said, raising her chin, "*Amnestia?*"

The man said, "Hush, Lola," but he turned to Slattery for his answer.

"Yes," Slattery replied.

Scorn seemed to ride the woman's mouth. She jerked her head and turned back to her washing. The man said, "You know The Kid?"

"The Kid?" Slattery said.

"*Sí.*"

Slattery frowned. If he said yes, then they would want to know how The Kid was, whether all went well with him. It was always like that. The Spanish idolized The Kid, but they would sink back into their silences and scorns, and he didn't want silence or scorn.

"Yes," he said. "I know The Kid."

The woman came away from her washing, her eyes large. The sluggishness dropped from her face. Her breath seemed quicker.

"Where?" she said softly. "Where is he? Is he all right?"

"Lola," the man said. "*Quieto!*"

Slattery said, "He's all right. He's fine."

The woman approached Slattery. She put her hand to her breast, heaving beneath the low-cut beaded blouse. She smiled. "You must not mind me, señor. We had heard—otherwise."

"No," Slattery said. "He's all right. There's nothing wrong with him."

"Would you like some wine?" the man said.

"No," Slattery said. He felt he was speaking harshly. He couldn't help it. "I've got to go. The horse—"

The man said, "I will tell my boy to saddle up the horse for you."

"The bay?"

"*Sí.*"

"How much?"

The man put his hand on Slattery's arm. He looked

once at the gunbelt. He said, "My horse for your horse. Even trade. That is how we do it."

"Your horse is better, fresher than mine."

The man said, "Please. You have done us an honor."

Slattery said, "*Gracías*." He watched the little boy, naked still except for silver spurs strapped to his brown feet, while he transferred Slattery's saddle. Then Slattery nodded to the man and his wife. He held out his right hand to the man and they shook hands. Slattery noticed that the man's hand was three shades darker than his own. Slattery mounted and turned in the saddle. He said, "*Gracías*," again, and then the man came quickly to the horse's side and said, "Listen to me. You cross bridge, southwest of capital. There is a hut about a hundred yards from bridge, not much bigger my *jacal* here. Off to left of road. Maybe back fifty, seventy-five yards, the *jacal*. Name is Lopez. You tell him Salusito say he should hide you—if you need."

Slattery said, "Thanks. I don't have to hide."

The man had a hand on Slattery's knee. "But if you have to."

Slattery kicked the bay savagely. "I said I don't have to hide." He knew he was snarling.

The man fell back. "*Sí*," he said. He made a little wave of his hand. "But remember. Lopez. Salusito say it is all right."

The woman called, "Go with God," and blew him a kiss. The man said, "Lola!" but she laughed.

Slattery worked his way to the river. They didn't understand. He couldn't involve anybody else. They had no idea of what they were saying, what they were offering him. They didn't believe he was going in for amnesty. No friend of The Kid would crawl to the governor and beg for mercy. They thought he was surely a friend of The Kid, maybe one of his gang. They thought he might need a hideout. Damn them, he thought. Why didn't they leave him alone?

It was dusk when he crossed the small bridge outside the capital. Earlier he had heard the faint yet clear tolling of the Angelus and he knew how close he was. He pushed harder, knowing that everything led to the center square where the governor's palace lay. With some freak good luck, he thought suddenly, he might be able to glide in at night, see the governor, find he had a chance of doing the job and getting away, all before anybody had seen him in strong daylight.

He shook his head. He didn't know the land that well. He felt tempted to search out Lopez, but he dismissed the thought. Lopez was nothing. He had no place in Slattery's life, in this job. Yet the thought of a lying-up place after the job was done kept working at Slattery. Especially in a land he didn't know too well. With a posse forming behind him, a lying-up place was very attractive. He thought for a brief stabbing moment of Watson, the stableman, singing one of the spirituals Slattery's mother had sung so often:

> *"Ah thought Ah heeed them say*
> *They was lions in the way . . ."*

He nodded. There'd be lions, all right. But he couldn't use Lopez. He just couldn't.

He rode along dry trampled grass, feeling the road start to mix with gravel and dirt. He saw the huddled adobe houses move by. Mud ovens like upside-down cups stood before each house. It was a city that had grown out of its own soil—like warts from its own skin. One of the oldest cities in the country, yet still untouched. Maybe that was why it was untouched, because it was so old. It had been here too long to be affected by the comings or goings of new peoples, new governors. It absorbed them all. Not a frame house in the whole city, not a brick house. Nothing but adobe. Slattery wondered if there was another city of its size anywhere in the world so conforming.

The adobe houses veered in, narrowing the roadway. Soon they came one after the other, one on top of the other, and the roadway was a city street. Women crowded the streets, carrying water from nearby wells in earthen jars on their heads. Donkeys plodded by, wood piled on their stolid backs. A Pueblo smoking a cornhusk cigarette sat at a corner.

Ahead of Slattery he could see where the narrow street opened up. It had to be the big square, the plaza. Ground lanterns and oil lamps threw small yellow islands of moted light into the hazier mauve of early light. He was headed toward the plaza. There was no other direction: each street led to the plaza. Cowhands walked the wooden planks or rode the narrow dirt street. Every man had a gun sagging at his belt, some two. Slattery watched a man ride up close and then veer past. The man's eyes had been on the ground. Other than the chattering vendors and the creaking wagons, there was a choked silence to the town. A Pueblo saw Slattery coming and held up a small blanket. Strings of turquoise were folded on the blanket. Slattery shook his head and the Pueblo waited for the next possible customer. A girl stepped out of a cantina, swiftly and cooly eyed Slattery, and then looked down the street, foot tapping. Two men staggered along the plankwalk—early drunks. They'd end up sleeping in the street, Slattery thought. But with the bartering and soliciting and the drinking, it was still a tight choked-up town.

He rode to the end of the street and looked at the plaza. Shops and saloons along one end. A series of hitching posts at another. The town mission side by side with the town jail. And along the far length of the plaza the governor's palace, just another long low adobe building. Then Slattery saw the cannons on the roof. A half-dozen men walked the center of the square, keeping it free of traffic.

They carried guns at their hips, rifles strapped to their shoulders. Deputies. Slattery studied them for a moment. Deputies or killers. Deputies and killers.

He jerked the bay's head suddenly and the animal turned a distressed eye back on this strange rider. Slattery said to a man on the plankwalk, "Any of these saloons worth a man's money?"

"Depends how thirsty you are," the man said and plowed past.

Slattery dismounted. He led the bay to a water trough and then to a post. He walked toward the first cantina he could see. A Pueblo stood at the doorway, his face foolishly drunken. Slattery said, "Go on home. Sleep it off." The Pueblo swung a clumsy fist and nearly fell down. Slattery pushed the batwing doors that seemed so incongruous in the wide baked-mud doorway.

The saloon was crowded, but it had the same intense quietude. Slattery felt they wanted to talk but weren't able to. Amnesty wasn't the huge success the governor probably liked to boast it to be. Nobody trusted anybody. He said to the bartender, a hard-faced man with gray flat eyes, "Rye whiskey," and the bartender said, "*Aguardiente* or beer. Slattery said, "*Aguardiente*," and the bartender poured pale rum into a shot glass.

Slattery hefted the glass and turned his back to the bar. There were a dozen small tables, crowded. The drunken Pueblo pushed open the batwing doors and a man got up and shoved him back out again. Slattery turned to the bartender. He said, "Trouble with Indians?"

The bartender shook his head quickly. "No trouble. We don't let 'em get drunk, so there's no trouble."

Slattery jerked his hand behind him. "He's drunk."

The bartender shrugged. "Didn't get it here. Most of them behave themselves. That one's a pest." Then he clamped his mouth shut as though he had talked too much already.

Slattery turned and saw the Pueblo stagger back in. He lurched forward to the center of the room, and he said, in thick tones, "You steal my land."

A man got up. He was tall thin-lipped, hawk-nosed: a hard-looking man. Slattery felt he had seen the man before, but he wasn't sure.

The American walked over to the Pueblo. "Pete," he said, "go on home. We don't like Indians in here." He turned to the crowd and said, "Ain't that right? None of these red niggers in here? Right?" A man said, "Right!" Somebody else said, "That's telling him, Charlie." Slattery wanted to get out of here. But if he walked across that open floor, they'd all spot him.

The Indian looked at the American. He said, "I here first."

"Yeah," the American said, "and you get out first too." He pushed the Indian, who fell to the floor, crawled aimlessly and got up. Another American rose from his table and pushed the Indian. He fell down again. A third got up and kicked him. It was getting to be a game. Slattery held his drink before his mouth, but he realized he wasn't drinking. He wasn't even breathing. The Pueblo got up and held his side and said, "I take you all. I take all you American pigs. I lick you all. Come on."

The three Americans looked at one another and grinned. The first—the one they called Charlie—slapped the Pueblo's face.

Slattery said from the bar, "Don't you think that's enough?'

Charlie turned to the bar and said, "You aim to buy in?"

Slattery walked two steps away from the bar, hugging the shadows. "No," he said. "I just think somebody ought to let the man go home now. He's had enough."

Charlie stared at Slattery and then turned around and kicked the Pueblo in the groin. The Pueblo bent forward.

Charlie brought up his knee and kicked the Indian in the face. He went down again, in a shriveled ball, moaning softly.

Slattery pulled the brim of his hat down and walked to the center of the room. He said mildly, "All right, I'll take him out of here." He felt naked in the middle of the room. He'd been safer, and smarter, back at the bar where the wall and low ceiling threw dappled shadows. He bent down and picked up the Indian and put him on his shoulder.

"What's it to you?" Charlie asked.

Slattery started walking to the door. He had to get out of here, quickly. Somebody outside would probably know where the Pueblo lived.

He had recognized the man they called Charlie. He'd seen him in Jackson County once, riding with The Kid. Charlie Savage—that's who he was.

Charlie said, "I said what's it to you?"

Slattery said over his shoulder, "Nothing. I just think the man ought to sleep it off at home."

Somebody said, "Indian lover," and Slattery turned, saying, "Watch your tongue, bucko."

"Well, I'll be damned," Charlie Savage said. "If it ain't Ben Slattery." He snapped his fingers. "Somebody get Chisholm."

5

"I'd never have believed it. Ben Slattery, wanting amnesty," Savage said.

Slattery said, "That's my business, Savage. I see you've turned yourself in."

They stood in the square, near the tree-lined portico. A single light glowed yellow from the interior of the palace. There was little to mark the palace as anything but another dobe house, except the fresh coat of gypsum.

Savage kept his hand on his gun butt. "That is," he said, "if you are asking out. Is that it, Slattery?"

A half-dozen men stood nearby, studying the new man with wary frankness. They'd heard this was Ben Slattery. They viewed him, their hands also close to or touching their six-guns, Slattery felt like a freak on display.

"Yes," he said. "I'm asking out. You don't think you could have just got me to come along with you if I weren't?" He stared at Savage, eyes unblinking, and the other man flinched and looked away for a moment. Then he shook his head. "How come you didn't just walk up to the governor's office and let him know about it? He's the one to see."

Slattery said, "I told you." He didn't like explaining himself to Savage. It rubbed him. "I didn't think Fallon would be up, working this late."

Savage spat onto the dusty cobbles of the plaza. "Hell, yes. He's up day and night. He takes this amnesty crap serious."

"And you don't?"

Savage laughed. "Don't tell anybody," he said. He slapped Slattery on the back. "It's just an easy out. I'm protected—we all are—but if anything ever starts popping and somebody needs an extra gun and is willing to pay heavy, why, Charlie Savage is his man."

Slattery stared at the deputy. He'd seen him briefly in the cattle war, riding with The Kid. Savage was a good man, quick, not a bad shot. And loyal to The Kid. Well, The Kid wouldn't think so. Not now. The Kid wouldn't think so at all.

They heard the horse's hoofs clattering into the square. Slattery turned and saw a fat man dismount heavily, panting. At first he thought it was Frick. Then he saw the flabbiness, the white pasty face. Next to him, Savage stiffened. He whispered to Slattery, "That's Chisholm. I'd give my eyeteeth for a shot at that bastard."

Slattery watched the fat man run up to them. A gold watch chain flopped on his black vest.

Chisholm stopped before the two men. He said to Savage, "Is this—the man?"

Slattery smiled thinly. "I'm Ben Slattery," he said. "I've come for amnesty." It was easy, lying to Chisholm. Chisholm looked like the kind of man you naturally lied to.

Chisholm said stiffly, "Good work, Savage," and Savage shrugged and turned his back on the man. "I'll take him in," Chisholm said.

"Suit yourself," Savage said. He started to walk away, and then he turned and came over to Slattery. He said, "You know, Ben, I don't like doing this, don't you. I mean, I don't relish turning men in."

Chisholm's eyes narrowed. He was a flabby-mouthed man, with small dark eyes. He said, "I thought he turned himself in."

Savage let his lip curl. He said, "Well, call it what you like," and he spun away, to the saloon. Slattery wondered whether Savage would beat up any more drunken Pueblos.

Chisholm turned to the deputies lounging in the square. He said, "All right, you men, keep moving. I've got him under control." Slattery wanted to laugh at this pompous fat man. Then Chisholm stared at Slattery and said quietly, "Ben Slattery, you may not know it and you may not believe it now, but I run this Territory." Slattery felt amazement wash over him. Maybe the man wasn't pompous at all. Maybe he really was powerful. Chisholm said, "The general sticks close to his office, signing papers. But I'm the one who brings him the papers. A man throws in with me he stands a fair chance of amounting to something."

"What's all that supposed to mean?" Slattery asked.

"Nothing," Chisholm said easily. "Or maybe something. I don't know. It all depends."

"On what?"

Chisholm's heavy shoulders raised and then fell. It was a delicate movement for so gross a man. There was finesse to Chisholm. He said, "It depends on whether I ever think I need a man to do a job, and whether a man ever feels he wants to get in solid with me."

Slattery felt a chill cross the square. He shivered and said, "What kind of job?"

Chisholm said pleasantly, "How the hell should I know? It all depends." And Slattery knew he wasn't going to go any further.

"You ready to see the general?" Chisholm said.

Slattery squared his shoulders. "Yes."

"Follow me," Chisholm said, walking with mincing, toed-in steps the way some fat men do. They went through the open gate and into the corridor. Slattery was surprised to see that the floor of the palace was earthen, except for crude mortar islands. The pillars and walls were hung with bright Indian blankets, to keep fresh whitewash from rubbing off on any man who lounged up against the inner side of the building. Hollow echoes sprang from the palace corridor as the two men walked, the governor's assistant and the outlaw turning himself in. Slattery wondered whether he could not pull it off right now. He could club

Chisholm from behind, drop the man senseless and silently to the ground. He could move in on the governor, beat the man to death with his gun butt. Then he could walk out of the palace and into the square, announce that he'd received his amnesty and been deputized. He'd move to his horse and be off. It was as simple as that. His hand moved to his gun butt, and from a dark shadow in the corridor a man said, "Don't do that, stranger." Slattery's hand dropped to his side. He'd never seen the man, in the darkness. There were lions in the way, all right, lurking in every cave. Chisholm turned his head and said, "You're not the first man who thought of doing it that way, Slattery. Forget it. You wouldn't get ten steps before they opened up on you."

Slattery said, "Habit, I guess," and he smiled blandly into the fat man's eyes. "A man just has to touch his gun ever so often."

Chisholm chuckled. "A bad habit, though. Especially when I'm the man in front of you. You disappoint me, Ben Slattery."

Slattery said, "Am I going to see the governor or not? I've ridden pretty hard today. I'd like to get this over with."

Chisholm stopped before a door. It loomed large before Slattery, thin yellow light slipping through the crack underneath. Slattery heard a faint scratching. Chisholm rapped on the door, and a man barked out, "Who's there?"

Chisholm said, "It's me, Governor. I've got a man seeking amnesty." Slattery heard the fawning quality in Chisholm's voice and he knew again he had misjudged him. Maybe men naturally lied to Chisholm. He too naturally lied to others. You'd seldom know where you stood with Chisholm.

Slattery heard a chair creak. From inside his office the governor said, "Very well, Mr. Chisholm. Let the man in." Chisholm opened the heavy oak door and said loudly,

"All right, Slattery." His hand reached toward Slattery's arm to grasp the man and propel him into the governor's office, but Slattery stared at Chisholm's hand and brushed it with his body as he walked past.

The governor said, "Slattery?" He stood straight, behind his desk, and Slattery saw eyes like hard blue rocks.

"That's right," he said.

"Ben Slattery?" the governor said, his voice tight, and Slattery felt the disgust, the loathing in the man's throat.

"That's right," he said. "Ben Slattery."

The governor came out from behind his desk. He stood two yards from Slattery, nostrils twitching, eyes flaming out. The man's hatred flowed over Slattery and filled every inch of the room. Behind them, the door closed quietly and Slattery heard Chisholm chuckle once, softly, before the footsteps receded.

The governor said, "You've come for amnesty?" Now it was astonishment Slattery heard.

"That's right." Slattery's mouth was dry.

"How come?" the governor breathed. "How come you've come for mercy? You, of all men?"

Rage thickened Slattery's voice. "Why not?" he said. This erect ice-cold man was ripping him apart, and Slattery didn't know why. White man. Authority. Maybe that was why. "Why not?" he said again, taking a step forward, his hands away from his sides, but clenched. A vein leaped in Slattery's temple. He said, "You've taken other men in and given 'em a clean slate."

Fallon said slowly, wonderingly, "Amnesty for Ben Slattery." Had he been insane when he thought of pardoning men for their crimes? Who was he, anyway, that he'd taken it upon himself to cleanse a man in the face of the law and before the eyes of other men? "You want to give up your gun, quit your side of the law and join ours?"

Slattery said "Ours? You don't mean ours, you mean yours, don't you Governor?"

"Ours," Fallon barked. "Mine and the rest of the law-abiding citizens of this Territory. You want to join us?"

Slattery was silent.

"What's wrong, Slattery?" Fallon snapped. "You come in for a clean slate and you expect to stand there like some dumb animal and hope I'll wave my wand. Is that it? Talk, by God. Right now. Why? Why are you here?"

"Amnesty," Slattery began, but the man cut him off with an impatient wave of his right arm.

"No. Not amnesty. I mean, why now?" Always, Fallon had to find out. Was it fear? Was it relief from a posse? Was it a brief resting place—this amnesty in the capital—until the next man needed an outlaw gun? Why?

"Because," Slattery said slowly, "I'm sick of the whole damn' business. Because I'm tired of it all." He stood straight and he knew he was telling the truth, even though it was a lie. Sure he was sick of it all. He had known that when he'd heard of amnesty for the first time, and he'd known it for sure when they'd offered him five thousand dollars for this job. The last job. He'd been overwhelmed with relief, with the sudden knowledge that he could pack it all in.

But still it was a lie, because now he wasn't seeking amnesty. He was seeking the easy way to put a bullet into Fallon's heart. Saliva formed under Slattery's tongue and his jaw muscles hurt, they were so tightly held.

And Fallon let out his own breath in a long, deep silent sigh. A man had come before him and admitted he was sick of bloodshed. Seven hundred outlaws had stood right here where Slattery was standing, and they'd lied and wheedled and sometimes snarled defiance, but never had one—until now—said he was sickened by what he'd done, and made Fallon believe it. Yes, Fallon nodded, this man meant it. You could see it in the tortured eyes.

He said quietly, "Man, how could you have done it?" For this was Ben Slattery. This was Slattery who stood off at Fort Heck, and no man in the capital would have dared go down there to flush him out. This was Ben Slattery, killer.

Slattery felt the blood leave his face. "Done what?" he asked.

"Kill," Fallon said. "Kill so often. Kill so coldly. Kill, for hire."

Slattery half turned. He thought: I'll just walk out now. They'll believe me. They'll believe I've been deputized, and I'll walk out and get on my horse. I'll go back to Fort Heck and I'll play the only game I know. No running away, no nothing.

But he knew he couldn't, because he still couldn't coldly chop down this man before him. It was one thing not being able to pull off a job; it was another thing turning chicken-hearted, running from it. Frick wouldn't stand for it. A man who could pay five thousand dollars for a job, could afford to pay anything to seek out Slattery for walking out on the job.

And anyway, if he did chop down Fallon—now—how far would he get? There had to be some sheet of paper from Fallon or a word passed into the corridor that the man was clean. No, Slattery thought sharply, not now. Not here.

Fallon said, "Come on, man. I'm waiting to hear."

Slattery shook his head. "I—I can't tell you." He felt the sweat popping out on his brow. "That's—my business." Great memories scraped at his heart.

Fallon stepped back. He was disappointed. Yet he hadn't really expected the man to talk. Still, this one was different. Then he asked the other question they never answered the way he wanted them to, he asked Slattery in a voice that was near a whisper. "Are you sorry for what you've done?"

Slattery's eyes closed for a moment. He let the memories come unhindered. No holding back now. His mind raced back, to where it all began. His eyes closed. He remembered ...

1854. Twenty-three years ago. He was a boy, fourteen. And all around him, the fields of snowy flakes. Cotton. The world was a cotton field. A man walked by, long whip in his hand. The whip raised and fell with a flat slapping noise, and somebody whimpered.

Still, everybody said it wasn't too bad. Ben Slattery didn't know. It was the only place he'd ever seen, the only world, a world of white pods and black hands.

It was Master William Kingston's plantation. Master Kingston was a fine man, Ben Slattery knew. Overseers may have carried whips and on occasions cracked them. They may have snarled out their abuse and obscene orders, and men may have cringed under them and sweated, but Master Kingston was a fine man. He never whipped anybody.

At night, the white world turned black. Ben Slattery rose up with his last basket of cotton, turned it in to the overseer, and walked to the tiny shack within the plantation fields, where he lived with his mother. Ben Slattery knew no other way, so it seemed all right, it seemed fair, he and his mother in a tiny shack, while across a patch of fragrant field, set on a tiny undulating knoll, was Master Kingston's mansion home. It seemed fair, yet when Ben Slattery caught his mother staring out of the open door of the shack (otherwise it was just too hot) toward the big house on the small hill, he wondered why she looked that way. So—distant.

His mother. Tall, so pale she seemed golden by day and like candlelight itself at night. Ben Slattery had heard an overseer nudge another one day in the fields, the overseer a new man, and he'd said, "I sure do like that high yaller," pointing to Ben Slattery's mother, and the other overseer, speaking out of tight lips, looked around quickly to see who was listening, seeing only the boy, and said, "Better not let the old man hear you talk like that." The first overseer said something, and the other one answered, "That's the way it shapes up to me," and then the two of them bent over, laughing like crazy, their lips wet.

Ben Slattery didn't care. He worked hard. He was a big boy, a good boy, his mother said. And at night, though Ben Slattery didn't know it was against the law until later, his mother read to him and taught him the letters and the numbers, until he, too, could read. It wasn't until even later than that he finally figured out how his mother had learned to read and write.

Sometimes the great tall blonde man—the master, himself—came late to the shack, staying half the night, and then leaving. And in the morning, his mother's eyes were misted and far off.

But mostly the world was a cotton field. Slattery put his hands through the soft puffs, piled it all into a basket, carried it proudly, refusing to stagger beneath the weight, listening to the awed overseer saying, "Look at that black boy. Just look at him. He's strong as an ox." And another overseer saying, "That's Ben Slattery. You know." And the two men nodded and smiled with their eyes.

Sometimes the world erupted. Ben Slattery hadn't been well one winter, his throat sore and his head throbbing, and in the field that following spring, he'd fallen down with a basket of cotton. An overseer, seeing the boy face down in the soil, not knowing which of the two hundred hands it was, kicked the boy and brought his whip snaking across the boy's back. Ben had rolled over, crying, and the overseer said, "Oh, my God. It's him."

Later that day, there was talk that Master Kingston had smashed the man's face and sent him packing. Nobody ever saw the overseer again, and nobody ever laid a hand on Ben Slattery again.

And the overseers were always careful to smile at the

boy when he walked past with his load.

Only William Kingston didn't smile when he saw the boy. It made Ben Slattery wonder. He worked even harder when Master Kingston stood near. And the master would walk away quickly, his face troubled. Ben Slattery thought it had to do with other things outside the plantation, things that belonged to that remote world outside the gates, beyond the sycamores, on the other side of the graveled roads where the creaking wagons of cotton rolled out of sight, the last thing Ben Slattery ever seeing being the mountain of fat whiteness on the backs of the wagons.

Always the cotton. Everything seemed to begin and end with the cotton. Breaking the field and planting the seed and reaping the snowy pods. Carrying the baskets, loading the wagons, watching them roll out of sight, pulled by straining mule teams, a black man saying with a bitter smile, "How come they don' make us do thet, too, pull them wagons?" And out there, somewhere, Ben Slattery didn't quite know where, were the rivers and the rails, the pressed cotton all squared up on wharves and piers, waiting to go to the corners of that other world, where men talked about opening up something called Nebraska and by-passing the Missouri Compromise and buying votes for western territory.

There was a girl, Frances Kingston, blonde as her father, slim as a young willow. She was Ben Slattery's age and she played with Ben Slattery, as all the white children of the plantation played with the black slave children, until they got to be "that" age. Frances Kingston came to his shack (though he never went into her house, and that was funny, Ben Slattery sometimes idly thought, but then he didn't know too many things and that just had to be one of the things he didn't know, a boy of fourteen). They played. They talked. Sometimes they even raced after each other, rolling on the ground, wrestling, crying out, "I gotcha, I gotcha" until one or the other begged to be let up.

Ben Slattery remembered how one day Frances Kingston came skipping into the shack, right after lunch. Ben and his mother resting up a few minutes before plunging back into the heat and dust of the fields, Ben's mother lying on her cot, one hand to her chest, kind of easing her breathing along. She'd been having aches and pains right along lately, rheumatism kind of pains, and a little rest at noon, her hand helping her breathing, seemed to uncoil the tightness somewhat.

Francey came in, her face flushed and warm, blonde curls dancing. Ben's mother had eyed the girl critically, looking at the long thin fair legs, the faint shaping out at hip and in at waist, and the tiny budding breasts, the swell of the girl's slender white throat.

She said to Francey, "You better beat it, honey. Us folks got to git out and wuhk." She hummed to herself—always singing, always, always, Ben remembered—staring at the blonde girl whose eyes held some sort of smoking mockery in them that Ben Slattery didn't understand.

Francey said, shaking her hair, "You can't chase me out."

Ben's mother had said, "I ain't a-chasing you, honey child. I'm just telling you what's what. Come on, Ben, we's got wuhk to do."

So Francey had skipped out, and Ben's mother had got off of the bed (but not before a single moan escaped her clenched teeth), and they'd gone to work. But while Ben Slattery bent and strained at the earth, he kept remembering the look of Francey's naked legs, flashing as she skipped off. It was a new thought, a disturbing, a pleasing one. That evening he stood outside the shack, staring at the huge white house, from which music sometimes drifted, and he imagined himself in the house with Francey. He started to walk away and his mother said, "Where you goin' to, son?" getting up on one elbow, the other hand still pressed against her chest. He said, "No place, Ma," and he kept walking.

Near the house he whistled softly, and almost instantly a window opened, and the blonde head looked down. "That you, Ben?" she said, and he said, "Yeah." She said, "What do you want?"

He said, "Come on down." His voice was suddenly thick. He wanted to swallow, couldn't.

"What for?"

"I dunno."

"Tell me."

"I dunno, I tell you. I jes' want you to. That's all."

She giggled, and Ben heard a voice say, "Who are you talking to, Francey?" and Francey said, "Nobody." The window closed.

Ben Slattery waited under a sycamore tree. He waited a half hour, and then he was going to go back (*where would it have ended, if he had gone back?*) when the girl suddenly popped up in front of him, said, "Boo! I sure scared you," and was off, running into the night.

He chased her. He caught her.

They lay exhausted, on a mashed-down stack of hay in the barn near the house where Master Kingston kept his mulch cows. They lay on their backs, side by side, and Francey Kingston said, "When I'm big, I'm going to go round the world in a big boat."

Ben Slattery said, "So'm I."

The girl giggled. "Silly," she said. "You can't."

"Why can't I?"

"You just can't."

"Why?"

"'Cause you're black."

He propped himself. A lantern threw pale light on the girl's exquisite face. He stared at it. He said, "You ain't any lighter than me."

She giggled. "Silly. That's not what counts. You just can't."

For a moment, the borders that held Slattery within one world, wrapped in soft cotton, threatened to crumple and catapult the boy into that other dim dark world.

He leaned back. "Who wants to go round the world, anyway?" he said,

"Sour grapes."

"Ain't not."

"Is so."

"Ain't not."

"I say it is."

He sat up again, angry. He put his hand on the girl's mouth and said, "You say that again, and I'll hush your mouth good for you."

She tried to shrug loose of his hand, but his fingers cut in and held her by the jaw. She grabbed his wrists and tried to wrestle him away. But suddenly he was much stronger. It had never been that way, but suddenly he was much bigger, much more powerful than the girl. He could feel the strength of his own body, and with a gleeful rage, he rolled over on top of her, got to his knees, and straddled her slender writhing body inside his muscular legs. He said, "I can do anything you can. I can read. I can write. I'm stronger."

She struggled briefly. She said, "You let me up, Ben Slattery."

"Uh-uh." He was enjoying himself hugely. "Not until you say I can go round the world too."

"Can't," she panted. "Can't, can't, can't. You're a nigger and you can't."

It was as if some dike in his brain suddenly collapsed, rotted through.

Sure he'd known he was black and she was white. His mother was Negro, and the girl's mother and father were white. He'd known it, and he'd known he lived in a tiny shack and she lived in a great mansion from which music wafted (but so too did music fill his own shack, his mother's husky contralto crooning him to sleep, for years and years, music all around), so there wasn't much difference there. Just a little. He'd known there was this little difference. Yet he'd never really believed it. Now, he did.

He put his hands to the side of the girl's blonde head and he raised up her head four inches from the hay floor. He cradled her skull and he wanted to smash it down, against the floor.

And she took her hands from his wrists and laced them around his neck, pulled gently on his neck and said softly,

"I'm sorry, Ben." He moved forward, toward her, until the shadow of his face covered hers.

William Kingston and his wife Agatha walked into the barn.

They'd come to see a new calf, to show it off to guests who'd come down from Virginia, people they were proud to have at their home, good folk, rich folk, aristocratic, correct.

William Kingston said, "Who's that—*what!*" Then he whirled swiftly and said, "Aggie, get out of here." Agatha Kingston left with their guests, all of them talking fast, trying to cover what they had seen, none of them terribly sure what it was on the barn floor, but somehow guessing.

William Kingston had stood there, one long awful moment, while he went nearly mad. Guilt was like a knife inside. The son he had secretly begetted by a slave and his own blonde daughter of his own lawful marriage and union, lying together.

Then the fury turned aside the guilt (or perhaps it was the guilt that spawned the fury) and William Kingston reached down a great white hand and dragged the boy to his feet. The girl cowered where she crouched, whimpering softly, trying to smooth her clothes, knowing (without knowing) that she had done some terrible wrong.

The boy stood, staring up at Kingston in puzzlement and fear. The man was so enraged. It didn't make sense. What had he done?

Kingston drew back his fist, and with the passion of years of shame and guilt, he smashed the boy's face. The boy fell and got up, blood dripping from the corner of his mouth.

But nothing was doing Kingston any good. He kept trying to say to himself, a black boy, and it made him angry, but it wasn't enough and it wasn't the truth.

The truth of his rage was that the black boy was his own son. And this sin, far greater than the other, just couldn't be punched out of sight. He'd crawled into Cora Slattery's bed, night after night, when it was so pitch dark a man couldn't see the color of his hand before his eyes. It was something he couldn't help, a force that drew him to the shack where the living proof of his sinful passions slumbered in another cot. But always at night. He couldn't stop, but he could keep it buried from sight.

Now he could twist his own eyes from their sockets, he'd still never get over the sight of this boy and his daughter.

He wanted to rid himself of the sight. He'd kill the boy, that would do the trick, he thought, his mind crumbling beneath the weight of its own sin. He groped behind him, fingers finding a pitchfork. He raised it, aimed it at the defenseless boy before him. But he couldn't quite kill Ben Slattery, because the crime wasn't really the boy's. So he made a jab with the fork, his fingers wet with sweat, and the boy swerved back, throwing up a hand. There was a tiny nicking pain at the boy's wrist, but he didn't really feel it.

The pitchfork fell from Kingston's nerveless fingers, and lay between them.

The moment was passing. Kingston had not come to

grips with the weight that now seemed about to burst his very skull. He couldn't stand it any longer. He felt his body begin to shake, and he knew his mouth was open and his lips were moving, but he had absolutely no control over the words he said.

He felt like some great ox, just clubbed and already dead, but refusing to fall. The shaking was so great.

He said quietly, his face a pale dead glow in the barn, "You mustn't kiss that boy, Francey. He's your brother."

There, he thought, hearing the words as if spoken by someone else. I've explained it all clearly, and the whole thing will disappear. I've made it very simple. He closed his eyes, knowing that when he opened them, it would be over.

He opened his eyes and there was the boy, before him. He put out a hand to keep himself from falling, the shaking was so bad again, and Ben Slattery stared at the hand, the hair at Kingston's knuckles like golden tufts. Then he looked at his own hands, saw first they were nearly the same color, but not quite. He kept his eyes down, while everything seemed to strike home at once. Everything was nearly the same, but not quite. He was almost white. Not quite. He could do nearly anything Francey Kingston could do. Not quite.

He wanted very badly to do something about what had just happened and what he had just heard. But he couldn't. He'd been a slave for fourteen years. He said, "I'm sorry, Master Kingston," and he walked past the big blond man and to the shack where he lived with his mother and where he knew he belonged.

He walked in, and his mother turned a contorted face to him and said in a voice nowhere as loud as a whisper, "Son, son, I been callin' you and callin' you. Git a doctor, I'm sick."

He fled, screaming.

The doctor had come, but the rheumatic heart had already burst. She lay on her cot, the hands still pressing the rib cage up and down, breathing, but more dead than alive.

William Kingston stood next to the cot. Ben Slattery stood on the other side, his dying mother between them.

The doctor had looked swiftly at all three of them, summed it up in a quick nod, and then did what he could. He said, once, irritably, "If I'd been here a little earlier," and then he cut it off. But Kingston had looked quickly at Ben Slattery and, when their eyes met, Kingston could hardly bear the hate that flowed at him and into him.

When it was over, a little before midnight, Kingston said wearily, "I think you'd better look at that boy's wrist. He's—cut himself."

The doctor unwrapped the handkerchief Ben Slattery had tied about his bleeding arm. "God," he said, "how'd that happen?"

But nobody answered him.

After the funeral, an overseer found the boy crying under a tree and took him to the big house. Kingston wanted to see him.

It was the first time Ben Slattery was ever in the house.

Kingston stood in a huge room—a library, Ben Slattery learned later—and he said, without looking up when the boy entered the room, "Sit down, Ben." Ben sat. Kingston held a piece of paper in his hand. "Here," he said. "If anybody stops you, show them this. You're free." He wanted to say much more, but he couldn't, nor did the boy let him, staring like a lump of stone. He gave the boy five dollars and he gave him a horse, hating what he was doing and therefore hating the boy for making him do it, and he sent the boy out.

The cool disciplined hatred did not begin until the gates closed. He was outside, for the first time in his life, on the other side of the barrier that marked the free man from the caged.

He rode the red clay roads, amazed to find the horizon still so distant, never dreaming that the far-off rivers and wharves were really so far off. He had no idea of where he was headed. Away, was his only direction.

When he heard people, he pulled the horse to the side of the road or, if there was brush, he and the horse melted into it and out of sight, his fingers clutching the paper Kingston had given him.

But nobody seemed to care.

He wasn't always able to slink into shadows; he wasn't always able to hide. Sometimes he passed people, on foot, on horse, in wagons. Some of them looked at him and looked away. One or two waved their hands in mild un-thinking greeting. Some smiled.

Nobody knew.

For fourteen years he'd been black. He'd lived in a shack because that shack was owned by a white man. He was owned by the same white man. His mother was owned by the same white man. He worked in a cotton field be-cause he had to. It wasn't hard and he didn't mind, and he still remembered how the white overseers had nodded in admiration at the way he carried his filled baskets of cotton fluff. But even if he had minded, he would have still worked there. He had no choice. He belonged to the white man.

And then one day, he no longer belonged to the white man. He was free.

He stopped at a farmhouse, fingers still holding the piece of paper buried in a pocket, and knocked at the backdoor. He said, "Ma'am, I'm looking for work. I'm a strong boy." The woman took him to her husband, who put Ben to work cutting wood. He worked there for a week, and then he left, with a little money, and he kept moving, away.

Nobody ever stopped him.

That was when the hate began to grow large, like a hard iron bar inside. There wasn't any real difference that anybody could see, yet he had been made to live as though there were, for fourteen years.

Once he tried to tell himself he ought to be glad he wasn't real black, because he'd never be able to pass himself off this way, but it didn't make him feel any better. It made him feel worse, more coldly angry. It made him so angry that it twisted him around in his saddle, his eyes searching for Master Kingston's plantation. He knew he'd never settled with Master Kingston for what had happened. Sometimes he thought he could forgive Master Kingston everything—the fourteen years and everything, the whole awful moment in the barn, the stabbed wrist— but he couldn't forgive him that Ben Slattery's mother had been calling him and calling him, and Ben Slattery hadn't heard her. He couldn't forgive that, especially when he remembered the doctor saying, "If I'd been here a little earlier."

That was Master Kingston's fault, and it made Ben Slattery so angry he wanted to go back and kill the man. But he had no idea where Kingston was, where the plantation was. Behind him, that was all he knew. He plodded on, away.

And sometimes he'd wake up at night, silently screaming, remembering the way his hands looked and the way Kingston's hands looked, so alike, but not quite. The next morning he'd slip away from wherever he'd been living and working. He'd move, again. Away. And the hate kept growing. Soon, that's all there was. Just hate. Hate, named Ben Slattery. Hate for white men, for authority.

..."Sorry?" he said, opening his eyes, looking at Fallon. Revulsion passed through him. This was a white man. This was authority. He waited for the hatred for this man to seep into him. Nothing happened. "I don't know.

Maybe. I don't know. It's—hard to say."

Fallon nodded. "Give me your gun."

Slattery stared at the governor's extended hand, and he remembered Kingston with the pitchfork. He said stupidly, "I thought we were supposed to keep our guns."

"We?" Fallon said, his voice mocking Slattery. "Who's we? You working with some gang, Slattery?"

Slattery flushed. "No. I meant the men who come in for amnesty."

Fallon persisted. "You're not in cahoots with The Kid, are you, Slattery? You two use the same saloon, down at Fort Heck. This isn't some plot hatched between you two, is it?"

Slattery forced himself to grin. It was funny, in a way. "No," he said. "I've known The Kid for two or three years, but not that way. We never worked together. I still thought men asking amnesty kept their guns."

Fallon turned his back. "Some do. Some don't. Some just get their pardons and take off. I thought that's the way you'd do it. The men who insist on keeping their guns, have to work with us. Is that the way it's going to be with you? You have to keep that damn' gun?"

Slattery looked at the .45. He touched it with his finger tips. "Yeah," he said softly, "I have to keep it."

Fallon whirled. "What for?" he snapped.

Slattery shrugged. "You never know," he said, evading the man's eyes. They were like dagger points. "I—I wouldn't know how to get along without it."

Fallon's voice softened. "Try, Slattery. Why don't you try?"

He swallowed. "I can't."

"Why not?"

Blood pounded in Slattery's throat. "Damn it," he roared, "I can't."

Fallon's lip curled in contempt. That's all they were, noise and a gun. Take it away from them, and they were like the cannons overhead, rusted, futile, empty. "All right," he said crisply. "You can keep your gun. But first we have a little ceremony. You'll probably think me a fool, but I still like to feel you've turned in your gun and we've turned it back to you." He didn't do it with all of them, just some of them, those Fallon thought he might reach. It was the least he could do. It put the outlaw in the hands of the law, and defenseless, for a brief moment. Then the law, in its gentle greatness, was able to hand the gun back. He'd explained it to Chisholm once when he'd first started amnesty, and Chisholm had smiled and said, "Like playing God, ain't it, Governor?" Fallon had wanted to slap the man's face.

Slattery said slowly, "That sounds pretty sensible to me. It might teach a man something."

Fallon said, "Give me your gun then. Let's see what it teaches you."

Slattery's hand strayed back to the holster. He touched the butt, felt the cool reassuring metal. Then he slipped the gun clear, spun it on his trigger finger in the trigger guard and handed it butt-first to Fallon. "Take it," he said indifferently.

Fallon took the gun, seeing he'd lost the man somehow. Well, he'd come farther with Slattery than he had with most. The man had seemed sorry. He understood about turning his gun in. Fallon wished to hell he knew why a man like Slattery had bought into the gun business.

Fallon looked down at the gun. He said, "No notches?"

Slattery stiffened. "In my head," Slattery said.

"You count them?"

"No," Slattery said. "Not really. But I guess I remember."

"That's an awful thing to remember."

"Other people have awful things to remember too," Slattery said impatiently, thinking of a man named Kingston who'd made a slave of his own son.

Fallon nodded. "I guess they have." He was thinking of Chickamauga. "Here," he said, passing the gun back to Slattery.

Slattery slipped the gun into the holster and absently patted the butt. Fallon's eyes narrowed and the loathing for the man crawled back. Slattery said, "Is that it?"

Fallon said, "Not quite."

Slattery felt a quiver of fear. Not quite. Nothing was ever finished. "What else?"

Fallon said, in a voice stripped of emotion, a tired dull voice, "I hereby deputize you under the laws of the Territory ..." He droned on and Slattery listened, in astonishment. It was over.

He said, when Fallon had stopped talking, "You mean I'm now a deputy of this Territory?"

"That's right."

"How about the rest of the country? How about crimes committed in other states?"

"Not many ask that," Fallon said. "You're a smart man, Slattery. I've been able to get a blanket pardon for you men. It's good in every state and territory in the Union."

Fallon went back to his desk and picked up a small blank sheet of paper. Swiftly he scrawled Ben Slattery's amnesty. He handed the sheet to Slattery. "There," he said. "You're free."

Slattery stared at the sheet of paper in his hand. Next to the white paper, his hand looked dirty.

6

Chisholm stood at the portico, facing the square, his heavy back to Slattery. But the big man spun quickly and laughed a quick grunting sound when Slattery started to stride onto the dusty cobbles of the plaza.

"You got it," he said, looking at the piece of paper in Slattery's hand, pale and flickering before the dying oil lanterns that ringed the open area.

"I got it," Slattery said.

Chisholm watched a sentry stroll the cobbles. He said quietly, "What do you think of the old man?"

Slattery said, "You're a busybody, Chisholm," and started to walk by, toward the hitching posts.

Chisholm chuckled and tagged along, mopping his brow with a large silk bandanna. He had to take three steps to each one of Slattery's. "I am," he agreed pleasantly. "What do you think of him?"

Slattery said, "Shut up, Chisholm. I remember you from Jackson County. I know how busy you were then. That's what I think of you."

Chisholm laughed again. Slattery wondered what it took to rub the man wrong. The governor's assistant put his hand on Slattery's arm. He said, "Kind of curious, coming from you. I mean, a killer smearing a man who maybe picked up a cow or two running around loose."

Slattery pulled his arm from under the man's hand. "Chisholm," he said, his voice low and flat, but carrying across the cobbles, and the sentry stopped his indolent pacing and let his fingers trail to his gun butt, "listen to me. If amnesty means anything, you better watch that tongue of yours. You tell me you run this place. All right. Then you know what amnesty means. I'm not a killer. Get that? I'm not a killer."

Chisholm started to grin and then stared again at the man. He said, "By God, you take this stuff seriously."

"Don't you? Or are you figuring some way to steal more cows?"

Chisholm pulled back and Slattery knew he had stung him. Chisholm said stiffly, "There's amnesty for stolen cows too. The governor's putting an end to cow stealing. All men who have cows on their grass can consider them their cows, as soon as Fallon signs the order. It's all drawn up, waiting."

Slattery swore quietly. "So you're in the same class as me and the rest of us. Not a damn' bit better. What do you know? And you're trying to make me feel filthy. You're a fat swine, Chisholm."

Slattery watched his eyes become pig-small and hard. The pupils turned black. Chisholm said, "You're heading for trouble, friend."

"Not from you," Slattery said. "You don't look like trouble to me. I'll just make sure I don't turn my back when I'm near you."

Chisholm regained his composure swiftly. "I don't shoot men in the back," he said. "That's not my line."

"No," Slattery said. "I guess it's not. I guess you're more the kind who hires men to shoot men in the back."

Chisholm nodded, the eyes like tiny black points. "That's right," he said. "Remember that. You'll never know when a man's behind you whether I put him there."

Slattery's hand twitched. In the old days, he'd have beat the man's face bloody for saying a thing like that. In the old days. He said, lightly, "Chisholm, from what you say, amnesty for cows doesn't go into effect until the governor signs it. I'd walk easy until then, if I were you."

Slattery had no real idea of what he meant, but had he known he'd have got the reaction he got, he'd have said it the way he had, when he had.

Chisholm started a heavy oath, cut it short, raised his

right arm as if he were going to punch Slattery, dropped his arm heavily to his side, the big meaty hand slapping the meatier thigh. Then he said, through a mouth suddenly bloodless, lips like silver scissors, "Nothing will stop that amnesty order. Those cows are mine."

"Well," Slattery breathed. "Well. So the governor is protecting cow thieves too. No wonder you nudged yourself so quick and close to Fallon. You really are a fat swine."

Chisholm said thickly, "You better watch yourself, Slattery. I swear, you better."

"Or?"

The fat man raised a hand to Slattery's face. "Or I'll—I'll—" He cut it short, panting. "Get out of here, Slattery. Just stay out of my way."

Slattery nodded. He said pleasantly, "Good night, Chisholm," and walked off to his horse, feeling a bit better suddenly. He stood next to the bay, fingers drumming on the leather saddle horn. Then he patted the animal and went to the saddlebag and readied a nosebag of feed. He looped the bag over the horse's head and waited until the animal began munching. Then he walked away, toward the saloon where he had been drinking when he ran into Charlie Savage.

He walked through the batwings, hearing the room clam up a bit, knowing they knew him now, most of them, knowing he was Ben Slattery, sizing him, casing him. In the old days, there'd have been a warming feeling, knowing people knew who he was, even when he realized it was always better not to be known at all in his line of living. But Slattery knew he was a loner and, like all loners, he also knew he wanted to be in, not out. There was another reason too, Slattery knew, more important than a lonely man's need for acceptance by the tinhorn sloppy-eyed crowd that filled the barrooms of the Southwest. Slattery's hand crept to his left wrist and fingered the lumpy puffy dead tissue of skin. He looked at his wrist, and he saw instead the piece of paper that said he wasn't a killer any more. He balled up the paper and shoved it into a pocket. He said, "*Aguardiente.* The bartender hustled him a shot and walked away.

Slattery turned with his drink, feeling the good wood of the bar counter behind his back, nudging him. Nobody stood behind him now. He couldn't count the bartender. The bartender didn't wear a gun. The room was in front of Slattery, a strange motley of men, some honest, some dishonest, some both, and nearly all of them leeches of the United States Government and its Territorial hacks. He saw Charlie Savage, flush-faced, the mean hard look like a smear of pale blood across his eyeballs, and Slattery wondered how long Savage would stay within the confines of the law. Savage sat with two other men, their eyes lazy and hooded, shoulders hunched, mouths like razor slashes. Savage looked up then, feeling the weight of Slattery's eyes, and he waved his hand. "Come here," he said, importantly, letting the room know he was equals with Ben Slattery and maybe even more than equals.

Slattery shrugged and carried his drink over to the table. Now he was in the center of the room, under the gun, but he didn't care. Not caring was another new feeling. He figured he was just tired. He sat.

Savage said, "Slattery, this here runt is Eddie Rico." Slattery looked at the tall skinny man on Savage's right. The thin slash of mouth moved and the man said, "Slattery," and Slattery nodded. "And this fellow is Fats Jefferson." Slattery nodded at the round-faced heavy-jowled youngster. The butts of .45s were table-top high, within reach. They looked like men who had to have their guns within reach. But they didn't have the look of the men at McCall's saloon. The Kid would have run them out of here just by walking through the batwing door.

Savage said, "You see the governor?"

Slattery nodded. "I'm in," he said. "Now let's stop talking about it. I'm tired of having people ask me."

Rico said, "That's how we all felt, at first," and Fats Jefferson smiled and nodded.

Slattery knew what was happening. He was being lumped with them. Savage had set the pace, ordering him to their table. Now the others were whittling him to their size. He felt contempt for them, then contempt for himself. Who was he, anyway? What was this in him, a feeling of superiority for being in the elite? Elite of what? Of killers that's what. He downed his drink and said to Fats Jefferson, because he looked the easiest, "Run on up there, boy, and fill it up." He poked his empty at the chubby young man. Jefferson stared at the glass and then got up and brought Slattery his drink.

Savage said, "What do you hear from The Kid, Slattery?"

Slattery shook his head. "Mind your business."

Savage flushed. "I was with The Kid. Don't forget that."

"And I wasn't," Slattery said. "I never had to be. Don't forget that."

Savage's fingers gripped the table top. Then he relaxed and said, "What's on tap now, Ben? Going out west?"

Slattery shrugged. "No. What for?"

Rico said, "Man, there's money out there like fruit ripe for picking."

Slattery thought of the five grand he'd have within a week. "Sonny," he said, "there's money here too. For the right men."

Savage snorted. "Like hell there is. Cattlemen's money. And one man's got that all nicely corralled."

"Chisholm," Fats Jefferson said, making it sound like a dirty word.

Slattery said, "Doesn't anybody give Chisholm any trouble?"

Savage said, "They try, maybe, but they don't get far. He's in too solid with the governor."

Rico said, "He's a cow thief and the governor's protecting him. Nobody else stands a chance."

Slattery thought of the Mexican family in the sheep town near the Pintada. Pinning their hopes on The Kid. Hoping they'd get back some of that rich graze where Chisholm and the rest of the beef men now had their cows: siding with outlaws just because they felt the government had sided with the cowmen who had stolen their land. They made it all so simple, the Spanish sheepherders. A man like Slattery came by and they immediately tabbed him as one of themselves. They had an underground railway of sorts, leading to a man named Lopez, where Slattery, or anybody fighting the men in the capital, could take refuge. But what good would it do? What would a man accomplish? Only if he started a cattle war, got the cattlemen fighting, upset the government and got a weaker man into the plaza. Then—maybe —the little man, the sheeper and the little cowpuncher, the nester, might find himself with a quarter section of decent land again, instead of thin grass and crumbling rock on the wrong side of the hill.

Slattery said, "No big cattlemen around here trying to cut up on Chisholm?"

Fats Jefferson looked around quickly. Then he bent his head and said, "They tell me there's a group of ranchers from Jackson County trying to get their cows back from Chisholm. They say he stole fifteen or twenty thousand head during the wars. They want 'em back."

Slattery said, "Can't say I blame them."

Rico said, "They call themselves some sort of Cattlemen's Association. They've brought in a man named Frick—that his name, Fats?—to rod the outfit. Least, that's what I hear."

Slattery said, "Frick?" Both Jefferson and Rico nodded. "How they going about it?" Slattery asked.

Rico spread his hands. "All I know is what I hear down

the old grapevine."

Savage said, "I know how I'd go about it. I'd gyp-pin-nacle that bastard Chisholm, that's what I'd do."

Slattery said carefully, "And that would leave the governor. Then what?" Granted a man could station himself behind some gypsum hill and could ambush Chisholm, where would that leave you? These men were fools.

Savage snarled. "Who the hell cares? I'd have cut down Chisholm."

Slattery said, "If I were Fallon, and somebody shot down my right-hand man, I'd just get a little tougher myself."

The others were silent and Slattery knew they agreed with him. Frick wasn't gunning for Chisholm. He just wanted Fallon out of the way. Some of the admiration he'd felt for Fallon had dissipated. The man backed Chisholm, and Chisholm was a cow thief. When Fallon wrote out his amnesty for cows and put it in effect, Frick and his group would be through. Jefferson said Chisholm stole fifteen or twenty thousand head of cattle during the Jackson Wars. Cows were bringing twenty dollars, twenty-two-fifty at the rails in Abilene. If Fats Jefferson was right, that'd be over three hundred thousand dollars. A fortune was at stake. No wonder, then, that Frick could afford five thousand dollars for this job. Cow empires pivoted on Slattery and his gun.

He said to Savage, "Where does this Frick hang out?"

Savage looked closely at Slattery. "Does most of his drinking at a bar on Cajon Street. That's the next street over. Why?"

Slattery shrugged. "I think I met him once. I might want to look him up. Short skinny fellow with a mustache?"

Jefferson shook his head. "No. Big guy. Clean shaven."

Slattery grinned. "Wrong Frick. How about Fallon? Does he live in that palace?"

Savage said, "Sure. Where else?"

"Alone?"

Fats Jefferson smirked. "With his daughter." He licked his lips. "Man, she's a piece of flesh."

"No wife?" Slattery said.

Rico said, "Widower. What's it to you, Slattery?"

"Nothing. I was just wondering how come he was working there so late. But since he lives there, I guess it adds up." He didn't know how awkward it sounded, but he didn't think they'd see through it. The Kid, maybe, but not these fools. He got up and said to Jefferson, "I'll repay that favor, boy. Give me your empty," and he swiftly strode to the bar, refilled the glasses and returned to the table. Jefferson's face was flushed, delighted Slattery had carried his drink to him. Jefferson said, "They tell me, Slattery, you draw as fast as The Kid."

Savage measured Slattery, eyes narrowed. "That so, Ben?"

Slattery said easily, "I don't know. We never drew against each other."

Rico said, "It is true you don't have a trigger? That you just snap the hammer?"

Slattery said, irritation laced into his voice "Don't be chumps." He took his black gun out and laid it on the table and Jefferson moved his fingers toward it and then dropped them into his lap. The gun looked heavy and huge, lying naked on the table.

Rico said, "No sights? How come?"

Savage said, "They snag. Who needs sights anyway? It's just a question of getting the gun out first. At three feet, who needs sights? Right, Ben?"

Slattery stared at the gun and then hefted it and slipped it back into his holster. The gun disgusted him. So did putting it on display. It was bravado. He was full of bravado lately. That act last night, with the glasses in McCall's saloon. What was he trying to prove? That he wasn't afraid of The Kid? He downed his drink quickly, realizing he was drinking too much and too fast. There was a rubbery feeling in his thighs. He said, "I guess that does me. It's been a long day." He stood up, knowing for sure how unsteady he was.

Savage studied him and said, "Where you sleeping, Slattery? Hotel?"

Slattery waved his hand. "Out there."

"What for? Need the price of a room?"

Slattery said, "Don't suck up to me, Savage. I don't like it." He walked away, feeling his back muscles tighten as he passed Savage, and then he was nearing the door. A bandy-legged cowpuncher got in his way and Slattery shoved him aside, the man saying, "Hey, who you shoving?" Slattery said, "You, bucko, want to make something of it?" The man growled and faded into the shadows and Slattery wandered into the chill night. But there was no sleep now, he knew. He found Cajon Street and another cantina, and this one served rye whisky as well as rum. He had three ryes before he stumbled out, glassy-eyed and knowing for sure he wouldn't be able to walk far enough or straight enough to find his horse, but walking anyway, and finding instead another cantina.

The rest was a whirling red smear in his mind, in weaving patches and long gray blanks. He remembered a bartender saying, "No more for now, Slattery," and Slattery reached across the bar and took the bottle from the man's hand and tilted it to his mouth. When he put it down again, an inch of whisky had gone.

He remembered a girl, sitting cross-legged outside the cantina, stirring a hot bowl of chili with a big spoon, and looking up at Slattery with a flashing smile, her head bent so that her brown breasts lolled against the low-cut *camisa*. She had said, "Chili, señor?" and he'd said, "No," just staring at the brown breasts, the girl letting him stare, thinking he would change his mind. But he didn't, and she said, "*Barata*. Cockroach."

He wandered down the street, smiling foolishly, until he found another cantina. He was bone-achingly tired but he wasn't sleepy and he wasn't getting any drunker. He didn't think he could get any drunker.

It was in the sixth or seventh cantina on Cajon Street that he found Frick, sitting alone at a rear table, a glass of beer in front of him, half full. Slattery saw the big graying man in the sourdough jacket, knew him instantly, and knew somehow that Frick was one of the things he'd been looking for that night. There were other things too, but none quite as easy to put a handle to as Frick.

Frick glanced up as Slattery's weaving shadow fell across his table, and his brow furrowed when he saw how drunk the man was. He looked around first, and then realized it didn't matter. Sitting in the saloon, he'd heard men talking about Slattery, how the man had come up for his amnesty. Everybody in the saloon seemed to know it, so he could know it as well. He said, "Sit down, man, before you fall down." Slattery sat.

"You made it pretty damn' fast," Frick said.

"That's how I work. I saw him."

Frick leaned forward. "Good," he said. "I figured you had. The whole town must be talking about you."

Slattery smirked, like a schoolboy. He felt like strutting. He said, "I've got amnesty."

Frick nodded, "That was the way I thought you'd do it."

Slattery said stupidly, "I'm free, Fallon says. Ain't that funny?" Frick laughed a hollow laugh. Slattery said, "No, it's not." Then he looked at Frick, wondering whether Frick minded he was drunk. Well, to hell with him. He was free to get drunk anyway, even if he wasn't free to do anything else.

Frick said quietly, "When do you think you'll do it?"

"How the hell should I know? I just saw him, I told you."

"Soon? It's got to be soon, you know. I—we—want it over with."

"So do I," Slattery said. He waved a finger in Frick's face. "I know why you want it so quick."

Frick shrugged. "If you'd asked at that saloon at Fort Heck, I'd have told you. You didn't want to hear me then."

"That was then," Slattery said. "I must have changed my mind."

"Just so you don't change it on the job," Frick said.

"Watch and see," Slattery said.

Frick nodded. "I will, all right. That's what I'm doing up here."

Slattery said shrewdly, "You aiming for Chisholm, too?"

Frick started and then said, "Shut up."

Slattery said, "You know, it doesn't quite jibe. It doesn't mesh." The words came out all slushed, but he knew what he was saying.

"What doesn't mesh?"

"You," Slattery said. "Wanting Fallon, not worrying about Chisholm."

"Suppose you leave Chisholm to me," Frick said.

"And if he gets in the way?" Slattery said.

Frick chewed his lip and then drank from his beer glass. "He won't," Frick said.

"But if he does?"

"I said he won't."

"And I heard you."

There was something fishy here, Slattery felt. Still, what was he trying to do? He had a job. There was no use trying to make it mushroom. Too many jobs had mushroomed on other men, got out of control. And a killer found himself in chains or dead. You begin with one man and you end with one man, if you're smart. Otherwise, you're gunning down bystanders, men who suddenly feel obliged to go diving for their guns. And the dead pile up, and maybe you're part of the pile. It was there that Slattery stood out, he knew. No bystanders. Never a witness. He wiped his brow with the back of his hand, trying to forget the one time—the first time—there'd been bystanders, witnesses.

Slattery said, "All right, have it your way," and Frick looked relieved. "I'll pull it off when Fallon's alone."

Frick nodded and said, "That's the way."

If Slattery had had a choice, he'd have made it Chisholm, and not Fallon, out of personal spite. But personal spite had no place here. "Just Fallon," he repeated.

Frick said, "And quickly. The governor might sign that order one of these days. You know what I'm talking about?"

Slattery winked. "Of course I do."

Frick got up. "You can find me in here most any night. If I'm not here, I'll probably be at home. I'm living at El Camino del Mar."

Slattery laughed and said, "What ocean is that?"

"You don't get drunk like this often, do you?" Frick asked.

"That's my business," Slattery said.

"No, it's not. It's my business too."

Frick walked out. Slattery watched him move with the importance of a big man, like a governor or a killer or a cattle boss. Slattery waited until the batwings stopped swinging. Then he stood up, found his balance and walked unsteadily to the bar. A man loomed in front of him and Slattery stumbled against him, and the man said, "Who the hell do you think you are?" Slattery said, "Ben Slattery."

He fell flat on his face then, and he never felt himself being carried to the door and thrown into the rutted street, landing heavily on his left shoulder and side.

7

The Kid forded the Pintada just before sundown, moving with unconscious grace, the sun glinting from his left front and bouncing off the glowing unlined face, the soft and beardless skin. He had watched the tiny dust spiral move along the river, sheltered at times by the cottonwoods but always visible to any one who wished to watch. And when the spiral was obscured, The Kid had spurred the gray mare until they stood on a high mesa, watching for the big rider and his gelding to come back into view. It had been shockingly easy, because Slattery hadn't seemed to care.

The Kid's face broke into a tiny sneer, scorn for the big man. This was Ben Slattery, a greenhorn, leaving a trail like the arroyos that cut deep furrows along the brown rocky soil of the sheep towns.

There was only one place Slattery was going. There was only one thing out there, in the direction Slattery rode: the capital. And in the capital there could be only one thing Slattery wanted: amnesty. Slattery had lied to The Kid, and The Kid was glad he had. There was no swerving now; it was a duel, and The Kid was even more glad that Slattery had showed him how good he was, with that trick shooting in One-Eye McCall's saloon. It would be no pushover, The Kid knew, and that was good. It had been a long time—in The Kid's way of marking time— that he hadn't had a pushover. He remembered the Texan named Brant who'd been the last—number nineteen. He'd kept up his promise, one for every year of his life. He was ahead of his promise. Eighteen years—nineteen kills. Slattery would be number twenty, unless somebody else got in his way before.

Slattery would be better than number nineteen had been,

better, probably, than any of them had been. Brant had been a fool, a Texan who thought like all Texans, that he was God's gift to the gun. He challenged The Kid in a barroom full of Texans, figuring The Kid wouldn't dare move. So The Kid had said "All right" and he put his hands behind his back. The giggle started to break through, pitched up almost scream-high, and Brant had goggled at him, not quite believing The Kid was really dueling him, with his hands behind his back that way. So Brant moved slow, not wanting to break the tableau of The Kid, motionless, defenseless. And The Kid waited until Brant's right hand, all fumble and jitter, reached his holster. Then The Kid moved, and Brant started to tremble, seeing The Kid's right hand like a streak of light. Brant got his gun out, fell to his knees, grabbing the gun with both hands to hold it steady and The Kid kept right on giggling, laughing now, tears spilling down his cheeks. He shot Brant four times in the throat. The man's head had bent back like a twisted chicken's.

Then The Kid stopped laughing and looked at the shocked crowd. They'd never before seen a man scared to death. He looked down at his .45 and sheathed it. He said, "That was four rounds, in case you didn't count 'em." He didn't add what they knew: there was another round in the gun. The Kid, like most of them, carried five rounds at all times. The gun rested on the single empty chamber so he wouldn't find himself stumbling on horseback and shooting his fool leg off. Slattery was different; he carried six rounds because Slattery weighed the chances of his falling off or accidentally discharging his gun, against the need to have every round he could carry, and he chose to carry six rounds, not five.

The Kid had walked out of the Texas barroom after Brant and rode back to McCall's. Nobody followed him. Nobody ever had. He'd never known a posse on his back.

Now the gray mare found a footing of pine needles, dry

and spongy. They rode, wedded, The Kid's lean legs gripping the bulging sides of the mare. She was a good horse, slow and slouch-gaited and with incredible wind. She never tuckered out, but then The Kid knew he was a light burden, and he knew too that he seldom ran the horse hard. He'd never had to.

He followed Slattery's tracks toward a stinking sheep town, pocking the hills like a series of small mounds of dung. He called out, "Hello, greasers," and he waited.

A man poked his head out of his *jacal*, and The Kid took off his black low-brimmed Philadelphia Stetson that had set him back twenty-five dollars. The yellow hair glinted in the sun. The man gulped and said, "*Quien es?*" knowing who it was.

The Kid said, "Me, that's who. The Kid." The man came out, his hands as far from his sides as he could get them. The Kid laughed and said, "Not me, pal. I don't have anything against you. I'm just checking up on a friend of mine, riding through here earlier."

The man said, "I see no rider today." The Kid tapped his holster and the man said, "Oh, you mean the man who rode up to Salusito and swapped his horse?"

"You remember right, pal," The Kid said.

The man waved his arm toward the next *jacal*. "Salusito. He and his wife sold him a horse."

The Kid said, to be dead sure, "Big man? Around noon?" The man nodded and licked his lips.

The Kid took a silver dollar from his pocket and spun it in the air and caught it. Then he turned it over, staring at it while the man kept licking his lips. The Kid said, "Thanks," and sailed the heavy coin to the dirt at the man's feet. The man scrambled and clutched the dollar and said, "God bless you, Kid, God bless you."

The Kid dismounted and said, "Mind my horse."

The man looked as if The Kid had given him another dollar. He ran to the mare and led it to a water trough, stared in and cursed wildly. "Dolores, Dolores, come quick," he cried, and the mica door of the mud hut was pushed aside and a young girl, maybe fifteen or sixteen, stooped her head and came out. The girl was as tall as The Kid, slender and olive-skinned, her body curving into the lush ripe roundness of a Spanish woman, but not yet overblown. She moved slowly to her father, knowing The Kid was staring at her. She'd been listening from the door and she knew who he was. The father said, "Get water, quick. This is The Kid's horse," and the girl's head moved with languid poise toward the blond boy. The Kid nodded, his eyes coldly mocking, and the girl was flustered. "Quick," her father said, and she fled to the spring. The Kid watched her, while she bent and worked the pump and then she came back toward them, a bucket of water on her head, her body swaying unconsciously, the flaring hips rolling gently. The girl moved to the trough and emptied the bucket, and she said to her father, "More?" He shook his head and led the horse to the galvanized iron trough.

The Kid said, "Thanks, pal. Watch her." He walked away from the girl who was not used to seeing men walk away so unconcerned and she chewed on her lip, staring with dark smoldering eyes at the boy. The father said, "Dolores," and the girl didn't move. "Dolores," he said again, more sharply, and the girl, still watching The Kid, said, "What is it?" If The Kid went up to the capital, she would go up, too. She would collect the money from the villagers to take up to Lopez, so he could buy more guns. It was time, again, that they brought some money to Lopez. Yes, she would volunteer to go, that is if The Kid were going up to the capital. Her father said, "That is The Kid, you understand?"

The girl nodded impatiently. He was The Kid, and she was a sheeper's daughter. Still, all the *Americanos* had always looked at her with the full blade of lust on their faces, frank with desire. Never had she returned their looks. But this boy had spurned her and it angered her. Of course, it was more than anger, more than vanity—it was The Kid. He was like a young god. And yet, she thought, so little, so delicate, so boyish. She pictured herself cradling the blond head to her swelling breast. She walked away from the picture, into the *jacal*, to the kitchen, where she helped her mother with the supper. Frijoles and chili. *Atole*. Always the same.

The Kid stood outside Salusito's *jacal*. He said, "Salusito?" A man poked his head out, saw The Kid and came out, gravely. He said to The Kid, "A second honor today. Even greater than the first."

"You sold Ben Slattery a horse?" The Kid said.

Salusito said, "No, Kid. I traded a man—he may have been Ben Slattery, I did not ask—my very best horse for his good but not-so-good horse. It was the least I could do for a friend and *compadre* of The Kid's."

The Kid ignored the man's obsequiousness. He said, "He say where he was riding?"

The man nodded.

"Where?"

It was something one did not discuss with others, another man's business, his directions, his plans. But this was The Kid, and naturally things were different with The Kid. Besides, Slattery had said he knew The Kid, and now The Kid was confirming this.

"To the capital, of course. Where else?"

"He say why?"

The man's face broke into a grin. "He say why, yes, but we know better, my wife and I. He say he go in for amnesty, but"—Salusito dared a wink at The Kid—"we know he go in to do some job or other. He ride like a man on a mission, a very important mission."

"Yeah," The Kid said, "he was on a mission all right. Dirty bastard."

The man sucked in his breath. He said falteringly, "He—not a friend of yours?"

"Sure," The Kid said, "we're great pals, Slattery and me. We got a date, him and me. I'm going to cut his heart out and feed it to your chickens." The Kid touched his gun belt fleetingly. Salusito wondered briefly if The Kid would cut his own heart out for treating the big man so well. Still, he had seemed a decent man, the big one.

The Kid was surely making a joke. Salusito said, "I—I told him about Lopez."

"Lopez?"

"*Sí*. Whenever a man comes by who must go to the capital but who is not of them, of the *Americanos* and their governor"—he seemed to spit out this last—"we tell him of Lopez. Lopez will put a man up, hide him out, feed him, rest his horse, give him a gun. Lopez has money. All the sheepers down here, we send money to Lopez to keep him financed so he can help any man who needs help."

What the hell? The Kid thought. Who the hell was Lopez? Some mush-headed do-gooder? Some sucker? Then The Kid grinned at Salusito. "Yeah," he said, "I forgot. Lopez. Sure. You told Slattery he could hide out there?"

"*Sí*."

"That's fine," The Kid said, and Salusito seemed relieved. He had been joking, The Kid. He and Slattery were friends. The Kid said, "Everybody down here knows Lopez? Everybody in all these damn' towns along here?"

"*Sí*."

Maybe he could drive Slattery to this refuge. Then The Kid could kill the man in front of Lopez, and Lopez would pass the word down to the poor sheepers. He took a dollar out of his pocket, and Salusito said gravely, "We no need The Kid's money. Just to know he is trying to get our land back for us, that is more than enough." The Kid masked his smile and squelched the giggle that threatened to rise from his throat. "Yeah," he said. "You'll get your land back. I swear you will." Six feet of it, per greaser. Didn't they smell the way things were shaping? They'd be lucky to hold this cruddy slope. The Americans were pouring out here. They'd drive Salusito farther into the desert, or into the six feet of dirt.

The Kid said, "I'll be riding now."

Salusito said, "You go up to the capital?" knowing a man didn't question The Kid, but fearing for his safety, a hundred deputies of the law waiting for such a prize as The Kid.

"That's right." The Kid replied. Solusito said, "Ride with care," and The Kid said, "Sure, they'll never touch me."

A little boy came out of Salusito's *jacal*, dark brown eyes huge with awe. Now he would have something to tell the others. This was The Kid, talking to his father. The boy risked a small wave of his hand, and The Kid looked at him and said, "Hi, vaquero," and the boy's heart filled so it nearly burst.

Then The Kid swaggered back toward the first *jacal* for his horse. The gray mare had been fed and doused with water. Water was like gold to these people, especially in this drought with summer not yet full on. But they had wet down The Kid's horse.

He climbed the horse, and the girl came away from the dobe side of the *jacal*, looking frankly at The Kid. The Kid said, "Follow me," and the girl's eyes grew large and then slumberous. She nodded. He rode slowly toward the junction of the Pintada and the Pecos, and then in the shade of the thick cottonwoods, their branches wrapped around one another in the embrace of starving lovers or grappling foes, The Kid turned and looked at the girl behind him. He said, "Where is this Lopez? Where's he live?"

The girl was startled. Then she said, "In the capital."

The Kid's lips flattened. "I know that," he snapped. "But where, goddammit?"

She said, head cocked, "I take you. I show you."

"The hell you will. Where is it?" he snorted.

The girl stared at The Kid. Was this why he wanted her to follow him? She said angrily, "Lopez is just beyond bridge, off to the left."

"Which bridge? East or west?"

"West," she said. "Surely you know—you said you knew Lopez."

"Yeah," he said softly. "But I forgot. Now I remember. Thanks." He started to turn his horse. The girl put out a hand and said, "Wait. Is that—don't you want—?"

The Kid grinned at her, the two front teeth sticking out like a rat's. Then he spat on the ground at her feet and wheeled his horse toward the junction of waters, thin and brown. He crossed over, hardly heeding the girl behind him and his eyes started to stare through dusk toward the northwest. It wasn't for him, this mingling of the flesh. He scorned it, rose above it. They didn't know, they didn't understand. This wasn't fulfillment. He'd tried it in the can joints in Texas, all smelling of buttermilk soap and lye, and he found no thrill in it.

He rode steadily as night drew a dark cloak about him, but when a crescent moon tilted its horn and spilled light on the piñon-pricked earth. The Kid moved directly into the soft yellow glow. A rising quality of excitement began to mount inside him. He and Slattery. There was the fulfillment, the only real fulfillment. His hands were moist on the reins and every so often he raised his right hand before his eyes, marveling at the way his fingers leaped and curled like a hawk's talons.

The Kid entered the city in blackest night, the moon just a feeble slice in the sky, the stars too high to shed light. He passed a woman on a corner—the last, most patient *puta* in the city, hoping some of the drunken bodies in the roadway would come to and need the solace of flesh—and he shook his head at her when she looked at him. Not that she could see his head shake, the black Stetson throwing his face into dense shadow. He wore a six-bit dark calico shirt and black California pants and straight-top leather boots, made by A. J. Luder in Kansas, blackened from the soot of a hot skillet. His boot heels were two inches high—not because he knew he was little and wanted to be big; others might think so, but The Kid knew this was nonsense, he was bigger than any of them— but high and pointed, the points no bigger than dimes, because with high-pointed bootheels a man could pivot on loose gravel or slick grass, find purchase in the dirt that lay below the surface of the ground. Once he'd ridden past a darkened street corner in a Texas cow town and he'd heard the faint rustle of a man clearing leather. The Kid had leaped from his horse without a thought, and the orange flame that looked like some rare desert flower sent its whining slug past his shoulder. Then he was landing, hitting hard and pivoting, nearly losing his balance, but not quite, his heels gripping and holding, and his gun had loosed its own pale blossom in the night, and a man coughed once, sagged to the ground, face first. The Kid had rolled him over with his toe. He had never seen the man before. It was, he recalled, number seven. Lucky number seven.

So he wore pointed heels, and he dressed in black and the night was his mate.

But what did it matter? He dressed in black and went out seeking his foes, face to face in blazing sunshine or under the swinging oil lanterns of saloons.

He moved steadily toward the plaza, not knowing where he'd find Slattery, but knowing he couldn't be one of these near-dead drunken carcasses littering the rutted roadways.

A wagon wheeled by, groaning, and The Kid smelled goat's cheese and onions. The vendor muttered to himself, and The Kid wondered what the vendor would think if The Kid suddenly dropped down in front of the man and lifted his black hat and showed his face to the man. He chuckled softly and the vendor whirled and said, "Dirty gringo," and The Kid grinned to himself. He neared the plaza, then pushed boldly into the square. He heard the heels of a man striking the cobbles and he knew it was a guard, posted in front of the governor's palace. The Kid touched the gray mare and the horse instantly froze. The noise on the cobbles seemed to hesitate, and then continued. The man was wary, but probably more sleepy. The Kid had no idea of what he was going to do, but he sensed that he would do something, that he had to do something.

He slid from the mare's back and bounced his right index finger against the horse's cold bony nose. The horse didn't move. The Kid waved the finger again and then glided away, toward the man's footsteps.

The Kid shut his eyes for a half minute or so, then opened them again. He was lucky, he knew, because he'd been traveling in pitch darkness, away from the lights of this gaudy nighttime city. The guard's eyes would be tired from the blare and glare of lanterns and street lamps. And The Kid was young, with a boy's strength of eye. When he opened his eyes, the dark gloom was less thick. He saw the bulky silhouette of the sentry, passing back and forth in a stumbling near-straight line. There was one light burning in the palace. The Kid stepped swiftly and silently until he was able to put the sentry's line of march directly between the far-off light and himself. For a second or two, in each direction, the sentry would be outlined by the faint light. It was all The Kid needed. He doubted he needed that much.

He loosed his gun from the holster, hefted it, made a

short clubbing motion, barrel first. Then he moved forward, toward the marching sentry. The man again hesitated, and The Kid froze, but the sentry had stopped to wipe his brow with his white bandanna. The neckerchief was like a flag, it was so large. The Kid scoffed at such falderal. A man needed a kerchief to mop his brow or remove cinders from his eye or scrape dirt from a wound, but not a tablecloth. Fops, that was what they were. He straightened up and walked over to the sentry who was carefully wrapping the kerchief about his neck.

The Kid said, "Evening, guard," forgetting all his prior care, tossing discretion off with the bland unconcern of a man who knew he was not at all little, but stood eleven feet high. He said, "Quiet here, ain't it?" The guard said, "You ain't kidding, friend," and The Kid said pleasantly, "You know who I am?"

The guard said, "No. Who the hell are you?"

The Kid shook his head. He said, "That's too bad. It's always better when they know me." He giggled and then stepped back and said, "I'll be damned—" Then the sentry relaxed, because it couldn't be what he thought it was. He said, "For a second you really had me going, friend. I thought you was—hell, I thought you were somebody else."

The Kid nodded. He said, "That's who I am. Somebody else. You're absolutely right. I'm The Kid." The guard laughed and said, "Sure, and I'm the governor's daughter." The Kid hit him hard across the temple with the barrel of his gun, breaking the man's scream in half.

He fell at The Kid's feet. The Kid bent down and listened for the man's breath. He straightened up. Then he bent again, and with a knife from his pistol belt, slashed the guard's shirt from his back. He turned the man over, and then very carefully, not cutting more than an eighth-inch deep, he printed in large letters with his knife, KID. He didn't think the man would bleed too much. He hadn't cut that deeply. When he was finished, he pressed down on the man's back, under the arms, feeling for pressure spots to help staunch the flow of blood. He kept the pressure on for a minute or two. Then he got up and walked away.

He thought it was a nice way to introduce himself to the Territorial capital.

He went back to his horse and found the mare nuzzling up to a bay gelding, a handsome lean horse. The Kid wondered who owned such a fine animal. He rode into the night, whistling softly through his two front bucked teeth.

In the one lighted room in the governor's palace, Fallon looked up briefly from his work, hearing the short scream and then the distant sound of a man falling. It was a sound he knew well and at first he was alarmed, thinking of men dying at Chickamauga. Then he muttered softly, "Another drunken brawl." There were drunks every morning when he walked his way through the waking streets, and if any one thing caused the Indians and Spanish to continue despising the Americans, it was this disgusting drunkenness. Sometimes Fallon wondered how far the hatred went; he sat on a Territory that was 90 per cent Indian and Spanish. Too many Americans, yes, even governors, had been massacred by pushed-around Pueblos and land-lost Spanish. The seething discontent was there, lying like a tinderbox beneath the placid and surface docility. And with the drought and the oncoming summer heat, it would get worse, not better.

He had leaned forward to the last fragments of work when the heavy door creaked open, and Martha stood there, a robe wrapped about her nightgown. She said, "Dad," reproachfully. He said, "All right, dear, I'll quit soon."

She came into the room blonde and lovely, blue-eyed, sleep softening her face, She must have waked, too, at the sound outside, and then had heard her father working, or maybe saw the light. Fallon said, "It'll be only a minute or two."

She said, "That's what you said at eleven, Dad. That was nearly three hours back. Now. You'll have to stop now. Tomorrow will be soon enough."

"Don't badger me, dear," her father said. "You're just like your mother." And the memory turned inside him but didn't hurt. It had finally stopped hurting, and that was good, because a man couldn't do his work, plagued by grief.

She said, "I'm not badgering you, Dad. It's for your own good."

He sighed. "That's what Mother always said. What is there about men that women have to baby them?"

She smiled softly. "Go to bed. Now you've got a new thought to worry over in bed."

He stared at her. He wondered whether she heard him at night, restless in his bedclothes, still pondering the problems that bubbled beneath the face of this war-torn land. To continue amnesty or not, letting the dregs come to the capital, where the danger of Spanish and Indian uprising was always present and where a little gunfire could detonate the tinderbox. To sign Chisholm's cow order or not— no, not Chisholm's, his own, he couldn't shove the responsibility to a man just because the man had pushed the idea—to sign the order and once and for all end the squabbling between cowmen over who owned what cattle, and maybe begin more than squabbling in its stead. To call in the troops and finish off Fort Heck and the rest of the dank murderous holes where The Kid and the others still lay. And beyond his control, another problem, the summer looming ahead, dead and dry, waterless, grass burning wells dry.

No wonder he didn't want to go to bed.

"All right," he said, getting up. He looked at the girl.

This was another problem. A girl of twenty, in a land of clashing brute elements. Not the place, surely, for Martha. But where, then? Back East, where he'd never really know how she was faring? And, he grinned ruefully, if he ever dared suggest sending her back, she'd defy him. She was his problem, but so too was he hers. She ought to be married, he thought irrelevantly, and wondered where she'd find a mate out here.

He walked to the door with her, and outside he heard a horse move off, and then a faint rustling sound, of maybe a man rubbing up against a dobe wall or crawling on the cobbles. He frowned. "Honey, I have to go outside and check the sentries."

Martha said, "I'll go with you, then. You're not going to start working on something new."

He looked at her. "You can't go out there, like that."

She shook her head, the long blonde hair swirling softly. "Why not? The way they look at me with all my clothes on is bad enough. This robe hides anything."

She walked ahead of him, long-legged and erect, and they moved into the square.

It was Fallon who stumbled over the body, the man moaning so softly it might have been just his broken breathing. Fallon scratched a match to flame, saw the caked blood and the crude message and instantly blew out the match. He said huskily, "Martha—can you take his legs?" and the girl said, "Of course, Dad," bending and picking up the man's boots. "Into the house," Fallon panted. "Nobody's to hear of this." The Kid. The Kid had come to the capital.

They moved under the burden of the man's near-dead weight, back into the palace, and to a rear seldom-used guest room. They laid the man on a bed, on his stomach. Fallon said, "Can you watch him? I mean, it won't bother you—?"

"Just go and come back as fast as you can. It bothers

me, but I can stand it," Martha said.

Fallon went outside to find his horse and rout some doctor out of bed. He hoped the doctor wouldn't be too drunk.

8

Frick and the three men who sat in his parlor heard the horseman ride by. One of the ranchers, his eyes gritty with lack of sleep, said, "Another damn' drunk going home," and another rancher said, "By God I wish it was me."

Frick lighted a cigar and took a sip of brandy. It had been an hour, maybe an hour and a half since he saw Slattery in the bar. Instantly he had gone and rounded up those Jackson County ranchers who were in the capital.

He said. "Go on home if you want to. Nobody's forcing you to go into this. I thought you men wanted me to help you get your cows back. That right, Hughes?"

The second rancher rubbed his hand through iron-gray bristling hair. He said, "You know we want them cows back. But couldn't they just sit where they were one more night?"

Frick laughed pleasantly. "They'll sit there. But we can't. Least, I don't think so."

"Get to it, then," Hughes said. "Smits and Whitaker and I want to get an hour of sleep, anyway. What the hell is this all about? You've got us all here now. What is it that couldn't wait until morning?"

Frick blew out a graceful cylinder of blue-white smoke. The room was warm, nearly stuffy. Outside, the Territory night was chilly, as it always was after the sun set, but inside the dobe walls were three feet thick. A fire had just begun to catch in the flagstone fireplace, dry shavings cut from the pitchy heart of pine crackling up and heating the heavy logs. The men sat in stiff high-backed oak chairs. Bright Indian blankets ran up the gypsum-coated walls and Indian rugs lay carelessly over the mortared floors. He said quietly, "Slattery's in town."

Hughes leaned forward, his breath coming out in a whoosh. "So soon?"

The others were intent, watching Frick.

Frick nodded. "I told you he was our man. He's come in and seen the governor already—"

"He's done it?" Smits said. Smits was a barrel-chested man with skinny short legs. He'd lost five thousand head in the Jackson Country wars. He swore that Chisholm had most of them.

"No," Frick said. "Not that fast. He's seen Fallon, got his amnesty"—the men broke into grins at that—"and now he's just waiting his chance. He says he'll pull it off as soon as he gets a clean shot at the man."

Hughes stared at the fire. Then he raised his head. "Frick, I take my hat off to you. I didn't think it could be lined up that fast."

From the corner of the room, Whitaker, a wispy-voiced man with pale eyes, said "It's not done yet." Smits nodded, his mouth a grim line.

"It's not," Frick said, "and that's why we're here. Gentlemen, I'm doing what I can do. I've got the man we all decided was the right man—"

"The man you decided," Hughes said.

Frick shrugged. "I decided or all of us, there's no difference. Nobody had any other suggestion. We've got our man up here, and he's ready to go. You're paying me decent money for my services."

"Pull it off the way you said you would and you'll be worth every cent of it," Hughes said.

"At least," Whitaker added, from the corner. He was a grave expressionless man who'd lost two sons in the Jackson wars, shot down at night by one of the raiding rustling teams that terrorized the country.

Frick continued, "And I want to do my best for you. But no matter, even if Slattery kills Fallon—"

"If?" Hughes said crisply.

"When," Frick corrected himself. "When Slattery kills Fallon, we'll still have Chisholm to deal with. Even Slattery is aware of this, and he's been up here just a few hours. Chisholm will automatically take over the governorship, until another men is appointed by President Hayes. Chisholm'll sign that order faster than Fallon ever would."

Smits stood up. He took an enormous breath and said, "We've been over that before, Frick. We can't turn this thing into a slaughterhouse. We can't afford war. We're bled dry. We're short of funds, and after we pay you and Slattery we'll be flatter than this rug." His heavy foot mashed the carpet into the mortar floor. "Fallon is the man we need out of the way. It's his order, no matter if Chisholm did think it up. While Fallon's alive, it's his problem. If he signs the order, we're sunk. We've got to put him away before it's signed." He turned to the others. "Is that right, boys?"

The other two men nodded, their eyes flicking back and forth, from Smits to Frick.

Smits said, "So Fallon is our major and immediate problem. He must not sign that order. Now I'm fairly confident Chisholm won't sign the order you think he'll sign so quick."

"Why won't he?" Frick said.

Smits hesitated. Then he said, "Because he's a filthy coward. He won't have the nerve. He'll guess why Fallon's been killed, or even if he doesn't guess he'll wonder a little. And when Chiz starts wondering, he's going to remember a lot of men who've sworn to kill him if he ever tried any shenanigans again."

Whitaker said quietly, "If Chisholm makes a move for that pen, to sign that order, I'll kill him myself."

Frick shook his head. "And that will start the whole affair boiling again. No sir. It doesn't make sense. Why, when I was up in Montana and I was called in to settle the differences between the cowmen and the sheepers—called in by the cowmen, of course—I saw to it the biggest sheeper was wiped out. I saw to it the man most responsible for sheep being on the range just wasn't going to be around any longer to cause any trouble. Now you've got Chisholm, causing all the trouble, and you're taking a chance he won't sign an order that would make him a rich man for good. I wish I had your confidence that Chisholm wouldn't sign that order. I just don't."

Hughes slapped his hands against his knees and stood up. "Gentlemen," he said, facing the two ranchers, his back to Frick, "I think we ought to bring this out in the open. I don't see that we stand to gain anything by not letting Frick know the whole score."

Frick let a ghost of a smile whisk across his face. Even Slattery had smelled that there was more to the plot. Frick said dryly "I think you'd better, too. Let me in on your little secret."

Smits looked at Whitaker and Whitaker nodded faintly. Smits said, "All right, Hughes, tell him."

Hughes said, "Frick, there's nothing to worry about. Chisholm won't be able to sign that order. He's being replaced. I have it from a man close to the President himself. There'll be a new man out here in a week. Chisholm is through. In fact, he's been replaced already, but correspondence and political red tape being what they are, he hasn't heard. Nor has Fallon. You have my word, however, that I am telling the truth."

Frick leaned back in his chair. As simple as that. The pressure of the wars and the grievances of too many people in Jackson County had finally reached Washington. It was about time.

Hughes said, "And with Chisholm out of his job, and

Fallon dead, it ought to be easy to bring pressure on any new man in the capital to look into the cattle-stealing problem. But if Fallon signs the order, even if Chiz is out on his ear, it's going to be tougher than hell to get the order countermanded. Fallon is a respected man. They'll think it is his solution to the cow problem. Some people here may sneer at amnesty, but back in Washington they like it, no matter what you hear to the contrary. This place hasn't been so quiet and well-run in two centuries. Fallon commands attention back East. He must not live long enough to sign the order. Is that clear?"

Frick rubbed his jaw. These men were better organized, more powerful than he thought. He nodded. "I'll get an audience with Fallon myself," he said. "I'll ask that he delay a little longer on the order. I've pressured him by mail. Now I think I'll see him. Just in case it takes Slattery longer than the next few days."

"Why should it?" Smits said.

"He's going to have to get the man alone some place, out in the open. Chisholm follows the governor like a sheep dog. And—" He broke it off, rubbing his knuckles.

"And what?" Hughes said. Hughes was the shrewd one, Frick knew. Hughes was a hawk.

Frick said, "Slattery was drunk tonight. That's all."

Whitaker leaned forward. "A man can get drunk, Frick. What are you saying?"

Frick shook his head. "I don't really know." He didn't know. Slattery just didn't seem quite the man tonight he'd seemed at Fort Heck.

Hughes said, "I think you ought to put a man on Slattery, Frick. Keep him under surveillance."

Frick squinted, wondering. Slattery wouldn't like that. But it would be safer, knowing if Slattery was dogging the governor. Because if Slattery fouled up, there'd be a hundred men around the governor, protecting him. Now was the time. Fallon was vulnerable. He suspected nothing, other than the rumbling of discontented Pueblos complaining of the heat or of Americans hexing the rain gods. "How?" Frick said.

Hughes snorted. "Hell, man, you were able to dig up Slattery. Dig up another man, just to shadow him, let us know if Slattery's trying to bring it to an end."

"But why wouldn't he?" Frick said. "He's getting five thousand dollars for the job."

Hughes smiled thinly. "I wouldn't know. You're the one who raised the doubts. Pay some fool a few dollars just to watch Ben Slattery. He'll be flattered."

Frick nodded. He didn't like it, because it meant another man would be cutting into the deal. Not much of a cut, but some. Not that the money mattered. It didn't. It was the spreading of the word that bothered Frick. Yet the man needn't know why he was watching Slattery. Frick would tell him that Slattery was really spying on the rest of the pardoned men. Something like that. Not enough to have the man want to gun down Slattery. Just enough to make him keep his eye on Slattery. Frick would figure it. He always did.

"All right," he said. "Don't worry about the money. I'll find a man to watch him."

Hughes said, "Money? Of course we won't worry about it. We don't have any to worry about."

Frick smiled. They were all the same. They wanted the biggest job done, a job that would net each of them tens of thousands of dollars. But they had to play it cheap. Sure they didn't have the money they used to. But men who could go straight to President Hayes—maybe through a senator or a few congressmen—had to have palm-paving money.

"That's it, then," Frick said.

The three men stood. Smits yawned. "I feel better," he said. "I thought something had come up to spoil this thing."

Hughes said, "I'll feel better when it's done. I think I'll see Fallon, too. Just to keep the pressure on. Good night, Frick. Get that man on Slattery. Pronto now."

Frick nodded. He walked the men to the door and out through the great *zaguan* gates of the vestibule. Hughes looked up at the stars and the thinning moon. "Nice night," he said pleasantly.

The men mounted, and rode quietly off.

9

The sun was like a hammerhead on Slattery's back. He opened his mouth, tasted dirt, and put his hands to the ground, palms flat. He'd fallen asleep in the cotton field. They'd be on him with a whip in a minute. Master Kingston would stare his cold dislike and then hurry off. He had to get up and get back to work. Ma would raise holy heck with him. He pushed himself away from the ground and pain tore from his shoulder to his finger tips. He saw the mixture of gravel and loose dirt, and he smelled the smell of cowtown, and he remembered.

He stood brushing his clothes, his left shoulder and side badly bruised. He straightened his hat. He reached to his holster and saw he still had his gun. He felt his side pocket, a handkerchief wrapped around a few bills and some silver coins. He faced the length of the street, leading into the open square, bright with passing wagons and mules. The early morning din of commerce was rising. But the gun-hung deputies already walking the planks built up off the street were grimly quiet.

Slattery went to the hitching post. The bay gelding stood patiently. Slattery fed the horse and led him to a trough. Then he went back to the saddlebag and took out his razor. He cupped water into his hands, rubbed his cheeks and shaved, the icy water pulling his skin tight as a drumhead. He felt better, hearing the harsh scrape of the blade against bristly skin. The sting and the jolting pain in his left side roused Slattery. He shaved and thought of how he would do the job. There was an unsteadiness to the business—another new and strange feeling—and Slattery knew he had to hurry before he found himself over-whelmed by it all. He'd stake out the plaza this morning, watch for Fallon, see when he moved out into the open, if he moved alone, how far from the plaza's arsenal of watching men he went. He stood next to the bay, and he watched the portico of the palace. It was a new way to work, out in the open. He had the right to stand there, the right to wear a gun in front of the law. He could move without fear of reprisal, or at least without much chance of reprisal until he pulled off the job. Then there'd be reprisal, of course. Then he'd have to move, fast and sure. Two bridges led out of town; one to the southwest, one to the southeast. Fort Heck was to the southeast. Still, if they knew it was Slattery, they'd quickly put out a roadblock at the bridge, both bridges probably. Fast, he'd have to be fast.

His stomach rolled once and he thought he was going to be sick. Then he remembered he hadn't eaten in half a day. No wonder he'd got so drunk. He grinned and shook his head. That was a joke. He'd got so drunk because he drank a gallon of rotgut. That's why.

He figured he could risk a quick bite to eat. There were cans of tomatoes and strips of jerky in his saddlebag. But somehow he was sick of eating out of his saddlebag. He wanted to sit down at a table or a counter and have some-body toss the chow down in front of him. He felt his money again. Enough. And there always was Frick. He could go to Frick and explain how short he was. Frick would advance him a couple of dollars out of the five thousand he'd soon owe Slattery.

He started to move away from the edge of the square when a man stepped out of the palace. He was a short bustling man with a nervous quick step. He carried a black satchel. He walked to the hitching post, looking behind him once, and then he reached for the reins of the horse four away from Slattery's. Slattery strolled close and said, "Morning, Doc," and the man said shortly, without looking up, "Good morning." He got on the horse and Slattery said, "Got a patient in the palace? Governor's not sick, is he?"

The doctor looked at Slattery, and Slattery saw alarm on the man's face. Then the man shrugged, and said, tight-lipped, "No. Not the governor. One of his damn' deputies." He jerked on the reins and the horse raised his head, nearly clouting the doctor between the eyes. The man was nervous, that was sure. Then the horse was steadied, and clopping down a narrow street. Slattery looked back at the palace, and his heart leaped and seemed about to burst in his throat.

The girl was young, maybe twenty, twenty-one years old. She was very blonde and pale, and reed-slim, yet with the subtle curves of womanhood beneath her pale cotton dress. She was tall. So much like another girl—like another girl would have been, and probably had been, at this same age. Slattery moved closer. The girl saw him, and her eyes narrowed. There was smoke in her eyes. Her mouth was wide, the lips full. Her nose was slender and straight. She raised a hand and pushed the heavy blonde hair from her cheek, in a movement graceful and direct. The sculptured lines of her face were like her father's. Slattery knew she was Fallon's daughter. Someone—Fats Jefferson, be remembered—had said Fallon lived alone with his daughter and that she was "a piece of flesh." Well, she was. But more. Coolly regal. So much like the other blonde girl, years ago. Slattery tried not to think of Frances Kingston, but he couldn't help it. He remembered her two arms around his neck, drawing him close, his body pressed down against her young breasts, her mouth opening to his.

Now he saw this girl ahead of him, ten yards away, and he stopped walking, standing there, wondering what he had intended to do, he, Ben Slattery, walking up to the governor's daughter.

Then he kept right on walking, and he said, "Morning, Miss Fallon, nice day."

The girl looked at him and then down at his holster. She said, "Is it?"

"The Governor up?" he asked.

The girl said, "Naturally."

Slattery said, "He's sure a hard worker. I thought maybe he might have worked himself sick or something. I mean, the doctor. But the doctor told me it was a deputy."

The girl started. Her right hand went to her mouth, knuckles pressed against her teeth. She said, "What do you mean?"

Slattery fought back the frown. He hadn't said anything. A man was sick. What was she so upset about? He just wanted to talk, to find out what he could about the governor, find out if and when he ever moved away from that damned office. He said, "I mean just that. We sure wouldn't want to hear the governor was sick. He'll be out riding, later?"

"I—I imagine." She tilted her head. "What's this all about? Who are you, anyway?"

"Just a man who's quit being what he used to be, thanks to the governor.'

The girl stood silently. She didn't know whether to believe the big man in front of her. She studied his face, found nothing there but tired lines around dark eyes, a skin darkened by the sun and more lines at the heavy mouth. A good-looking man, in a big animal way. Yet there was something else. She said, "What's your name?"

"Slattery, ma'm, Ben Slattery."

The name meant little. She'd heard it, didn't know where,

dismissed it. She said, "I'll tell the governor how concerned you are about his health," and this time it was he who started and she who wondered what she had said to make the big man so edgy. He put his hand to his hat brim and started to move away, but now she was curious. She said, "Ben Slattery? You had something to do with—with the Jackson wars?"

"Not much," he said. "I'll be moving off now. I haven't eaten anything this morning. I—"

"Neither have I," the girl said. "My name is Martha Fallon."

"Yes, ma'm."

She was amused, a bit, by the big man's manners, his near-groveling and scraping. She said, "I'd very much like to have some breakfast." She'd had coffee in the huge stone kitchen, but she'd been too tired then, too upset to eat. The sudden shocking events of the middle of the night, the poor man's back carved with a knife, the frightened lonely hour she'd spent while her father searched the dim town for a doctor, finally routing one out to clean the wound and give the man some morphine so he'd sleep. And this morning, when the man waked feverish, she'd had to ride out and find the doctor again, a waspish man who'd had three hours sleep and acted it. Well, she hadn't had even that much.

She looked at the big awkward man and she found herself slipping easily into a coquettish way, an old habit so long disused she thought she'd forgotten she'd ever been like that. It had been years since she saw a man so obviously smitten. Yet was he? It piqued her. She knew the man was rough, but then they all were, her father had so warned her when she insisted on coming out with him, and it was so. But rough or not, she needed company and this man was eying her with the wary polite covetousness that so pleased any woman.

She said, "They don't really approve of women walking

into any of the restaurants alone. I'm sure it would be much better if you accompanied me. We can talk there too."

He fidgeted and then he said brusquely, the obsequiousness vanished, "Miss Fallon, you don't know me. I'm Ben Slattery. I've done a lot of things no young lady would approve of."

She suddenly had to take him under a new dimension. The manners had fled. But instead of making him less appealing, it only made him more so. She said, "There are hardly any people out here who haven't done things I'd really approve of. But I'm my father's daughter, and if he believes in amnesty for outlaws, then so do I. You said before that you were a man who had quit being what he used to be, didn't you?"

Slattery stood silently. Then he said clearly, "That's right." He wanted to kick himself. The girl was willing to talk to him. He could learn what he had to learn, to do his job. He stared at her blonde beauty, and then down at his dark hairy hands. Black and white. He said angrily, "Let's go then."

The girl said, "My, you're a strange one," and she slipped her hand under his arm, feeling the hard tense muscle. He acted as though he hadn't seen a woman it ten years. She felt foolish, almost giddy. She said, "The hotel? There's a decent restaurant there, they say."

He said, "Fine. Any place," and she looked at his face, the jaw muscles so tight she wondered if his teeth ached.

They walked into the hotel—the town's only large decent hotel—and into the high barnlike eating room. A Spanish woman with an apron around her middle stared at them, her mouth curling in obvious disapproval. Ben Slattery said, "You sure now?" The girl made an impatient sound and said, "Don't be a prude. What's wrong with this?" He said, "Nothing, I guess," and the lie plunged to his heart. They sat.

The woman said, "So?"

Martha Fallon said, "What—what do you have?"

The woman said mechanically, "Chili and frijoles with red peppers. *Atole*. Tortillas."

"Eggs?" the girl asked.

"No eggs this morning."

Slattery said, "Wait a minute. Go back there and rout up some eggs. Fry 'em and turn 'em once, light. Bring us some potatoes, hash fried. Sourdough biscuits. Coffee. Make sure the biscuits are fresh. Nice and light."

The woman said, "No eggs. We have no eggs this morning—" and Slattery said flatly, "Find some." He looked at Martha Fallon and he said, "Does the governor worry much how they run the saloons and restaurants? Or doesn't he have enough time?"

The girl smiled quickly. "Not yet. But Father says he'll get around to it soon. He has been upset over the way some of the restaurant people take advantage of their patrons."

Slattery said, "Shouldn't be surprised if he clamps down real quick."

The woman fled, and Martha Fallon laughed, delighted.

"Oh, you put the fear of God in her."

"You did. Not me. She didn't know you were Fallon's daughter. You've never eaten here?"

She smiled wistfully. "I've never eaten anywhere in this town except in the palace. Father and I eat our suppers together, but he's up before me, usually, and at work by the time I'm having breakfast. So I eat that alone, and usually skip the midday meal. This is—the first time I've eaten out." She felt a tiny heating of her cheeks. She was being ridiculously pleased by eating with this big dark man. She wondered casually just what he'd done. Probably some minor infraction. Maybe gambling or brawling.

Slattery's fingers drummed the table top. Behind him he heard a man's footsteps and he turned quickly. A man stood there, staring at the room, and then the man ducked back out. He was a big man, with snaggle teeth. Slattery said, "Looking for somebody, I guess."

"I guess," she said. "But he didn't find him."

Maybe, Slattery thought. Maybe he didn't. Maybe he did.

He said, "Pretty lonely for you, then?"

She nodded.

"Your father, he's too busy most of the time to spend time with you?"

It was a roundabout way of asking for a date, she thought. But then he seemed to be a roundabout man. She said, "That's right. It's been a long six months."

"You ride?" he asked.

"Sure," she said. "Does a person have much choice?"

"Guess not," Slattery said. "You and the governor do much riding together."

"Occasionally. Sometimes in the evening he and I ride out of town, over toward Mr. Chisholm's spread."

"That's the ranch to the west, north a little ways? Big piece of grass?"

She nodded. "Mr. Chisholm owns nearly all that land out there." She waved her hand in a vague westerly direction. "Lots of cows."

"I've heard," he said dryly.

The girl laughed nervously. "Everybody acts that way about Mr. Chisholm."

"Miss Fallon," Slattery said, "from what I know—and I admit I'm a hell, pardon, a heck of a one to be talking about another man—but Chisholm is a filthy cow thief. If any one man is to blame for the upset down in Jackson County, it's your father's man Chisholm."

The girl colored. She snapped, "He's not my father's man. Dad had no choice. Chisholm was the only man who knew the Territory and its problems when Dad got out here. Mr. Chisholm was appointed by people back in

Washington. Dad was glad to find a man with Mr. Chisholm's experience and knowledge." But the words sounded tinny in her ears.

"And if your father leaves this job, for any reason, I guess Chiz will be acting governor?" Slattery asked.

The girl shrugged. "I don't know. Dad's not going anywhere."

Slattery's right leg twitched. "I mean," he said, "if the government decides he's done a good job here and he's needed elsewhere, to do the same kind of job."

The girl dismissed the discussion. It was too hypothetical to play with. It wasn't going to happen. She sat quietly and the food arrived, with a flourish. There was a small basket of blueberry muffins on the side. Slattery looked up at the Spanish woman. She said, "I made them myself."

They ate quietly. Slattery wondered over what had been said. Fallon rode occasionally with his daughter. Mostly out to the west, toward Chisholm's spread. Anything else? Just that Fallon hadn't really asked for Chisholm; he'd been handed the man. But now that Fallon was so strongly in control of the capital, and of the Territory, Slattery wondered what the relationship was between the two men. Chisholm had boasted of his power to Slattery last night. The man said he ran the Territory. Now Slattery wondered. Was Chiz desperate? Was he trying to prove something, by bluster? The man had finesse. It could be. Chisholm might just be finding himself outside of things, on the fringe, hanging on. The amnesty for stolen cows would save his skin.

Slattery said, "Your father ever talk about Chisholm's idea of letting bygones be bygones on the rustled cattle?"

"He's mentioned it."

"How's he feel about it, the governor, I mean?"

She made a motion with her hand. "Like so. Sometimes he feels it might not be a bad idea, that it would end the problem once and for all. Like—" She paused, and he said gruffly, "Like amnesty for outlaws."

Martha Fallon nodded tentatively. "Yes, the same sort of thing. But then at other times he wonders whether he just couldn't get around to investigating and finding out as well as he could who owned which cows."

"That would be a big job. Take an awful lot of time."

"I know. Dad knows, too."

So Fallon still hadn't decided. Now Chisholm's desperation became pronounced.

He felt the girl's eyes on him, and he looked up. Martha Fallon said clearly, "Mr. Slattery, are you interested in having this meal with me or are you trying to pump me for information?"

Slattery grinned. "Ma'm, nothing has pleased me more in years than this little chat with you."

"With me? Or the words I'm saying."

"With you. It's been an awful long time since I sat with a young lady this way."

Martha Fallon was silent. He wasn't really interested in her. He was a man, like most of them out here, she supposed, who seldom saw an attractive girl. She knew she was attractive. She also knew that to these men almost any girl would be attractive. So it wasn't herself; it was that she was a woman. It could have been any woman.

They finished the meal, and Slattery said to the Spanish woman, "How much?"

She bowed and said, "For the governor's daughter and her young man, nothing."

Slattery looked quickly at Martha Fallon. Then he put two bits on the table. The Spanish woman's eyes opened wide. "*Gracias,*" she said.

They walked outside. Slattery said, "It pays to know you, it seems."

Martha Fallon said quietly, facing the big man, "And to be thought my young man."

He stared at her. He said, his voice thick, "About that ride—would you be free now?"

The girl started to shake her head. She ought to go back—the man who'd been hurt. But then she knew there would always be something. Worrying mostly about her father. Her father didn't need such worrying. He could take care of himself. And the wounded man would be all right. The doctor said the fever was nothing, the cuts superficial. She said, "Yes, I would. I am."

They strode together, back to the hitching post, and Slattery said, "This is my horse. Where's yours?"

"At the official stables, behind the palace."

Slattery took his horse by the reins and walked the animal, the girl alongside. They pushed past the squalling throng in the plaza, through the open portico and to the rear of the building, where the government stables were located. The girl went into the stable and came out with a handsome steeldust mare. There was a big C on the horse's rump. The girl got up and said "One of Chisholm's horses. A gift to the United States Government." Slattery nodded. It was a fine animal. Chisholm had an eye, probably, for only fine animals.

He got up, surprised at the pain that still streaked his left side and shoulder. They rode through a street running west, the girl slightly ahead, and Slattery watched her neat quick movements, keeping her horse at a high amble. Slattery didn't see much ambling or high racking, with Western horses; the girl had done her riding back East, in English saddles. It was the way Master Kingston had rode, and Francey.

They pushed past the thinning rows of dobe houses, the faces of the Spanish masked with polite impassiveness as they looked up at the riders. Slattery felt the implacable hostility. He wondered whether Martha Fallon noticed it, too.

Then they were clopping across the bridge and out into

the cattle country that ranged down from the sloping hills of the Sangre de Cristo. He moved his bay alongside her mare and he said, "Chisholm's spread?"

She nodded.

"Where's his ranch house?"

She pointed to the northwest. "You can't see it from here."

The grass flowed ahead of them, miles of rippling land, but sunburned and stippled brown. Blood and thievery had won this grass, and the sun was stealing it away. The land needed rain, badly. He said, "How long has Chisholm had all this?"

She put a finger to her chin. "I guess he's owned his spread a few years now. But nothing this size until—oh, about six or eight months ago. He bought up all the land that was available. Had to. What with his new big herd."

Slattery shook his head. For the first time he saw himself and The Kid and the rest in a different light. They weren't the movers or the doers. They were the tools, moved by others for other men's ends. Chisholm stripped Slattery down to his true level: hired hand. Like any other rider on his spread, a thirty-dollar-and-found man. Except that Slattery's hand came higher priced. There was no other difference.

"Where's it all end?" he asked.

The girl pointed, again to the northwest. "It's all fenced except for this opening at the bridge, and at the other end on the north slope where the grass runs into the canyon wall. Must be a hundred-foot dropoff there. That's the north limit. The fences run out to the west a good ways." She pointed toward the horizon where white clouds lay like snowballs or giant pods of cotton.

"We're inside the fences. Does Chisholm care?"

The girl shrugged her lovely slender shoulders. Slattery studied her, the exquisite line from her chin to her throat, the poised head.

"Are you sure?" he said. Slattery was irritated at the cringing quality to his voice. He was trespassing.

"I'm sure. Mr. Chisholm has told me I'm always welcome."

"He married?"

The girl swung her head to Slattery and laughed huskily. "No."

"No wonder."

They were back at the former basis again, and Slattery was glad. He breathed in the sweet spring air. Oat and barley grass dotted the range, the tiny spikes pearled with shiny granular seeds. Ahead of them Slattery saw a rider, half a mile off, wave a hand at the girl, and then plod along after a bawling cow. The girl waved back. She said, "Chisholm's hired new hands recently."

"What for?"

"He's branding everything. He wants to be ready ahead of time for the official count in November."

The man was brazen. Or, again, desperate. Slattery said, "Seems to me he takes a lot for granted."

"That's Mr. Chisholm for you."

"You don't really like him, do you?"

"Mr. Slattery," she said, "I hate his guts."

Slattery felt better. He said, "Your father doesn't though."

"Dad doesn't hate anybody. Could he, doing what he's doing?"

The words stabbed Slattery. "No," he said dully. "I guess he couldn't." She had reduced him to killer again. He said, "Your father ride this way when he goes to see Chisholm?"

"He gets enough chance to see Chisholm in the palace."

"Never rides out here, for the exercise?"

"Sometimes. My, you're prying."

"I'm just trying to figure your father and Chisholm. Somehow there seems to be a difference between granting amnesty to outlaws, even to killers, and doing business with Chisholm, a cow thief. I may be all crazy about this, but that's how I feel. Your father gives us amnesty, but he doesn't then put us on a throne in the palace."

The girl was stung. "Suppose you ask the governor about it. I'm sick of your damn' insinuations."

He put out his hand. "All right. Suppose I do ask him. Tell your father Ben Slattery wants to talk to him about cattle amnesty. Tell him Ben Slattery knows a lot about the men who lost their herds to Chisholm."

She stared at him, anger blazing in her smoky blue eyes. Her nostrils flared. "I will," she said hotly.

"Fine. Tell him to ride out here tomorrow—" Why tomorrow? he thought. Why not today? "Tonight in fact. I'll be here."

"Why here?"

"Why not? It's wide open. Nobody could bother us. Tell him Ben Slattery will be here this evening, right after the Angelus. You got that?"

Her mouth was thin, bitter. "You've just been using me, haven't you? All the time, it was to get me to tell you about my father."

"Sure," he said. "That's all. Who the hell needs you?"

She leaned forward and raised her hand. She slapped Slattery's face, a stinging shot. He just sat there, mocking her, and she raised her hand again and struck at him. But this time he caught her wrist, twisted it cruelly and she let out a little gasp of pain. He looked at her arm, held by his heavy hand. The horses fidgeted, came together and trumpeted. The girl tried to pull away. Slattery tightened his fingers, drew the girl back toward him. He pulled her close and slid his right arm around her waist and pressed the girl against his chest. He lowered his mouth and found her lips, thin, hard, tight-shut. She wouldn't relax, even when she quit struggling, afraid of falling, afraid of rousing the nervous horses.

He released her suddenly and she straightened in her seat. She whispered, "You're an animal."

"That's right," he said.

"Tell me, what did you do? What did you have to get amnesty for?"

"Ask your father."

"I'm asking you. You afraid to answer me? Or do you just hurt the arms of women?"

"I killed."

"What?" she said stupidly, the color gone from her face.

"I killed. I was a killer. I shot men dead, for a price."

She sat, shocked, immobile. Then her lips moved, but no sound came out. "Why?" she mouthed.

"Because I'm Negro," he said.

The girl recoiled. Her hand went to her mouth.

"Wipe it off," he said. "That's right, wipe it off. A black man kissed you. You're contaminated. How did it taste? Dirty? Black? Sure I'm an animal—a black animal. I kissed you, and you're contaminated."

Her mouth worked again for words, her eyes large and dumbstruck.

"You—you poor miserable thing," she said. The horror was still there, but bewilderment had mingled with it, and another look which Slattery didn't want to be pity.

"You're all twisted, aren't you?"

"Why not?" he snarled. "Why shouldn't I be? You ride where you want to because you're the governor's daughter. In the restaurant they get down on their damn' knees because you're the governor's daughter. You're a white goddess to those poor Spanish. I saw how they treated you."

She said softly, "They thought you were my young man."

"But I knew better," he said. "I knew what I was. I know what I am. I can't be anybody's young man."

She looked at his face closely, studied him, the bright sun bringing out the rich ruddy color that lay below his skin. "You've crossed. You're so light. Nobody could ever tell."

"My father was white. My mother mulatto."

"You're practically white then. Nearly all white."

"But not quite!" he spat out. "When I kissed you, I was white. Now I'm black. Don't I smell different all of a sudden, don't I look different? Don't I act different?"

She said quietly, "When you kissed me, you were white and you were insolent. Now I know you're Negro, and you're not. If you'd like, you can kiss me again."

His hands twitched at his sides. "Stop it, damn you! Stop being sorry for me. You don't know what you're doing." He turned quickly, back toward the east. Ahead of him, a quarter mile off, a rider moved indolently across the grass. Instantly Slattery felt alarm. He said, forgetting everything that had just happened, "You know that man, you ever see him before?"

She said, "What man? Oh! No. But Chisholm has so many new hands."

"Sure, and they're all working like dogs to get those cows branded. He's flower-gazing."

"What's it to you?"

He slapped his holster and she winced. "That's what it means to me. I can't let people get behind me like that." The man looked up and then started trotting slowly toward the bridge. "Go on," Slattery said softly. "Go on."

The girl watched Slattery. His face was intent, tautly drawn, the jaw lean and bunched with muscles. He leaned forward, hands at his horse's reins, heels drawn out, ready to drive their points into the gelding's flanks. He was carved of pale bronze, and her heart caught, watching him. He was magnificent and huge, and terribly frightening.

He said, "I'm going to follow him, after he gets a start. You stay here."

"Why here?"

"I don't want you in the way. I don't want you to get hurt."

Slattery kept watching the man move off at a slow trot. Once the man turned his head and looked back. The horse's pace seemed to quicken slightly.

"Why don't you want me to get hurt?" the girl said. She wanted to wipe out all of the other madness that had come upon them, the knowledge that he was a killer.

He didn't seem to have heard her, his eyes focused on the retreating rider. He held his stilled pose for a long moment, and then he turned, his weight shifting in the saddle. He said, "Because that's the least I owe you."

"You don't owe me a thing," she said softly.

He turned his head away, slowly, mechanically. Then he said, "Tell your father I'll be riding here this evening." He jabbed his heels, and the gelding, glad to be away from the tight-reined tension, went careening over the crackling grass, his streaming mane like the wind in Slattery 's face.

The girl sat still as death, watching.

Slattery closed the gap to a hundred yards before the rider realized he was being pursued. Then he bent low and tore toward the bridge. But the bay was closing the distance with every stride. The horse ahead was a chestnut and the rider appeared to be a big man, with thickly hunched shoulders and heavy hams. Slattery whittled the distance to fifty yards, then checked the gelding slightly so he could keep the gap that way. He wanted the man to move into town ahead of Slattery. If it was the way it shaped up, then the man was working for somebody. Nobody was likely to ride behind Slattery like that. He caught himself. Nobody but The Kid. The Kid was very likely to ride behind him like that. But this wasn't The Kid. Had the man wanted to ambush Slattery, he wouldn't have picked open range. No, it had to be a man who wanted to keep Slattery in view, to see what he was doing.

The man hit the bridge, the sound of the clattering planks reaching Slattery. Then he wheeled to his left and disappeared up a narrow roadway, and Slattery kicked the gelding and leaned forward with increased tempo. They drummed across the bridge and made the left-hand turn. Slattery knew he was taking a chance when he moved onto the same street as the other rider, but it still didn't look like an ambush job. He started up the street. There wasn't a rider on it.

He said to a woman, peering into the mud oven before her house, "What is this street?"

The woman turned and said, "Del Mar."

Slattery jerked the horse to a rearing stop and walked him slowly up the street. Frick's street. El Camino del Mar. Ahead loomed a larger newly coated house. There was a hitching post, but the horse wasn't a chestnut. Still, it looked familiar. Slattery moved between two buildings to the rear alley that ran behind El Camino del Mar. There, behind the house, stood the chestnut, his flanks heaving. Slattery grinned. He walked his horse to the chestnut and dismounted. He rubbed his left shoulder, the pain high in the joint. That's what he got, letting himself get so sodden they had to throw him into the rock-hard road. His ribs still ached and his head throbbed. He was in rough shape for a brawl, but he didn't see that he had much choice. He didn't care much either. Other things were more important. Fallon would be riding out—he'd bet on it—this evening. By evening, he'd wind it up.

He waited, standing near the chestnut. His own bay had worked his way to shade and was quietly munching dry grass. The chestnut was too blown to move.

He waited ten minutes. Then a man came around the side of the house, his back pressed tight to the dobe wall, his eyes pointed toward the main street. He backed until he reached the corner of the house, and then he quickly ducked behind the house, closed his eyes and let out a huge sigh. He opened his eyes. Slattery said, "You're pretty damn' dumb, bucko."

The man was big, even bigger than Slattery had thought, a horse-toothed man with a punched-around face, a brawler. Frick had picked him quickly, Slattery knew, but Frick had a good eye for men. This one looked right for the job, big and dumb. The man's eyes flitted to Slattery's gun belt.

He said, "What do you mean?"

Slattery waved an impatient hand. "Frick glad to hear how hard I was working?"

The man's mouth opened and his right hand crept an inch toward his pistol.

Slattery said, "Don't do it, bucko. It ain't worth it. What'd he pay you, ten bucks?" The man's eyes opened wide. "It ain't worth ten bucks, getting killed."

The man said, "You ain't got nothing on me."

Slattery patted the chestnut. "Your horse talked."

The man squinted and said, "Yeah?"

Slattery walked toward the man. "Yeah. Come on. Get away from the wall." Slattery rotated his left arm, feeling the pain in his shoulder, not caring. A man can stay boxed in just so long—then he either breaks out or he strangles. "Come on," he said impatiently, and the man moved a long stride away from the wall. Slattery reached up quickly and pulled the man's hat brim down with his right hand, the left hand snaking the .45 out of the man's holster. The man pushed Slattery away, and took off his hat. His face was mean and Slattery knew he was a tough one. "Give me my gun," the man said.

"Take it back," Slattery said, and the man lowered his head and charged.

Slattery stepped to the side and flipped the gun behind him into the grass. It landed with a small thud and the man straightened and started for it. Slattery drifted to the man's side and drove a fist into his ribs. The man said,

"Oof," his mouth a round hole, and he started to sag. But then he shut his mouth and forgot the gun, driving into Slattery. He got inside this time and rammed his right hand against Slattery's chest. Slattery felt as though a horse had dropped on him. He moved away from the man, knowing his own gun and gun belt were bogging him down, but unable to do anything about it. The man waved at Slattery and said, "You wanted fight. Come on."

Slattery stopped the words with a pumping left hand into the man's horsy teeth. The punch sent shock bolting to Slattery's shoulder. Slattery moved to his right, trying to suck the man with him. The man raised both arms wide and moved in, low, trying to grab Slattery by the middle. Slattery chopped his right fist against the man's thick arms and butted his shoulder into the man's battered face. He felt the nose give and blood began to trickle from the man's nostril. Slattery took a deep breath and waved his left fist. The man pulled away. Slattery waved it again, and the man again pulled his head toward Slattery's right. Slattery swung his left a third time in a sweeping circle, pummeling the man's cheek and sending him reeling toward Slattery's striking right fist. He had timed it right. The sound was of an ax striking tree, a meaty sound. The man grunted and looked at Slattery with amusement, and then he fell, face forward. Slattery stood over him, waiting. The man wasn't moving.

Slattery went to his horse and drew a canteen of water from the saddlebag. He splashed water on the man's head, and then rolled him over and splashed more on his face. The man tried to pull away from the water, his eyelids fluttering. Slattery nodded and started to walk toward the house.

Frick stood there. He said, "Very nice. That was very nice."

"You want the same?" Slattery said.

Frick eyed Slattery. "I'm not sure you could give me the same, but I don't aim to find out. Brawling is for punks."

"Stop hiring punks then."

Frick shrugged. "It seemed like a smart notion." He looked down at the writhing figure on the ground, soft moans coming from the battered face. "Guess it was too. He did his job."

Slattery said, "I don't like men on my back."

"Sorry. Next time I'll remember," Frick said.

"What'd he tell you?"

Frick toed the moving man. "Get up," he said crisply. The man struggled to his knees, started to go down again, got his hands under him and pushed himself up, swaying. His jaw hung loose from its hinge. "Go on," Frick said. The man stared at Slattery and started for him, but his knees gave and he sagged again. Slattery reached his arms under the man and wrestled him to his horse. He shoved the man up into the saddle. Then Slattery grabbed the reins of the chestnut.

He said to Frick, "What'd you pay the man?"

Frick said, "Ten bucks."

Slattery shook his head, his mouth scornful. "Give him ten more. He's got to have that jaw fixed."

Frick smiled thinly. He reached into his pocket and drew out some bills. He shoved a bill into the man's trouser pocket and then punched the chestnut in the side. The horse pulled away from Slattery, the rider lurching badly but hanging on.

Frick said, "You're a soft-hearted man."

Slattery stiffened. "And you're a prying bastard. What'd he tell you?"

"He said you worked your way into Martha Fallon's graces, shall we say?—and went off on a nice long ride with her. That was pretty slick."

Slattery said, "You satisfied?"

Frick cocked his head. "Yes and no," he said. "Yes,

what you did with Martha Fallon. I assume you were trying to figure some way of luring her old man out of that damn' office of his—he's a regular bird-dog, isn't he? I got in to see him this morning. He must be glued to that desk. I don't envy you your job, getting him away from there."

"What aren't you satisfied with?"

The big cattleman squinted into Slattery's face. "I can't quite finger it," he said. "There's something about you—like making me give that thickheaded fool another ten dollars. When a man takes a job, he takes the responsibilities with it."

"But you paid him the extra ten," Slattery said wickedly.

Frick nodded. "That's the part about you I like. You're soft-hearted, all right. But you're tough, too. I could have told you to go to hell, but I didn't see the sense in finding out whether I could lick you. By the way, how's your left arm?"

Slattery's hand went automatically to his shoulder. The man was crafty. "All right," he said. "Just a little stiff. It won't stop me. You saw that."

"Now suppose you tell me what went on with Martha Fallon. I mean," sarcasm riding his words, "outside of the romantic angle."

Slattery said, "Get another man on my back tonight. You'll find out."

Frick looked around quickly. "You've lined it up?"

"Yes."

"Good for you."

"Thanks."

"You—want to tell me?"

"No."

"You're a hard man to do business with."

"So are you. I don't want anybody around me from now on. Get that?"

Frick nodded. "All right."

"I mean it. If I'm going to do a job on Fallon, it won't matter much to me if I do a job on a couple of other people too."

Frick grinned. "You are tough."

"That surprise you?"

"In a way."

"Fool," Slattery said as he got up on his horse. "I don't think I trust you, Frick."

"Now what's that mean?"

"I want that check tonight. Have it ready."

Frick smiled. "Sure. Why not? It's a postdated check."

Slattery's eyes narrowed. He snapped, "Then write it out right now. I may not get a chance after the job is done to pick it up."

Frick said smoothly, "I can't help you out. I don't have any checks with me, blank checks."

Slattery stared at the man. He thought he was lying, but he couldn't prove it. He said, "All right. Get a check then. Start looking for one right away. I'll be back this afternoon. Have it ready."

"All right," Frick said.

"I mean it. I'll be around. You'd better have it."

"Do I have a choice?"

"No," Slattery said. He wheeled his horse and started back toward the bridge. He moved slowly and several times turned his head. There was no one behind him. Frick's house passed out of sight. Slattery saw the bridge ahead of him. Off to his right was Lopez, a man Slattery had never seen. Lopez was in a good position to help.

Fallon would have to pass this way, go across the bridge, to enter Chisholm's range. Slattery could watch from Lopez' house, wait until Fallon went by, maybe even have a fair crack at him from the house itself. He chewed on his lip. That would mean involving Lopez. People might talk. They'd find out where the shot came from. The shelter of the law threw the job into a strangely different perspective.

A narrow rock-littered path led directly to the house. A two-wheeled *carreta* was turned upside down, next to the shack. A lean dog yipped nervously at Slattery's horse's legs. Slattery dismounted. "Lopez," he called softly.

A rough wooden door pushed open on rusty hinges. A wizened dark-skinned old man looked out inquisitively.

Slattery said, "Tell Lopez there's a man would like to see him."

The old man nodded. "I am Lopez," he said. "I am pleased to meet you. You wish to come in?"

Slattery said, "My horse?"

"My son will take him. Come in. Your name?"

"Ben Slattery."

The man's back seemed to stiffen. Slattery followed him inside. A boy of fifteen or sixteen, bare to the waist, was sharpening a knife against stone. He looked up at Slattery, measuring him. "*Americano*," he said, his eyes flickering with contempt.

"*Fugitivo*," Lopez said. "Take care of his horse." The boy smiled at Slattery, as if to apologize, and went by. Lopez turned. "Welcome, Ben Slattery. My house is at your disposal."

Slattery looked about him. Benches ran along the wall, draped with threadbare blankets. A pine settle. A sagging highback chair. Two cots. Slattery wondered what good this man could do in the Spanish dream of reconquest.

Lopez followed Slattery's eyes. He said, "Nothing, eh?" He chuckled gummily. He pulled an old rug from the earth floor. He reached down and with his hand scraped away a layer of dirt. A small iron ring winked up at Slattery. Lopez pulled on the ring. The floor rose. "Trap door," he said, looking up, still pleased with himself. "Look."

Slattery bent down. There were a dozen trunks in the hole beneath the house.

Lopez said, "Rifles. Dynamite. Ammunition. Revolvers. Enough for two hundred men. More, every day." Slattery shook his head. He whistled softly.

Lopez let the door fall shut. "You had no idea, eh?"

"No," Slattery said.

"Few have."

"What good's it going to do you?"

The man drew himself erect. "We are being driven from our land."

"You can take your grievance to the governor."

The man laughed, a hollow barking sound. "Of course. And he tells us how sorry he is."

Slattery was silent. The steady conquest of a nation, from border to border, meant the steady uprooting of others who stood in the way. Yet what else was there? The Americans were opening up the land. The railroads were slicing vast expanses of raw nothingness. Towns were springing up. Mining and banking and ranching, small businesses in town, jobs for men with strong backs or for men who could ride or for men who could just add ciphers on a sheet of banking paper. Men and money and materials, in an unending stream.

And Lopez had two hundred guns to stop the stream. It was pathetic.

Lopez said, "You do not think we can do it?"

"Win back your land?"

"Yes."

"No, I don't think you can. It's suicide."

The man smiled humorlessly. "Better suicide than surrender. Why are you still hiding from the law? Why haven't you quit, too?"

Slattery said, "I've got my amnesty."

The man smiled. "Of course. That is smart. Now you can do whatever it is you have come up here to do. No?"

"Yes. You heard about me?"

"From Salusito. From the young girl who lives next to

Salusito."

Slattery didn't remember any young girl. But there had been several dobe houses. They must have watched him ride up and haggle for the horse. Salusito must have talked to some of his neighbors. It didn't matter.

Slattery said, "All I want is to use this house tonight. From later afternoon on, until evening. Until after the Angelus. All right?"

"For as long as you want it."

Slattery nodded. There was nothing else here. He didn't want to discourage Lopez, yet if he talked with him, he would not be able to hide his feeling that Lopez was fighting a hopeless battle. It surprised him that Lopez did not realize how hopeless it was. "Thank you," he said. He got ready to leave.

Lopez put out a knobby-wristed arm. "Wait," he said. "You do not approve?"

Slattery paused. "Sure. You put pressure on the bastards in charge, maybe they'll relent a little, slow down their grabbing. That's something."

The man made a mouth. "No, that is nothing. That is charity. We are not looking for charity. We are not beggars. We want what is ours."

"Well, you might make them see it your way."

Lopez kept his thin fingers lightly on Slattery's arm. He held them there a half minute. Then he let his arm drop. It was a decisive moment. He had apparently made up his mind about Slattery. He said, "You have strange attitude for a man outside the law."

"Maybe."

"We had hopes," Lopez said, "when Salusito sent word you were coming here. The great Ben Slattery."

"But now—?" The man bowed slightly. He spoke stiffly. "It is always a pleasure to have the great Ben Slattery use our small facilities." He turned and stared through the mica window. "Meanwhile we shall keep at it."

"That's fine."

The man spun, angry. "The Kid would not talk like that! The Kid would see what we are doing. He would help. He would do everything he could. He would fight for us. The Kid, he understands us and our problems."

"Sure," Slattery said. Always The Kid. The two were equated, The Kid and the Spanish dream. If only Lopez and the others saw The Kid, as he was.

Lopez could not hide the sneer. "You wish to use my house this afternoon and evening. You will be hiding, after finishing your mission?"

He shook his head. "No. Waiting so I can do my mission."

"You will do it from here?"

"Maybe."

The man shook his head, almost in pity. "The Kid would not do it that way. He would not wait until dark, to strike from cover. The Kid, he goes face to face."

"We all work our own way. You work under cover."

"I am an old man. But you—" He shook his head again.

The legend of The Kid's bravery was the fabric on which Lopez had spun his dream. The Kid epitomized breathtaking courage.

Slattery said wearily, "Maybe you're right. I think you've got The Kid figured out wrong. I think you'd see it different, if you ever met The Kid."

Lopez smiled a small secret smile. "We shall see," he said. "Meanwhile, please do not forget that Lopez is honored to turn over his house to you."

"I won't forget. I can't thank you enough. I don't like involving you this way."

"That is nothing." The words were automatic now. He led Slattery to the door. The big man ducked through. His horse stood in front of him, fresh and content. Behind him the door creaked shut.

Inside the *jacal*, Lopez went swiftly to the tiny kitchen.

"Dolores?" he whispered.

"*Sí?*" The girl appeared, white-faced, her beauty a pale glow.

"You can go tell The Kid that Slattery will be here, today. Late afternoon and evening. You know?"

"*Sí*. I tell The Kid."

"Wait until Slattery is gone, out of sight. Wait here, five minutes."

"*Sí*." The girl sat patiently, yet inside she was filled with excitement. She would soon be seeing The Kid again. Ever since she had followed him up, she had been waiting to see him. She had gone straight to Lopez, with the money from her village, but more, to tell him The Kid was on his way to the capital. Lopez had fixed a place for her to sleep, in the kitchen. Then in the middle of the night, while she slept, The Kid had arrived at Lopez' for a minute. All he wanted to know was where Ben Slattery was. Now Lopez and Dolores could tell him. The Kid would be waiting for word on the other side of the town, in the grove of cottonwoods near the southeast bridge. The Kid said he wanted to surprise his old friend, Ben Slattery. It would be an eventful meeting, tomorrow. Maybe The Kid could persuade Slattery to see things the way they, Lopez and The Kid saw them. Dolores hoped so. More, she merely hoped to see The Kid, be around him. It angered her that he had been so cold to her. She wanted to try again.

10

It had been a bad day for Fallon from the start. The man's cruelly carved back, the letters in blood announcing that The Kid was here in the capital. Then Frick, all smiles and unctuous good nature, trying to persuade Fallon not to sign the cattle order, and somehow only succeeding in angering the governor with implicit threats of violence. Fallon had received Frick and heard him out, and once the man had retreated down the broken-snake corridor of whiners and wheedlers, Fallon's hand had leaped for his pen. He'd wanted to sign the order on the spot. He hadn't, but that was because Fallon could still control his angry impulses. But damn the man, and his bluff way. Frick had boasted of driving some poor sheepers off Montana graze when the sheep were threatening to ruin the grass for cows. Frick pictured himself an intelligent potent intermediary. Chisholm was a cow thief, all right, but what was Frick? A powerful, meddlesome agent for powerful, meddlesome people.

Then the daily complaints had started pouring in. They seemed different somehow, today. There was a backbone to the Pueblo grousing of poisoned water, stolen land, rainless seasons, raped daughters. And the peons, eyes glinting, mouths like down-turned scimitars. Prouder, they seemed, harder. They had sloughed off their indifference, their seeming hopelessness, their cringing hand-rubbing insinuation.

More, too. The Kid was here. And Slattery was here. Fallon could not get over the feeling that somehow the two acts were related. What might The Kid and Slattery be concocting, between them? The town was full of outlaws, ex-outlaws. Four or five hundred, in or about the plaza every day. Suppose they just took it upon themselves to wrest control of the capital, raze the palace, massacre himself? What for? Fallon didn't know, but then he never really knew the outlaw mind. That was why he wanted to make it a law-abiding mind. Then he'd be able to understand it. And suppose it were all one, the Spanish, the Pueblos, The Kid and Slattery, and a few hundred ex-outlaws—by God, that would be armed insurrection, and it would take a division of federal troops to stop it.

He shook his head. With a wish and a modicum of faith, he'd been trying to run a Territory that—maybe— ought all along to have been run with guns and troops.

He called out savagely, "Chisholm! Goddammit, where are you?"

The door opened. But it wasn't Chisholm. It was a deputy—an outlaw, Fallon thought swiftly.

"Sorry, General," the man said. "He ain't out here."

"What's your name?"

"Rico, General."

"Well, Rico, I want a job done,"

The man stood, eyes curious, guarded.

"Find a man named Savage and send him in to me."

"Charlie Savage?" The face was bland, a careful mask,

"That's his name. I want to see him. You know him?"

"I know him. I'll get him." The man wheeled out.

Fallon leaned over his desk. Chisholm had been in at the beginning of the day's work. Then after he'd brought Fallon the mail he'd disappeared. Now Fallon got up and walked briskly to the door, flung it open. Instantly the corridor quieted and then boiled over. Hands clawed for him, voices raised. "*Gobernador Fal-yon*," they cried. It was more than a cry, more than a plea.

Fallon put his hands on his hips. "Shut up," he said quietly. "I'll be back in a few minutes. If you want to see me, wait here. I'll be right back."

He turned and walked away from them, to the rear guest room where the injured man lay on his stomach.

He walked over to the bed, dim light slipping through the shaded windows.

"How is it, Jones?" he said.

"All right," the man said weakly. There was a watery look to the man's eye, his cheek pressed against a pillow, half his face showing. His mouth trembled. Fear had leaped at him last night—this morning—and entered his body.

"Any pain?"

"A little."

"You'll be up in a day or two."

The man shuddered. "I—I want to get away from here."

"You'll be able to ride within a week."

Fallon watched the large moist eye. It seemed to be searching for something. Jones said, "How'm I going to— get along—for those four or five days after I'm up?"

"You want to stay hidden here until you're fit to ride?"

The man's head moved up and down. He started to cry softly. "You should have seen him, Governor. He—just stood there, telling me who he was. Not even trying to hide. He—he doesn't know what it is to be afraid."

"All men are afraid, Jones."

"Not—him. He's different."

Fallon said, "You can stay here. Nobody knows except my daughter and myself, and the doctor. The doctor won't talk."

"God bless you, Governor. I'll never forget this." He was crying again.

Fallon started to put his hand on the man's shoulder. Then the door behind him opened, and the man's body leaped in bed. Fallow whirled.

It was Martha.

She leaned against the closed door, her face ashen.

"Oh, Dad," she said.

He came toward her. "Don't come in here then," he said softly. "I told you not to bother yourself. We're taking care of the man."

She shook her head. "It's not—him. I know he'll be all right."

"What is it then?"

She stared down at the figure on the bed. She shook her head again.

Fallon said to the man, "Jones, I'm going back to my work now. I'll be looking in on you. We'll hustle you some lunch later."

"I'm not hungry," the man said.

"Nonsense," Fallon said. "You'll have to be strong."

The man shuddered again. "Yeah," he said. "Strong."

Fallon walked to the door. He took his daughter's hand, squeezed it. Now it was Martha. Each problem impinged on his strength. It was as though this day were a testing ground. They walked into the corridor.

Fallon said to the girl, "You tell me in my office?" The girl nodded, staring straight ahead. She'd suffered a shock of some sort. She moved slowly, with a jerky stiffness.

At the office door, Fallon had to push aside a clamoring peon. The man hissed at the governor, "You listen to us, you listen to us. Or—"

Fallon took his hand from the doorknob. "Or what?" he said, staring at the peon, expecting to see the man drop his eyes, falter, retreat to the turtleback obsequiousness he knew. Instead the man's eyes held firm, filled with hate. "You see," the peon said finally, and Fallon grunted and walked into his office, the girl clutching his arm.

"Now," he said. "What is it?"

"Slattery," she said. "He wants to see you. Today."

Fallon frowned. "What for?"

"About—about some cattlemen who lost their herds in Jackson County."

"Slattery?"

"How do you know?"

The girl's eyes dropped. "I—went riding with him."

"You?"

"Yes. I—didn't know. He started asking about the doctor and what the doctor had been doing here and—"

"He knew the doctor had been here?"

"He knew. He didn't seem to know the man had been hurt, or how, but he saw the doctor coming out this morning."

"He talked to you, is that it?"

"Yes."

"You rode someplace?"

"Out on Chisholm's grass a short ways."

"Why, what for? I don't understand you, Martha. How many times have I warned you? Don't you know these men are killers, crooks, cruel ruthless outlaws?"

She shook her head. "Please, Dad. No, I didn't know at first. Oh, he said something about amnesty, and I thought he'd committed some minor infraction, nothing serious. Somehow I wanted it to be something minor. He seemed—nice."

"Nice?" Fallon said, the amazement battling the disgust. "Ben Slattery's one of the worst killers in the entire Territory. Maybe the worst."

"Was," she said tonelessly. "Not is. He's got his amnesty. Hasn't he?"

"He has. But I don't trust him."

Martha Fallon shook her head. "Neither do I. He—he was asking so many questions about you. Finally I told him to ask you himself, in person, and he said, all right, he would, but not here in the palace, out there past the bridge, on Chisholm's grass. This evening. After the Angelus."

"What did you say?"

"I don't know. I don't remember. I think I told him I'd tell you."

Fallon made a fist. He pounded the desk top lightly. "By God, I'll be there. I'll get to this mess yet."

"Dad?"

The girl's voice was tortured. She'd not told him yet what was bothering her.

"What is it, child?"

"He's a Negro."

"Who?" Fallon asked, confused.

"Ben Slattery."

"Nonsense."

"But he is. He said so. He blames it all on that. That he's a Negro. It's like a war—to him."

Fallon tried to remember. A big man, tanned, dark hair. What else? Strong square-tipped fingers, heavy hands. What else? Nothing, that he could recall. "He wasn't trying to fool you, for some reason?"

She shook her head, the blonde hair falling across her cheek. She pushed it back, and Fallon saw the look on the girl's face. He said, "You feel sorry for him?"

"Yes. More than sorry. I—I want him to lick this thing. It's terrible, Dad. It's tearing him apart."

"Where is Slattery now?'

"I don't know. He went riding off, chasing somebody. There was a man riding behind us, and Slattery went off to find him, to see what he wanted."

Fallon grunted. The outlaws were tracking one another. He'd turned the capital of the whole Territory into a breeding ground for crime.

He turned away from her. She was a girl, his own daughter, in a frontier of hunted desperate men, and he ought to give her more than this brief word and a turned back. But he had no time for more. There was the feeling in Fallon that the Territory was alive and wriggling beneath his fingers, beneath the hand of the law. It must not get away. The heat was becoming unbearable.

He said, "Go to your room. I have work to do. You shouldn't have come out here. It was a mistake."

She glided away, turned once at the door. "There'll be

time enough later." And she went.

She understood, Fallon knew. That was enough. Time later to tend to her, to be father to his own daughter. Now she was—like the rest, Pueblo, peon, criminal, citizen— just another charge. He put her away and looked after his other charges.

There was another rap on the door. "Come in," he said, hoping it was Chisholm. It was Charlie Savage.

"What do you want?" Fallon said. The man's eyes squinted. "You sent for me, didn't you, General?"

Fallon pondered and then said, "Yes. Shut that damn' door. Come in. Sit down."

Savage sat, uncomfortable.

Fallon said, "When's the last you heard from The Kid?"

Savage shook his head. "I told you. I ain't heard from him in two months."

"You sure?"

"Dead sure."

"You know Ben Slattery?"

The man was wary. "Some."

"Work with him?"

Savage shook his head. "Nobody ever works with Ben Slattery."

"Nobody?"

"Nobody."

Fallon said, "I wish I could believe that."

"What do you mean, General?"

Fallon slapped his hand on the smooth desk top. "God-dammit, stop calling me General. You have to call me anything, call me Governor."

"Right, Governor."

Fallon leveled a finger at Savage. "You once said I could count you in to raid Fort Heck with a troop of federals."

The man paled slightly. "That's right."

"Suppose The Kid came up here? Would you lead a posse of men after him?"

"How many men?"

"A dozen. Fifteen. Twenty."

Savage said quietly, "I'd hate doing it. I don't like going up against The Kid."

Fallon's lip curled. "Not even with twenty others to help out?"

"You don't know The Kid."

Fallon wanted to laugh. Sure he knew The Kid. The Kid came at night like a ghost and he carved his name on men's backs, as easy as can be. The Kid was like everybody else, except he had no fear. Which made The Kid so different it was impossible to imagine him.

He said, "Savage, you do know The Kid. You rode with him. You know how he operates better than the rest of us do. I've got a hunch The Kid's around here. Don't ask me why. Don't tell anybody. You let it out, there's apt to be trouble here, and I'll hold you responsible. Only you and I know of this talk. So if the word leaks, you'll be in trouble. You get all that?"

Savage nodded, pale. "But why me?"

"You rode with The Kid," Fallon said again. "I want you to take fifteen or twenty men—if you need more, say so—and I want you to ride in twos and threes all over this town. I want you to search out every house, every alley, every saloon, the hotel, the backs of stores. I want you to flush out The Kid if you can. If you find him— What's the matter?"

"Nothing."

"If you find him, you're free to deal with him any way you want."

"No amnesty for The Kid?"

"If he wants it," Fallon barked. "But he doesn't. He'd have been here, if he wanted it." And he is here, and I know he doesn't want it, Fallon wanted to say.

"What do I tell the men who ride with me on this?"

"Tell them the governor wants the town searched, top

to bottom, for any criminal element hiding here. Don't mention The Kid. Just tell them there's an outlaw or two hiding out nearby, a man who doesn't want amnesty but aims to stir up trouble. Won't that do?"

Savage pushed out his lower lip. "It might," he said. He'd have to be careful. If he told the men what Fallon suggested, they might think it a lark. If he told them that it might blow up in their faces, they'd sure as hell resent it. He'd have to make it sound tough, but not too tough. He didn't like the spot he was in. Amnesty had its drawbacks. Well, at least he was in charge. He'd find a nice soft spot for himself. He'd keep out of town, he wouldn't find himself being sucked into Spanish homes or dark alleys, back rooms of cantinas. He said, "Can I pick my men?"

"Yes."

"All right. I want Ben Slattery. I want—"

Fallon's hand crashed against the desk. "No!" he said hotly. "Not Slattery. Anybody else, but not Slattery."

Savage frowned. "Why not Slattery? He's the best we got."

Fallon said, "Not Slattery. That's all I can say." Slattery and The Kid. He still wasn't sure they weren't hatching something.

Savage felt the first real prickle of fear. Slattery wanted to stick around the capital. Slattery had said—in the bar, last night—there was good money for the right man, right here. Slattery was up here, then, to make some money. And Fallon thought The Kid was up here too. The two together! Maybe Slattery was working with The Kid on some big job up here! A man looking for The Kid might find himself looking for Slattery, too. Savage would make damn' sure he didn't find them, either of them. He'd stay well out of town.

"All right," Savage said. "I'll find twenty others, without Slattery. When do you want me to start?"

"Right away. Report back here when you've got your boys lined up."

The mask slipped back over Savage's face. He said casually, "We'll need some extra ammunition, won't we?"

Fallon stiffened. "The hell you will. You're just looking for one man."

"Right," Savage said. He had tried. He wheeled to the door, raised his right hand in a small salute and went out.

Fallon felt better. If Slattery and The Kid posed a threat to the Territory, he'd know soon enough. And The Kid would find the capital a tougher place to live in by day than by night.

He walked to the door. He opened it and waited for the hubbub to subside. Then he said, "All right, who's next?"

A dark-eyed peon grabbed Fallon's arm. "I next," he said.

"Come in." He walked ahead of the man, back to his desk. "What is it?"

The peon jabbered in Spanish for a minute, then remembered and started all over again. He said, "My wife, she insulted by one your men. Big man. Yesterday night. Start in with her."

Fallon reached for a blank sheet of paper. "Name?" he said mechanically. "Wife's name ... Where do you live? ... Do you know the American? ... Can you describe him then? ... Did he assault her? I mean, did they have sexual relations? ... Was it rape? ..."

The questions droned on, the answers like machine-gun bullets. The governor listened and wrote. He would look into this as soon as—as soon as he finished looking into other things. Behind him, Fallon felt a pressure growing, like a very real weight on his shoulders.

11

Six hours.

Slattery strolled the street they called Main Street, bigger and wider than the other spokes leading to the plaza, his fingers stiff at his sides. He'd pull off the shot that would end the life of Fallon—that would do the job, he corrected himself fiercely—and he'd drop through the convenient trapdoor at Lopez' *jacal*. The horsebeats would drum into the evening and fade at night. At night he'd head west, Frick's check in his jeans.

He looked into a store window and carefully read the sign: DRY GOODS, MUSLINS, CASSIMERES, AL-PACAS; BOOTS AND SHOES; LADIES' AND GEN-TLEMEN'S PATRONAGE INVITED. The men's boots were Morocco-topped and studded with silver nailheads. The heel was too wide for moving swiftly. They looked like fops' shoes. The sign said $25.

He walked away from the plaza, down Main Street, studying the windows. Tinware, glassware, queensware, Philadelphia Chippendale furniture. A big sign: GRO-CERIES, from which the smell of coffee beans swept into the street before it merged with the smell of horse chips and sweat. Another sign: SPIRITUOUS LIQUORS, CHAMPAGNE, and the neatly lettered notice, *Army-connected personnel will do well to come in and examine our stock of fine beverages.*

The swill-makers knew who to call on. They could have added to the Army, the Territorial hacks who had turned in their guns, the poor Pueblos who had nothing better to do than brood over lost land and disappearing buffalo meat, and the landless peons who now chased their sheep over ever-dwindling rocky pastures.

Slattery passed an apothecary, the window filled with

calomel, rhubarb, camphor, Seidlitz powder. There was rattlesnake oil for rheumatism and buffalo gall for heartburn, wild-cherry bark tea for liver ills.

Slattery heard a horseman clop up behind him and wheel to a dust-kicking stop. He whirled, hand near his holster.

The rider was the man he'd seen with Charlie Savage, the one called Rico. Rico swept past and into a bar. Slattery stood his horse outside, then dismounted and quick-looped the bay to a post and went through the batwings. This was what he was trying not to do, but he knew he'd not be able to stop. He shouldn't drink too much before the job. A little to put him on edge, sharpen the senses, speed the reflexes, but no more. He never went into a job, sloppy. Once he'd killed while drunk, the first time, but that wasn't a job. That was—well, that was the first time he'd killed. Now he walked in, six hours to kill, less now, and knowing it was wrong.

He saw Rico standing off to the edge of the small early afternoon crowd, eying it. Then Rico nudged a man and spoke to him swiftly, quietly. The man shook his head and Rico nodded vigorously. The man said, quite clearly, "What the hell for?" Rico said, "Don't argue with me, man, it's the general's orders. Every man I tap."

The man stared at Rico, and Slattery edged closer. The man was heavy-set and bullheaded, with an ugly scar running from the tip of his right eyebrow to his right nostril. He said, "Take me to the general. I want to hear him say so."

"All right," Rico said. "Be in the plaza in ten minutes. I've got five or six to go. I'll be there. The rest of the men are falling in now."

Rico walked importantly away, and Slattery touched the man's arm as he went by. Rico turned and his eyes went flat and impassive.

"What's up, Rico?" Slattery said,

"Don't you know," Rico said.

"Posse?"

Rico squinted. "I ain't saying."

Slattery took his hand from Rico's arm. He said, "Suit yourself," and walked to the bar. He said to the bartender, "Beer," and the bartender poured him a glass and spooned off the top. Slattery held the cool glass and took a sip. Then he turned. Rico was gone. The other man was sitting by himself, finishing a drink, his head down and his eyes clouded. He wasn't drunk or even near drunk, Slattery could tell.

Slattery walked his beer over to the man's table. He said, "Can I sit, bucko?"

The man waved a hand. Then he looked up. "You're Slattery," he said. It wasn't a question.

"That's right." Slattery didn't ask the man's name. He said, "That Rico's hot about his posse, ain't he?"

"Yeah," the man said. He swore quietly and bitterly. "It's a hell of a deal, you ask me."

"It sure is," Slattery said agreeably, waiting.

"A man turns in his gun, that ought to be it. But now we got to chase down other men. Kind of turns a man's stomach."

"It does."

"And not even knowing who the hell we're chasing."

"Maybe his name wouldn't mean anything."

"No?" the other man said. He shot his eyes up at Slattery. "That's not how Rico tells it. Rico says he understands the man's damn' big."

"Riding in town someplace?"

"Rico says so. How the hell does he know?"

"Fallon," Slattery said flatly. "Fallon must have sent him out to round up the boys." Slattery held his glass to his mouth. Rico hadn't touched him for the job. Rico was working under orders. They had a posse forming, but Slattery was out. They were looking for a big man, but Slattery wasn't to be allowed in. Fallon didn't trust him.

But why? Then Slattery stiffened. "You think it's The Kid?"

The man's hand jerked. His eyes narrowed and he let out a long quiet whistle. "Friend," he said, "you may have something there." He nodded his head. "The Kid, eh? Sure, that's who it must be, The Kid. Who else?"

Nobody else. The Kid was here, and Slattery had known it all the time. The Kid had come up behind him, because The Kid hadn't bought his story at McCall's saloon, that Slattery wasn't interested in amnesty. The Kid had figured Slattery had just been trying to put The Kid off with a lie. Now The Kid was up here, and The Kid probably knew.

Slattery felt a grin touch his mouth. The Kid would learn that Slattery had his amnesty, and that would seal it. The Kid would search out Slattery. Slattery wouldn't be able to tell The Kid he'd got his amnesty because it helped slide him into a better spot to pull off his job. The Kid wouldn't wait for alibis. Well, that was all right. Slattery wasn't going to crawl.

Slattery put his beer glass down. It was even more important—now—that he not get sloppy. He said, "Thanks, bucko. Good luck," and walked out.

He rode toward the plaza, slowly, seeing a cluster of men milling on their horses. He saw Charlie Savage and Fats Jefferson. There were twelve or fifteen others. Then Rico came riding up, with three more men. Rico moved toward Savage. Savage nodded and then counted the men and looked down the streets, away from the plaza. Slattery moved to the edge of the cluster. He said to one of the men, "When we ride?"

"When Savage gives the word," the man said shortly.

Slattery nodded. It would be Savage in charge. Savage knew The Kid. Slattery turned his back and moved a distance away, but still close enough. Savage called out, "All right, men, we're ready. Rico and I will ride out to the east. We'll beat the brush from the bridge on in." A man near Slattery snorted quietly and said, "Sure, there's nothing out there." Savage said, "Fats Jefferson will take two of you to the west of town and work back in. Tony Quinlan here"—Slattery turned and saw a dark-faced man with broken teeth—"will wait here in the plaza with the rest of you until every man Rico's tapped shows up. Then he'll break you up into twos and threes. You'll go up and down every street, into the bars, into homes, into shops. You got that?"

"Yeah," the man near Slattery said quietly. "We got that. We walk in and get potted, that's what we get. What a game this is."

There was some grumbling and then Savage said, "Anybody don't like it, they can tell me. You don't want to ride, just say so." His eyes swept the crowd, and Slattery watched men flinch. He was hard, all right. But then he'd ridden with The Kid, and they all knew it, and it made them slow down when they wanted to talk back to him, now. Most of these men had worked alone, probably, little jobs, horse thieving, rustling.

A man let his horse take him away from the cluster. Savage saw the man and called out, "You, where you going?"

The man said, "No place," and Slattery heard shame streak the words. Slattery moved toward the man, his own hat pulled low, and he said, "Friend, this is a dirty business." The man said, "It is, but it really ain't worth crying over. We ain't gonna find anybody. Hell, a man could hide himself in a thousand places. Fifteen or twenty men ain't gonna find a man who don't want to be found."

Slattery shook his head. They didn't know The Kid. The Kid would just as soon they found him, come at him in twos and threes. They'd pile up before his gun. Slattery rode away from the cluster, and Savage lashed out, "You, on the bay. Where the hell you going?"

Slattery turned slowly, and deliberately shoved his hat

back from his brow. He stared at Savage and Savage said, "Oh."

Slattery said, "You want me, bucko?"

"Hell, no," Savage said, "we got enough without you." Then he turned to the rest and his words whipped the men. "I don't want to see another man move unless I tell him so. You sit here, get me? I'm in charge."

Slattery spun away and moved out of the square. At the edge of the square, he saw Fallon standing next to his daughter. Shock traveled through Slattery. Here was the man, the target. He nodded his head and said, "Afternoon, Miss Fallon." The girl's head moved in a tiny nod, but she didn't say anything.

"You want to see me, Slattery?" the governor said.

"Not here," Slattery said.

"Why not? What's wrong with here?" Fallon said.

Slattery said, "Not here. Not now. It'll have to wait. You don't want to hear me, then don't be out on Chisholm's grass this evening."

Fallon eyed the man coldly. "I'll be there," he said. He stood stock-still so that Slattery had to move his bay around him and into the narrow street.

Slattery looked at his hands. Everything was shaping up now. He clenched his hands and squeezed them. Like that. It was all there. Fallon would be on the grass, and Slattery would be either at Lopez' *jacal* or else out on the grass.

And with The Kid near, once the job was done, Slattery and The Kid would bring their own duel to its logical end. Then it would be over.

He knew, now, he could beat The Kid. Knowledge came like that to Slattery. It was sure as life. He never felt faster. He'd been standing still, up here, for hours, but now he was moving and he was making things move for him. He rode toward El Camino del Mar, and he found Frick's house.

Slattery called out, "Frick!" He heard movement inside,

and then Frick's head stared out through a mica window. Frick pushed open the door and stood between the house and its *zaguan* gates.

"What do you want?" he asked Slattery.

"The check," Slattery said. He snapped his fingers. "Now."

"How do I know you'll do the job?"

Slattery grinned crookedly. "You're postdating the check," he said softly. "Remember? Stop it tomorrow if you want to—if I don't do the job."

Now he had Frick where he'd wanted him all along. The man would have to go along. Slattery knew the check couldn't be traced to Frick. Slattery guessed how Frick worked. The man must have handed over five thousand dollars, or would hand over, to some innocent blind. The blind would not know or would pretend not to know where the money came from. Then the blind would do as he was told: write out a check for the five thousand, to Ben Slattery. They'd never trace it to Frick. Just to some poor sucker, doing a job for a few bucks.

Frick stared at Slattery, his eyes troubled. "How come you've got to have the check now?"

"I told you," he said harshly. "I won't have time to come around for it tonight. It'll be too hot for me. It'll be too hot for a helluva long time. It's got to be now." He took his gun from his holster. "Get it and bring it out. Don't even think of coming out with a gun in your hand."

"I'm not a punk," Frick said.

"Then get the money."

Frick stared at Slattery, measuring the man. He said, "You know, I think I'd like to find out whether you could take me."

"Any time," Slattery said indifferently. Frick was right. Brawling was for punks. Slattery didn't care one way or the other. Frick kept looking at Slattery. Slattery said again, "Any time." Frick grunted and went inside.

Slattery knew the man wouldn't pull a fast one. He had said back at Fort Heck he'd pay because Slattery was a killer. It still held.

Frick came out with an envelope. Slattery took the envelope and slipped the check out, looked at it quickly. The signature at the bottom of the check was that of a man named George L. Baxter. The name didn't mean a thing to Slattery. But Slattery knew there had to be such a man, just another tool, a middle man who'd never be linked to Frick.

He put the check back into the envelope. He'd seen enough. It was postdated, thirty days hence. The ink, dating the check, was still wet. Frick had just written in the date.

"Thanks," Slattery said. "See you in hell." He rode off.

12

The Kid lay under a cottonwood in thick brush, the brim of his hat covering his eyes from the afternoon sun. He was a half mile from the outskirts of the town, a mile and a half from the plaza. All morning he'd been waiting for the town to explode. He'd expected to see posses riding hell for breakfast in every direction. Nothing. He'd carved his calling card on the sentry's back, but nobody had picked it up. Or—The Kid was beginning to think— somebody had picked it up and put it away. They'd squelched his entrance. He'd have to figure another way.

He heard the sound of the horse and he rolled behind a tiny rise in the ground, beyond the river bank. Then he saw the girl's horse. He grinned.

"Kid?" the girl whispered.

"Here."

The girl sighed loudly. "I was so afraid you wouldn't be here."

"I'm here. What do you want?"

The girl got down from her horse. "Lopez, he tell me to come. He saw Ben Slattery."

The Kid began to giggle. "Where?"

"At Lopez' *jacal*. Slattery come there, to ask to hide out there."

The Kid frowned. "Hide out? What for?"

"They did not say."

The Kid plucked a blade of grass and ripped it lengthwise. Then he ripped it again. It was a game, to see how many times he could rip it its full length, before tearing it across. He started to rip it again, the third time. Three was the charm. He'd never been able to make the third tear, the full length. His fingers were very steady, very careful. What was Slattery hiding from? The man had his amnesty. The grass tore. "Anything else?"

"*Sí.* Ben Slattery will be at Lopez' again, late this afternoon."

"Good," The Kid breathed. "For how long? He say?"

"*Sí.* Until evening. He has—job to do."

"Job?"

The girl nodded. "He did not tell Lopez what sort job. Just say he no like to involve Lopez. Lopez say it no matter. Great honor."

The Kid was puzzled. Was he figuring Slattery wrong? He said, "Slattery get his amnesty?"

"*Sí.* Lopez ask him. He say *sí.*"

Then it didn't matter. The Kid didn't care. Maybe Slattery was working for the governor, to clamp down on Lopez. Yeah, maybe the governor was wise to this hideout business. Slattery would be just the one to do it too. Kee-rist, it was going to be fun, tangling with Slattery. He looked at the girl. "I'll be around Lopez' this afternoon."

"Good," the girl said. "You and Slattery, you do this job together?"

"Together," The Kid said solemnly. "Me and Slattery.

We're a team."

"You help Lopez?"

"Like he was my brother." The Kid started to giggle. His brother. His brother used to beat the bejabbers out of The Kid. One day The Kid got a knife. He held it up when his brother came at him. He said, "You hit me again, I'll stick this in your throat." His brother had looked at the knife and grinned. He thought The Kid was joking. The joke had been on him.

"I see you—later?"

"Sure," The Kid said.

"I stay with you—tonight?"

The Kid got up and walked over to the girl. He said, "You're a greaser bitch, you know that?"

"*Sí.*"

"You're dumb. *Sí?*"

"*Sí.*"

"You're not worth a damn to me, you know that?"

"*Sí.*"

The Kid giggled. "Beat it," he said. Kee-rist, she was a patient one.

Tonight, maybe earlier, she'd see The Kid go face to face with Ben Slattery. It would be something to remember, to tell the rest of the poor suckers. How Slattery was trying to sell out the Mexicans, how he was working for the Territory, to squash Lopez and his little uprising. And how The Kid had stepped in and challenged Slattery. Face to face. The only way.

The girl rode off. The Kid watched her disappear, toward the town. He was to the east of the capital. Lopez was to the west. He'd either have to go around in a long deep semicircle, far outside and to the south of the city, or else he could cross the bridge ahead, ride straight through to the plaza, keep on going west, and to Lopez, near the other bridge. The Kid didn't care. Either way, he'd make it. Nothing could stop him. He carved up a man in the plaza last night and they were all too paralyzed to do anything about it.

He went to sleep.

The noise that woke The Kid was a man's voice. The man was quite far off, at least three hundred yards, and The Kid was well hidden in brush, so he was not alarmed. The voice, however, put The Kid on edge. He'd heard it before.

The voice said, "I'll ride through here. Meet you at the cottonwood ahead. Then we'll take another breather." The man seemed to chuckle.

The Kid got up slowly and brushed leaves and loose dirt from his trousers. He adjusted his hat and reached for his gun, eased it out of the scabbard, to make sure it moved smoothly. Then he let it slip back in. He looked through the dense foliage and he saw a rider heading slowly toward the cottonwood behind which he'd been hiding. Off to the north The Kid heard another horseman. They were obviously looking for something, someone.

At first The Kid was disappointed. They hadn't been that paralyzed. They had a posse out, of sorts, looking for him. Then he felt elated. They were looking for him. It had to be. Who else? What else? It couldn't be anyone else.

The rider moving toward him had his head down, looking at the ground, seeing, probably, the torn grass where Dolores had come by. He bent more closely and then he straightened, stared ahead, and called softly, "Rico? Up here, man."

The Kid heard the other rider swerve his horse, and then crash through underbrush. The gray mare was tied to a tree, a hundred yards off. The mare wouldn't move, wouldn't make a sound. She never did. The Kid walked toward the mare. He'd recognized the first rider. It was Charlie Savage. An amused smile played across The Kid's face, making him look quite boyish. It was the face of a prankster. He picked up a rock, tossed it in the air and caught it in his small neat right hand. Then he started to cut to his left front, so that he would put the two riders in front of him. The second rider, a tall thin man with a .45 in his right hand, went by. The Kid looked at the man's face from a distance of twelve feet, hidden by brush, and he almost laughed aloud. The man was so frightened.

The Kid stepped onto the rider's trail, and the horse ahead flickered and started to turn his head, but the skinny rider just pulled it back and kept plugging along.

"Rico?" Charlie Savage said. "You coming?"

"Yeah," Rico said. "Keep your bladder dry. I'm coming." The voice was high and thin, like a squeak. The Kid just kept walking. He put his hat brim back and he felt the soft hair fall across the brow. He knew what others would have said, had they seen him: that he looked like a child, a face of impudence and humor. He stilled the laughter in his throat and he said, "Rico?" The tall thin man spun around, his mouth hanging open.

The .45 started to come up—it had to move a mere five inches to be level on The Kid's heart—but The Kid beat him cleanly, drawing and firing while the other man was still moving. Rico's .45 fell from his hand. Rico looked down at it, and then seemed to reach for it, bending low over the side of his horse. He kept bending, his right hand out. Finally he touched the gun with his hand. He never knew it. He never saw it or felt it. Blood ran into the parched broken grass.

The Kid said, "Charlie? I'm over here, Charlie."

He spun the .45 on his trigger finger, and Savage turned his animal broadside and leaped down, on the other side of the animal. Now he had the protection of the beast. He fired from under the horse's belly and the horse leaped to the side. Savage had to grab the rein and hold him in place.

The Kid stood at the edge of the trail, watching the

floundering rider and the horse. Savage was trying so hard to protect himself that he couldn't take time to aim. It was going to be so terribly simple that The Kid was disappointed. He said, "You looking for me, Charlie?"

The sob and the second round came nearly together, and this time a leaf hissed, three feet from The Kid's ear. He moved to the side and he said, "Come on out, Charlie. I want to talk to you."

There was silence for a brief moment, as though Savage was wondering if maybe The Kid really did want to talk. Then he pulled off his third shot. It landed in the dirt and the horse screamed and broke free, plunging away. Savage lay on the ground, the .45 pointed at The Kid. The Kid fired swiftly and broke Savage's wrist with his first round.

Then he said, "Come on, Charlie. Get up. Let's talk."

Savage shifted the .45 to his left hand and tried to hold it steady with the nerveless numb fingers of his right hand. But he was shaking and the fourth round went off to the left, missing badly. The Kid said impatiently, "Get up, Charlie. I can't shoot you this way."

Savage got to his feet and started to crawl for the brush. He had one round in his gun and five more rounds in the gun in his left scabbard. He had a dozen more rounds in his pistol belt. He knew he had no time to start reaching for the other gun. He had even less time to worry about fitting rounds into the chamber of his empty gun. He couldn't beat The Kid with his right hand. Now he had no right hand. He reached the brush and he panted, "All right. What do you want?"

The Kid said, "I just want to know why you quit, Charlie."

"Quit?" If he could keep The Kid off and talking for five or ten minutes, somebody would ride up. They'd have heard the gun duel. There were over fifteen men out there to the west. Surely two or three must have been close enough to have heard. Then tears formed in Savage's eyes. He had played it so smart. He'd left this whole east section to him and Rico, because he knew it was safe, he knew The Kid wouldn't be out here. Still, somebody might have heard. Somebody had to have heard. He could fire his fifth round if he heard anybody coming. Then they'd surely know where he was.

"Yeah," The Kid said. He sounded hurt. He said, "You shouldn't have turned in your gun to the governor like that, Charlie. Me and you, Charlie, we've been a team. Remember Jackson County?"

"Sure I remember," Charlie said hoarsely. "I waited, Kid. Hell, I waited two months. But you never showed."

"I was busy," The Kid said. "I been working on my own until I'd get a chance to get the boys together again. Now I'm here, Charlie. You should have waited."

Savage fought off the sob. He said, "I been working, too. Remember Chisholm? The big rancher who hired us and then took off, without paying?"

"Sure," The Kid said. "I remember him. He was the fat one."

"He's up here, Kid. He's got a big spread now. On the west side of town. You come in that way?"

"Yeah," The Kid said. "I came in that way. That's Chisholm's spread?"

"Yeah," Savage said. "Nearly twenty thousand acres. All his. And he's the governor's *segunda*. You know?"

"Chisholm? Well, whaddya know! Ain't that something! He's sure got it good, ain't he, Charlie?"

"Yeah," Savage said, quickly. "How's about—me and you, Kid—how's about us going on up there and burning him down? How's about it, Kid?"

How long? he thought. Didn't they hear? Weren't they coming?

"Naw," The Kid said.

"You don't want to get back at Chisholm?"

"Sure, *I* do." He waited, while the giggle started to

form. "You get that, Charlie?"

Savage said, "What's wrong, Kid?"

"Nothing at all," The Kid said. "Get up, Charlie. Face to face. The only way. Come on."

The Kid stepped out onto the trail, and Savage brought the .45 into position. He rested it against a low fork on a cottonwood, but when he started to squeeze, the barrel began to nose to the left. He strained to hold it tight. It kept nosing.

"Kid," he said. "Wait. Wait, Kid. Wait." The words were slobbering like wild animals spilling out of his throat. "I can't. My right hand's no good, see? I can't face you. It's not fair. My right hand's shot. Wait."

"Fair?" The Kid said. His face was perplexed. Of course it was fair. "We're face to face, ain't we? What else matters?"

Sweat began to run down Savage's eyes. It burned his eyes and he closed them for a second, feeling the scalding salt rub in. Then he opened them, and everything was terribly clear, unmoving. The Kid stood three feet away, looking larger than Savage had ever remembered seeing him, thinking at first, my God, he's growing, and then realizing that The Kid was walking up, but moving so quietly he'd missed seeing him. The Kid loomed very large and then The Kid's right foot seemed to raise toward Savage's face. The point of the boot hit the .45 at the barrel and turned it. It looped into the air and away from Savage.

Savage started to scrabble for his left gun but it snagged in the holster, his fingers shaking like trembling aspen. The Kid said, "Here," handing him The Kid's own gun. Then as Savage turned the gun and aimed it—he couldn't miss, he knew, at this range, even with a broken right wrist and a left hand that was numbed where The Kid had just kicked him—The Kid stepped in swiftly and smashed the rock he'd been holding into Savage's mouth.

Savage went down, the gun still in his hand, and The Kid turned the barrel until it pointed at Savage's broken and bloodied mouth. He said quietly to Savage, "You oughtn't to have done it, Charlie," and he pressed Savage's index finger against the trigger. The gun leaped. Savage's eyes rolled and stared whitely at The Kid. The Kid very carefully tugged at the eyelids and shut the man's eyes.

Then he picked up his gun and he walked to the gray mare, waiting stolidly in high grass. The Kid snapped off a blade of grass and got up on the horse. He sat quietly for a moment while he stripped the grass blade lengthwise. He stripped it down again without tearing it. He tried the third time, but it tore. He'd never been able to do it three times. Someday, he thought. This grass was too dry. He wondered idly if Chisholm's grass was this dry. It'd sure burn quick, if it were.

He pointed the mare toward town. There'd be a posse somewhere—there was one, that was sure—and The Kid felt like meeting it. He was up to twenty-one already. Then he thought of Slattery. He'd have to be careful. He wouldn't want to lose Slattery. All this gunshot. He'd be careful in town. Slattery was waiting.

13

Slattery thought he heard gunshot at the east edge of town, near the Pecos, but he wasn't sure. There was one shot and then a half minute later another shot, or a sound like a shot. Then two or three others, at short intervals. Finally, one more. Then silence.

He was meandering back and forth, watching with grim intentness the searching by Tony Quinlan and his small posse. It would take a month, this way. Even then, they weren't going to find The Kid unless The Kid so chose. He could be in the back room of one of the Spanish houses, hidden in a closet or in a cedar hope chest. And the way the men were racing in and then out, shaking their heads. They didn't want to find The Kid. Not one of them wanted to go up against The Kid. Slattery couldn't blame them. Ex-outlaws didn't make the best posse, Slattery knew. He doubted that Fallon knew it. Fallon wouldn't have known.

When the shots, or the noise like shots, sounded in early afternoon, Tony Quinlan and two men were coming out of a saloon. Slattery saw Quinlan raise his hand and swing his head to the east. He seemed to flinch with every shot. Then when the last round had become a tiny rolling echo of noise, Quinlan said very slowly, "They must have found him. That ends it, I guess." And he and the two men went marching back into the saloon.

Slattery started up the street toward the plaza to see how the governor had reacted to the firing. A man from behind Slattery said in a loud whisper, "Slattery!"

Slattery turned and saw Chisholm. The fat man's face was sweaty and lined with worry. Chisholm said, "In here, Slattery."

"What for?" Slattery said.

The fat deputy said, "In here, man! Don't just stand there." Slattery saw the worry break up the lines of fat. It was more than worry. He said to Chisholm, "You look like hell, bucko," and he followed him into a saloon, curiosity pushing him.

Chisholm moved to the side of the room, to a small table. He had three empties in front of him. A piece of paper lay face down on the table, sopping up spilled whiskey. The man stank from the whisky and from his nervous sweat.

Slattery said, "What the devil is eating you, Chisholm?"

The man turned his face toward Slattery, He spread his hands. He said, "Damn it, man, I been looking for you all day."

"What for?"

Chisholm twisted his hands, touched the paper on the table and said, "I need a man to do a job."

"What kind of job?" Slattery asked stiffly. Chisholm had mentioned a job, before. He'd been jaunty about it then. But that was before. Something had scared the guts out of the man.

"You know. Your kind of job." Chisholm's eyes slid to Slattery's pistol.

"I've got amnesty," Slattery said. "I don't do that kind of work any more."

Chisholm's face broke into the panic Slattery sensed was lurking beneath the gray tinge of worry. "You've got to—" Then Chisholm stopped and touched the paper and recoiled from it. He said, "I've got to find somebody."

"This place is full of somebodies," Slattery said. "I'm not on the market."

"But you've got to," Chisholm said again. "You don't understand. There's nobody else can do it."

Chisholm didn't know about The Kid, Slattery thought. The man must have been hiding out all morning, going from saloon to saloon with this sheet of paper that was driving him to terror.

Slattery said, "Somebody's got you scared."

Some of the shrewdness came back to Chisholm's face. "Nobody here," he said. "I can handle myself here."

Slattery looked at the paper, face down. "That?"

Chisholm nodded, his face sickly gray again. "I've got a friend in Washington," he began. He leaned forward. "I got lots of friends, Maybe you don't believe me. I've got powerful friends."

Yeah, Slattery thought, and they've got you scared to death. Some friends!

Chisholm picked up the letter and wiped it carefully. "They say I'm being replaced. There's rumor I'm being replaced."

"So?"

The man leaned back, erect. "I won't take it! I've worked like a dog for the governor, for the whole goddam Territory. He couldn't have got started without me next to him. And now he's knifing me."

"Fallon?"

"Who else?"

"He doesn't look the type." Fallon wouldn't have knifed Chisholm. He didn't operate that way.

"Then why are they talking about replacing me?"

"What's talk?" Slattery said. "Why worry about talk?" He started to get up, sick of the fat man and his tears.

Chisholm lumbered to his feet. He was half-stoned. He said, "Wait here. You've got to," waving a fat finger. He staggered to the bar, and Slattery sat again, watching, wondering. Chisholm came back with a drink. He sat down heavily and drank his drink and then looked at the empty with a foolishly vacant look, then looked back at the bar, wondering how come he'd walked that distance, back and forth, for a drink and now the drink was gone. Chisholm said, "You can't win that way," and he pushed the empty away from him. He said, "What did you say?"

Slattery said, "I didn't say anything. I said why worry about talk." Slattery hated sitting here, giving this slob advice, trying to comfort a man who'd run thousands of cows off other men's land and become rich in the process. But something was holding Slattery, and he started feeling the first spasm of horror, not knowing what it was, not knowing why he was sitting here, yet guessing, a little. "It's just a rumor. Forget it. That's all."

"No. That's not all. That's how it begins, somebody hears something and then somebody else hears it, and pretty soon everybody's talking about what a lousy job Chisholm must be doing. And then what began as a rumor has to be backed up. So the dirty lie is absolute truth."

"You got something there," Slattery said. The man was

smart. He was more than that. He'd had a decent streak in him, once, but it had been perverted along the way. Only decent men recognized how a lie became the truth. Slattery looked at his hands and then at the underneath of his left wrist.

Chisholm said, "What's that?"

Slattery said, "That was a lie, too. Now it's the truth."

"What're you talking about?"

"Nothing. So what will you do?" It didn't seem important, losing a job like Chisholm's.

Chisholm looked at Slattery, at his hands, big and composed, and then at the black gun protruding from the scabbard. He had a crafty look on his flabby face. He said, "I'll buy your gun."

"No."

"I'll give you five hundred dollars, for your gun."

"No."

"A thousand, then. A thousand dollars for you to do a job for me."

"Just for your position here, you'd have a man killed?"

The heavy head nodded, several times.

"Why?"

Chisholm took a breath. "You know my spread?"

Slattery nodded. "I rode out a ways on it today."

"You did? Why?"

Slattery shrugged. "I rode with Martha Fallon. She kind of led."

The swollen face broke into a grin. It was more a gargoyle's leer. He rubbed his hand. "A fine girl, that."

Slattery was silent. A girl worth loving. A girl worth a decent man. His mind said, *a decent white man*. He looked at his wrist. He said, "Why do you need to kill somebody?"

"I own twenty-two thousand acres out there. My men are branding my cows, tallying them. I think they'll tally over twenty thousand head. You know what cows get at the Kansas rails? You know what they're getting at the pens in Chicago?"

"Twenty-plus in Abilene. Near thirty at Chicago."

Chisholm nodded, his pig eyes glittering. "That's a lot of money, invested in those cows."

Slattery nodded. But they're not all yours, you filthy rustler.

"Nobody's taking that money away from me."

The spasm of horror passed through Slattery again. He still had no clear idea what it was, what caused it, but it made him want to get up swiftly and walk away from this panic-stricken fat man who was trying to save a fortune with another man's gun.

"Nobody," Chisholm said again. His eyes narrowed further, black-tipped. "I won't stand for it."

"You'll kill for it?"

He sat back, affronted, a drunken greedy man holding to a shred of dignity. "I won't kill. You will. Somebody will. I don't kill."

"You just steal cows."

The pig eyes blinked, opened. They were steady, unflinching. "That's right. You kill. I steal cows."

Slattery said, "What do you want?"

"I told you. I'll give you a thousand dollars."

"Not enough. You don't have enough to buy my gun."

The fat man took a deep breath. "I'll make it enough. You have no idea how much money I'd spend to save those cows."

"What's losing your job got to do with those cows?"

"You going to do this for me or not?"

"No. What's losing your job got to do with everything?"

"Two thousand dollars."

"No."

Chisholm looked around. The bar was far off. He raised his hand to his eyes and tried to steady himself. He said, husky-voiced, "Wait."

"No." Slattery said. "I'm leaving."

"Wait!" the man said. It was a shriek, and a few men turned their heads.

"No," Slattery said, getting up.

"Twenty-five hundred. Please. Dear God, you've got to!"

"No." He pushed Chisholm's hands away from his chest. He walked to the batwing doors, but Chisholm was after him. Slattery swung up on his horse. Chisholm said hoarsely, "Three thousand."

"No. You don't have enough to pay me."

"I'll make it enough. Just tell me what you want."

"Tell me what your job has to do with it all."

The man sobbed. "I'll give you five thousand dollars!" He was crying now, and Slattery felt disgust for Chisholm mix with pangs of horrror that were rising inside him.

"No," he said, jabbing his heels into the horse.

"Wait!" Chisholm screamed, "I'll tell you." Slattery reined the bay sharply and Chisholm ran, panting, to where the horse stood, fidgeting. "You know the cow order?"

Slattery stared with loathing at the man. "You mean the one Fallon hasn't signed yet, about making the cows on a man's graze that man's, no matter where they came from?"

Chisholm nodded. "That's the order," he said, almost relieved that he could talk about it. "I want to make sure it's signed."

"So talk to the governor about it."

"I have," he cried. "He won't sign it! He hasn't signed it and he won't sign it. I can tell. He'll never sign it. And now this"—he still clutched the soggy paper—"now this says I'm through. They'll get somebody else up here. And Fallon will never sign it, and his new assistant won't know how unfair it all is." He stopped talking and sat down on the street, tragic, grotesque. Riders passed him, staring with cruel amusement at the man in the black vest and the gold watch chain, sitting in dust and filth. He was crying now, without stopping.

"So he won't sign it," Slattery said. "You ought to have figured that when you stole those cows."

Chisholm raised his head. He said, "Ten thousand dollars. Fifteen thousand dollars. Please."

Slattery got off his horse. He bent down. He said, "You'll give me fifteen thousand dollars to kill some new man who might come out here and take your job?"

Amazement crawled across Chisholm's face. He stopped crying. He looked down and saw where he was. He got up and brushed himself off, looking at his clothes with a detached interest. He said quietly, "You'll take the money?"

"For killing a man I've never seen? Don't be a fool."

Chisholm grabbed Slattery by the head and dragged his ear close to his own stinking mouth. He whispered, "*For killing Fallon*. Then I'll sign the order. You'll take the money?"

The horror rose full to Slattery's throat. The horror was a physical thing in his throat, like gorge, a choking mass. His own hand twitched at his side. He pulled back, away from the leering drunken Chisholm. He wanted to empty his gun into the man's belly. He said, "You stole all those cows, didn't you? Practically not a one of them was yours."

"Yes. I stole them. You'll take the money?"

"You stand to lose three or four hundred thousand dollars, don't you? If they ever check carefully, I mean."

"Yes. I'll go to twenty-five thousand."

Slattery said, "Will you go to fifty thousand?"

The man didn't even blink. He didn't pause. He said quietly, in full control of himself, thinking he'd won the man over, "Yes, I'll go to fifty thousand, if you insist. But you must do it quickly. Is it a deal?" He reached out a hand.

Slattery looked at the hand. Somehow it always seemed to come down to the look of a man's hand reaching toward him, the color of a man's skin. Chisholm's hand was pasty white. Slattery got off his horse and he said, "With fifty thousand dollars, I could go any place in the world. Nobody would ever bother me again."

"That's right. You'll be free, with fifty thousand dollars."

Slattery drove his right fist six inches into Chisholm's belly. The man bent over, his eyes enormous, the eyeballs bulging in their sockets. His mouth opened for air, and then he collapsed to the street, his fat white hands slapping futilely on the dusty roadway like fish out of water.

Slattery got back on his horse. He could not shake the horror of what Chisholm had asked him to do. Chisholm wanted Slattery to kill a man he had already been hired to kill, for opposite reasons. The appalling irony of it sickened Slattery. He needed a drink, needed one very badly.

14

The Kid whistled softly in the high thin afternoon air. The river was turning like a sluggish brown snake, running down the hills at the northwest and The Kid followed the stream to the bridge at the east end of the capital. He stopped at the bridge and broke open his .45. He spun the revolving chamber and slipped in three rounds so there would be five bullets in the gun. He crossed the bridge and stopped again, reaching for the high grass that climbed from the river bank beneath a stand of willows. He plucked up a blade of grass and set it between his teeth. Then he plucked up another blade and stripped it down lengthwise. It tore in half horizontally. Too dry.

The winter had been milder than usual. The snows hadn't piled up in the canyons. Now the spring river was thinning under the hot May sun. The Kid plucked another blade of grass and studied it curiously, a grin forming at his mouth.

Chisholm's spread was around to the other side of town. The Kid wet his right forefinger and held it to the air. Wind dried his finger where it faced southeast. The Kid let the grin break large across his face. It was damned funny, how it worked out that way. The wind would blow straight across Chisholm's grass, racing the length of the graze. That would be the way a grass fire would go, gutting the cowman's range.

Everything was sweet, the grass at The Kid's lips, the breeze flapping his calico shirt, the delicious feeling of unopposed power. Savage had gone against him; Savage was dead. Slattery had gone against him; Slattery was ahead, ready to die. Chisholm had started the Jackson County wars and Chisholm had welshed on a job; Chisholm's grass was ahead of The Kid, prime for burning. It occurred to The Kid that there must be something different about himself, that these matters should all work out so well and so easily. For instance, the winter might have been filled with snows. The spring might have been rainy. The river could have been full. The runnels on Chisholm's graze then would have been brimful with good water. The grass would have been green and wet. He wouldn't have been able to exact this revenge from Chisholm.

And Slattery—Slattery might have been a coward, Slattery might have been afraid to face him. But Slattery wasn't a coward. Slattery would meet him, face to face.

He kicked the gray mare and the animal wheezed once and began to trot toward town.

He stopped at a general store, just east of the plaza. Nobody had paid him any attention, which was the way The

Kid had it figured. The streets were curiously empty and quiet. The Kid didn't want to be seen until he had done some or all of the jobs he had to do here in the capital. He rode with his hat pulled low and a bandanna around his jaw and mouth, ostensibly to keep the dust from gagging him.

He got off the mare and looped it carelessly to a post outside the general store. He strode to the plankwalk and through the swinging door. He moved to the rear of the store, where he saw kerosene lamps on display.

A high-collared black-jacketed clerk said, "May I help you?"

The Kid lowered the neckerchief from his mouth and said, "Yeah. I want some lamp fuel."

"Kerosene?" the clerk said.

The Kid grinned. "Sure. Kerosene. I need lots of it."

"Two-pint lamp?"

The Kid waved a hand. "I said lots of it. How do you sell it in big batches?"

"Half barrels, you mean?"

The Kid nodded. The mare would have to lug the barrels, but the mare could do it. She would have to. "Four," he said.

The clerk gaped at The Kid and said, "Four half barrels?"

"That's right." The Kid winked and grinned. "Big bonfire. Having a party." The clerk smiled fishily and rubbed his hands. The sound was like dry paper, crackling.

The Kid paid for the oil and then the clerk said, "May I help you load them into your wagon?"

The Kid said, "Yeah. You can help. Only I ain't got a wagon. My nag is carrying them."

The clerk smiled fishily again, not believing the boy, and then they went outside, carrying a half barrel at a time. They got the four barrels into the street, and the clerk looked at The Kid and saw he wasn't fooling. There was no wagon. He said, "No horse can carry that much."

The Kid said, "Start strapping them on," and they strapped the four half barrels to the horse's flanks. The mare turned her head sadly and neighed once, sadly, but she never moved her legs until the job was done.

The Kid sailed a dollar at the clerk. The clerk gaped at the dollar and said, "Thank you." He looked more closely at The Kid. The Kid checked the oil barrels and turned. He saw the clerk staring at him. The Kid said, "You know me?"

The clerk shook his head.

The Kid said, "I guess you don't. Some people think I look like The Kid."

The clerk smiled carefully and said, "Not at all."

The Kid said, "You ever see The Kid?"

The clerk said, "Well, not that I recall. But I'm sure—"

The Kid snarled, "Don't be so goddam sure." He got up on the mare and kicked the animal. The mare started walking, breathing heavily. The Kid felt like a farmer. Nobody was going to bother him, looking like this. He adjusted the bandanna again over his mouth, pulled the brim of his Stetson down. He entered the plaza, looked at the long low pile of baked mud that was the governor's palace. He saw a small cluster of riders near the portico, and a man with a silver mane of hair and silver mustache standing just inside the portico. The men were shuffling on their horses. The Kid smiled. It had to be the rest of the posse that had been crawling through brush, searching for somebody. He whistled through his silken bandanna, silently, headed away from the plaza, down a narrow roadway.

The road led downhill for a half mile or so, the streets nearly deserted under the scorching afternoon sun. The Kid kept touching the mare's sweaty neck, veins etched like distended worms beneath the drawn skin. The animal was scarcely making any time, but it didn't matter, because it would all add up just right. It always did.

The houses thinned out and then the westerly bridge loomed ahead. The Kid stared down at the river. It was barely a trickle. He looked for Lopez' *jacal*, saw it, wondered whether Slattery had reached it, and then kept going past. When he saw the double strands of barbed wire running to the west and to the north, he knew he was on Chisholm's graze.

The spread was like a right angle, with its arms of wire running west and north. The wire ran out of sight. Up ahead The Kid saw the sand-colored canyon walls rising at the northwest. Ahead, a half-dozen horsemen were riding down a small herd of cows. They got behind the cows and started moving them to the northwest. A heavy cloud of dust lay at the foot of the canyon cliffs. The Kid nodded. That must have been another herd, a big herd. Maybe all the cows Chisholm had. Yes, it would work that way. Chisholm was gathering his herd, for some reason or other, branding or disease-dipping or culling prior to shipping. The cloud of dust was enormous, The Kid saw. It was a hell of a herd of beef.

The Kid stopped the horse and started unstrapping the barrels of kerosene. He looked around, but the six riders had swept out of sight. An occasional wagon creaked across the bridge, behind The Kid, but he doubted anybody would notice him. He took one of the barrels of kerosene and kicked the calked strip from the edge of the barrel mouth. Then he lifted the lid until the strip tore loose. He picked up the barrel and started pouring kerosene in a long thin row, just inside the barbed wire. The wind remained steady and strong, a heavy flapping wind now, running from the southeast. The Kid watched the dirt greedily suck the liquid fuel. He tilted the barrel until it was nearly upside down, making sure every bit was used.

It was long hard slow work, wrestling the barrels. He

took the second barrel and walked two hundred yards ahead. He doused a second row of grass with the second barrel of fuel. He went back and wrestled a third barrel farther into the graze. He soaked down the grass, and repeated with the fourth barrel, working his way back and forth across the graze. With a wind and dry grass, the fire would blaze out of control in a handful of seconds.

The Kid finished wetting down the grass and picked up the empties and returned them to where the horse was slowly munching barley. The Kid watched the heaving flanks of the animal, saw the breathing return slowly to normal. He sat near the horse, patiently waiting, whistling. He kept ripping blades of grass lengthwise, wondering if he'd ever get one torn three times. Two was the limit. The sun was slipping down the intensely blue sky, toward the ringed clouds to the west.

Everything was inevitable, like the sun sinking through the high blue vault overhead. Nothing could be stopped now. He kept ripping grass.

15

Fallon said wearily, "We'll bury the men after sunset," and the ill-fated posse began to break up. The governor started to turn back to the palace. Then he stopped and said, "Who found the men?"

A rider from the middle of the group said, "I did,"

"Who? Step up here."

The man came forward, slowly.

"What's your name?"

"Jefferson."

"Jefferson," Fallon said. "That's an honest name."

"Yes, sir," the man said.

"Take a group of men to where you found the bodies, Jefferson. Just set there. I'll send a priest to join you, after the Angelus."

"Right, Governor," Jefferson said.

"That's all," Fallon said. "Go on back to whatever you were doing." Drinking, Fallon thought. They'd be brooding and drinking, the rest of the afternoon and night. They'd be seeing hobgoblins too. He didn't blame them. Two men, the best of the batch, shot dead. They didn't say they knew it was The Kid, the rest of them, but Fallon could see that they knew. Rico and Savage must have warned them it might be The Kid. Or maybe not. They just guessed. The Kid was a terrible man. The Kid and Slattery. Slattery might have done it, too. Slattery hadn't been in the posse. It could have been Slattery. He'd talk to Slattery about it, when he saw him.

He walked back to the office, pushing through the corridor. He walked past the waiting men, and his back was tight. He'd never felt this way, that a man might put a bullet in him. Not even in the war had he felt this way. He was frightened.

He paused at his desk and then quickly went to the door and flung it open. He said, "Next?" and when a Pueblo walked into the office, Fallon didn't bother closing the door. There was nobody up here to help him out, to keep order in the corridor. This way he'd know what was going on out there, with the door open. Chisholm had disappeared. Chisholm wasn't much help, but he knew how to bluster and bluff these poor beggars.

Fallon said to the Indian, "What's wrong?"

The Pueblo said, "You put a curse on the rain."

Fallon looked through the window at the high cloudless late-afternoon sky. He said softly, "I pray for rain, every night."

"You no pray right," the Pueblo insisted.

Fallon said, "You've got a hell of a nerve."

The Pueblo looked blank-faced.

Fallon said, "You people pray every day. You've got

your chants and your dances. I've heard your thunder drums and your gourd rattles all week. Maybe you're not praying right."

The Pueblo made a scoffing noise. "We pray right. But you have put a curse on our prayers."

"I'll see to it we don't any more," Fallon said dryly.

The Pueblo blinked, and Fallon wanted to cut his tongue out. The Pueblos were an ill-humored lot. Now the Indian could go back and tell his people that the Long-Haired One had admitted he had been hexing the rain gods. It had been a foolish bit of irony. He said, "I'm only making a joke. A very bad joke, I'm afraid."

The Indian stared more closely at the governor. Fallon knew he was digging himself in deeper, joking about a matter of life and death to the Pueblos. It was a serious mistake. This was a day of mistakes. Death rode that wind outside. Fallon watched the Territorial flag flapping on the jailhouse across the plaza. It pointed stiffly out, from the southeast to the northwest. It was a rain wind. The first rain wind in weeks. He said to the Indian, very solemnly, "I will bring you a rain by nightfall."

The Pueblo grunted and lowered his eyes. When he raised them, they were crafty. The Indian said, "The rain gods need a sacrifice."

The bloody savages, Fallon thought. He said, "You've got one. Two of my men were murdered a few hours ago."

The Indian cocked his head and smiled. It was a brown-toothed smile and his bad breath swept over Fallon. "That is good. But a fresh sacrifice would be even better."

Fallon said, "Get out." The man thought he was clever. Then Fallon leaned back and risked a small smile. In a way, he was. The more white men who died by one another's guns, the fewer white enemies to deal with. They never forgot, the Pueblo, no, or the Spanish, either. They never forgot and they never forgave. It had been only twenty years ago that they massacred an American governor and his entire family scalping the children while they still lived. Of course, the retribution had been awful, total. The Indians and Spanish had been massacred in their villages, on the trails, tending their sheep, the innocent with the guilty, twenty innocent to each guilty. It had been horrible and complete. Now the mixed Indian and Spanish blood lay quiet, passive. Their strength was lower than ever before. Still, they remembered when the Pueblo was the lord of the great river and the land all about it, and they remembered when the Spanish came up from the south and the east, to claim the land for their king, six thousand miles away.

Now the white man held sway, the white American. But the Pueblo never forgot. Nor did the Spanish. Fallon felt the fear quicken inside.

He started to yell "Chisholm!" but he remembered Chisholm wasn't around. He said, "Next? Who's next?" and a big man in high riding boots walked in. He said, "I guess I am. What a stinking mob that is out there!"

Fallon studied the new man. He looked at the trim build, the lean jaw and big-knuckled hands. He said, "Your name?"

"Hughes, John Hughes."

"Rancher?"

The man laughed. "Right the first time. May I sit?"

Fallon felt uneasy. The man was too casual. He said, "Sit." The man sat, folded his hands in his lap. He wore no gun belt, no gun. Hughes watched Fallon's eyes and then he opened his arms wide. "No hideout weapon, either," he said. "Care to search me?"

Fallon flushed. "No," he said. "I'm just edgy."

The big man took a cigar from his high pocket, removed the brown wrapping paper and lighted up. He said, "Those beggars out there, eh?"

"That's right," Fallon said evenly. "That's all I see, beggars. What do you want?"

The man nodded, but his eyes narrowed and he stopped smiling. He said, "Right again. I'm a beggar too. I'm begging you not to let this place blow up in everybody's face."

Fallon felt himself go tense. "What do you mean?"

"I'm a rancher. Used to be a big rancher." Hughes paused. "I come from Jackson County."

Fallon grunted. "You know Frick?" he said, and this time the other man started. Fallon grinned and said, "Frick was in this morning. He said the same thing. What are you boys getting at?"

The man shrugged. "You know then. Frick and the rest of us don't want to see our cows lost for good. We'd like to help you form a protection association for ranchers in the Territory."

"Protection from what?"

"From thieves," Hughes said.

"There's no thieving going on now, that I know of."

"No-o-o," Hughes said slowly. "I can't say there is. But there has been. And there could be more." He studied his cigar, rolling it in his fingers. He let the ash drop to the mortar floor.

"What would your protection group do?"

"Count cows," Hughes said flatly. "Just count cows."

"And after they're counted?"

The hands spread and Hughes let his lower lip jut. "Return those cows which don't belong where they are now."

"Nice impartial association, you'd be," Fallon said icily.

"You and your men count right along with us. We'd just be part of the group."

"And if I didn't go along with the way you wanted those cows disposed. Then what?"

Hughes said quietly, "I'm prepared to turn over to you a bank draft for twenty-five thousand dollars."

Fallon leaped from his chair. "Get the hell out of here," he said. "You think you can buy anything. You can't buy a man's honor."

Hughes got up. "We will not tolerate letting our cows disappear from us. Abner Chisholm has stolen twenty thousand head of cattle, our cattle. We want them back. Where does honor come in there? Who's honorable, the man who sits in the governor's chair and protects Chisholm? Or the men who want their own cows and their own money returned?"

"How do I know you're telling me the truth?"

"Join us," Hughes said pleasantly. "Come along with us. We'll prove those cows are ours. We'll show you bills of lading for the purchase of beef. We've got men who are experts at reading blotched brands. Men who just wet their hands and rub a cow's skin, and reveal the original brand. We'll slaughter a few cows and skin them. You'll read the original brand on the underneath of the pelt. We'll bring men forward who will testify as to how many cows each of our ranchers had, how many Chisholm had—how few, I should say. Men who have nothing to gain by so testifying."

Fallon's lip curled. "Then why did you just try to bribe me?"

Hughes puffed on the cigar and reluctantly put it out against his heel. "It would have been an easy way," he said finally.

"You're a frank man," Fallon said.

"I am."

"And a liar."

"See here," Hughes said. "You don't quite understand me. I'm not just asking you to come along. I'm telling you. You don't seem to understand. If you don't see this our way, with or without the money I offered you, then I'll go higher. You understand that?"

Fallon nodded. "I understand. You're pretty damn' sure of yourself, aren't you? Got lots of friends back East, is that it?"

Hughes nodded, his eyes grave, watching.

"You think I care about this job? You think I care that much that I'd play ball with a man who tries to bribe me and who threatens to have me replaced?"

"Not threatening. Promising. I can do it."

Fallon bent his head. His hand went through the papers on the desk. He came up with the cow amnesty order. He said, "See this?"

Hughes nodded.

"That's the order making a man legal owner of all cows on his graze."

Hughes said, "It's not signed."

"Not yet," Fallon said. He was panting now, beside himself. This man would actually throw the county back into cattle war. He had as much as said so. And with the Pueblo and Spanish hatred seemingly growing each day, with Slattery and The Kid, one or the other or both, murdering his deputies, Fallon knew that insurrection could follow on the heels of unrest and gunfire. He could, with one stroke of his pen, add to that unrest. He could sign the cow amnesty and make Hughes and Frick and the rest of their mob so incensed they'd strike at Chisholm in an instant. It would be war, ranchers buying guns, deputies turned back to outlaws. Amnesty for cows would mean the end of amnesty for men. It would mean war. It would mean the end of Fallon's job.

And yet Fallon wanted, more than anything he could think of, to sign that order.

"Not yet," he said. "It's not signed yet," his voice low and filled with contempt. The man was so shrewd. Oh, Fallon could see it now, he was so shrewd. He'd baited the governor, pushed at him until Fallon was forced to the wall. But Hughes, like Frick before him, was playing on the governor's reputation as an honest man, a man who hated war and bloodshed.

Hughes said, "And you won't sign it, will you?"

Fallon let the sheet of paper drop from his fingers. "I wish I had the guts," he said.

Hughes came forward and around the desk. He said, "Listen to me, Governor. Chisholm's not worth it."

"You are?" Fallon asked.

Hughes colored instantly. "I'm a hell of a sight more reputable than that fat thief."

It was a terrible world, Fallon knew. You had to weigh thieves against extortioners and decide which was better, which was worse. Where were the blacks and whites of things? He said slowly, "I haven't made up my mind. I'm still not sure."

Hughes relaxed. He said, "I can't ask more of any man." He walked away from Fallon, an easy-striding man, smooth as glass. He was so sure of himself, Fallon knew. Fallon said wickedly, "I mean it. I still may sign that paper. Chisholm said he'd offer me twenty-five thousand dollars, if I sign it." It was worth the deceit just to see Hughes stumble at the doorway and turn around, white-faced. Then Hughes smiled easily and said, "That ought to make it easier for you to decide. Now you know what a crook Chisholm is—and a briber, too. Good afternoon, Governor." The door closed.

Fallon sat weakly at the desk. Honest men couldn't play the part of liars.

He said, "Next?" and the door opened. A Mexican walked in, apologetically. Fallon looked at the man and he said, reaching for another sheet of paper, "What's wrong?"

The Mexican said, "*Americanos*, they kill my chickens."

"When?" Fallon said, writing.

"Yesterday."

"Where? ... Your name? ... Which Americans? ..."

An hour later, Fallon went to the corridor. He said, "That's all for now." A Mexican said, "I wait three hours."

Fallon said, "I'm sorry. Tomorrow." The Mexican said, "Always tomorrow," and Fallon said, again, "I'm sorry." Then he chewed on his lip. "Wait," he said. "I'll be back here, tonight, in my office. If you wish, try then."

The small line of petitioners shuffled off, and Fallon watched them. They were barefoot, dirty, their clothes in tatters. They were complacent, quiet, mildly embittered. Had he been reading stiffening hatred in them that wasn't there? He watched them turn the corner and pass through the portico. He walked behind them and saw one of them raise a hand and point to a dark speck to the east. The Mexican jabbered something and another Mexican looked up. A Pueblo joined them and they all pointed and stared at the sky. Fallon looked at the flag atop the jail. It still blew ahead, pushed by the southeasterly rain wind. A heavy moist heat filled the plaza. The day darkened slightly, though the sun still stood at the lip of the sky, a faint orange ball.

Behind the governor, Martha Fallon slipped through the portico. She watched her father. It looked for a moment as though he were praying. Then she walked up to him and put a hand on his arm.

He turned and said, "It's going to rain." It sounded almost as though somebody had blessed the world.

"When?"

Fallon shrugged. "An hour or two. This evening or night. Before morning, for sure."

"You finished your work now?"

"For the day."

"Come back and have supper with me," she said.

Fallon frowned. "Is it that late?" He remembered Slattery and their engagement on Chisholm's grass. He said, "I've got to ride a bit."

Martha Fallon smiled wistfully and said, "I know you do. I'm the one that told you. To see that killer."

Fallon shook his head. "Former killer," he said. The

day had played him like some taut-stringed instrument. But nothing really had happened. Threats from cattlemen, threats from poor Indians, threats from tatterdemalion peons. No more. He caught himself short. Yes, more. Two men had died. He started to stride to the rear stables.

"I'm going along with you," Martha Fallon said.

He said, over his shoulder, "Don't be silly," and the girl hurried and grabbed his arm. "I'm not silly," she said. "I'm going with you."

He turned and stared at her. She was as tall as he, her eyes as blue, and softer. But she stood erect, unmoving, unyielding. He remembered, long ago, how another woman had looked, choosing to share his life without complaint. He said pettishly, "All right, all right. Come on, then."

They walked to their horses and mounted, and moved slowly toward the dying sun.

16

"You're a talkative cuss," the bartender said. He poured another shot of rye whisky into Slattery's glass. The big man with the deep tan had been drinking steadily at the bar for two hours, without showing it the slightest.

Slattery said, "I been too damn' quiet, too damn' long."

"That kind of life don't make for much small talk."

Slattery nodded and drank. He said, "You don't know how it is, by yourself, living inside yourself, years and years."

The bartender never seemed to answer questions like that. He said, "Now the governor's made you an honest man, you feel better. Is that it?"

"Better and worse." Slattery turned over his left wrist. He said to the bartender, "You know how I got that?"

The bartender shook his head.

"A man stuck a pitchfork in me." Liar. It wasn't a man, it was his father. It wasn't his father, it was a white man.

"Lucky he didn't stick it someplace else."

"Lucky? I don't think I've ever been lucky in my life." He said to the bartender, "What time is it?'

The bartender tugged a big watch from his pants pocket. "Five thirty."

Half hour to Angelus. Half hour to Fallon. Half hour to the job. Half hour, more or less, to The Kid.

"Did I ever tell you how I got started?" he asked.

The bartender stepped back. "No," he said. "Don't want to hear, either. By God, you've got a loose tongue."

Slattery drank and pushed his empty at the bartender. The bartender said, "No. No more from me. Go someplace else."

Slattery walked out. Nobody ever wanted to know how he got started. He wanted to grab the first passing peon and hold him by the collar while he told the man. It all started, see, because a white man stuck a fork in my left wrist. The white man was my father. And I was black. So I became a white man, myself. See?

No.

He got up on his horse and pointed the animal west. He ambled slowly to Lopez' *jacal*. Ahead of the shack was the bridge and ahead of the bridge was Chisholm's spread, as big as the land itself. A gray horse moved on the grass of Chisholm's range, riderless, and Slattery smiled a thin knowing smile.

He stopped the bay outside the *jacal* and called softly, "Hello, house."

Lopez opened the door and held it wide for him. "Slattery, come in. We have been waiting."

"Who?" Slattery said. Not yet. He wasn't ready yet.

"Dolores and I."

Slattery nodded and walked in. Lopez went to the bay

and led the horse to water. Then he looped the animal with lots of rope.

Slattery sat on a pine bench. He saw the girl, across the room, dark and lovely. He said, "Why are you waiting?"

The girl looked at Lopez, coming back through the door. Slattery said, enjoying himself, "You're waiting for The Kid, eh?" Lopez raised his brows at the girl.

Dolores said, "No. Why should I be here waiting for The Kid?"

Slattery said, "Because. That's why. The Kid's coming to meet me here. Didn't you know?"

Lopez said, "We thought it was to be surprise. We didn't know—"

Slattery said, "What's down in that cellar, underneath the floor, Lopez?"

The ancient Mexican said, "Guns. Ammunition. Like I told you. Nearly three hundred guns."

"Two hundred," Slattery said. "Last time you said two hundred. What's really down there?"

"What do you mean?"

"You've been bleeding those poor people a long time now, haven't you, Lopez?"

The man stiffened. "I do not understand." Lopez turned to Dolores. "Do not listen. He is not a man, not like The Kid."

Slattery grinned. "That's true," he said. "You are. You've got them all buffaloed, just like The Kid."

Lopez said, "Wait till The Kid gets here. I would like to hear you talk like that to him."

Dolores nodded, huge eyes burning.

Slattery said, "They send you money, don't they?"

Lopez said guardedly, "Yes."

"You've got them all lined up, all the sheepers out there."

"They want to help. They do what they can."

"Sure," Slattery said. "But what do you do?"

"I buy guns. I buy ammunition. I prepare for the day

we strike back."

Slattery said wickedly, "Take me down there then. Open those trunks. Let's see how prepared you are. Let's count the guns."

Lopez said, "I do not have to defend myself to you."

"Right. Just to them. Take Dolores down there. Count the guns with Dolores."

Dolores raised a hand. "Lopez is an honest man," she said. "He need not defend himself to me, either."

Slattery stared at them. All together. He always was the outsider. He said, "What a sweet racket you've got. Keeps you fed, keeps you clothed."

Lopez waved his right hand. He said mildly, "I live so rich, you see. My palace."

The man's quiet sarcasm stabbed Slattery. He looked about him. It was a hut not unlike the tiny shack on the plantation where he'd been born and where he lived and where he slaved. Yet Slattery knew that things were not always as they seemed. He said, "If I'm wrong, I'll apologize. I don't think I am wrong. I think you've convinced those people down there you really intend to do something you know in your heart you can't do. You know as well as I there's no chance for revolt any more. It's too late. You can't turn back the clock."

"We nearly did it, twenty years ago."

Slattery grinned thinly. "That was a long time back. This child here wasn't even born. Things have happened since then. You know it, Lopez. You're not fooling me."

Lopez was silent. The girl looked questioningly at the old man, then at Slattery.

Slattery said, "If this were straight, if you were on the level, I'd have heard about it. Me or The Kid or Vulka or Wilson or one of us, down at Heck. If you were really fighting the law, you'd have come to the outlaws themselves for help. But you didn't. I never heard of you. The Kid never heard of you, I'll bet, and The Kid knows the

Spanish pretty damn' well. You're faking, Lopez, and you know it. What's in those trunks down there?"

Lopez turned away and walked to the wall. He said, "The Americans, they take away my land. They leave me with nothing. You know?"

"Sure," Slattery said.

"They steal my grass, drive off my sheep. Now, I live here where my fathers lived and where their fathers lived, where we have always lived. I have in my veins the blood of the Spanish kings. You know?"

"Sure," Slattery said. "I know. What's down there, Lopez?"

The man whirled. Tears glistened in his eyes. "You no understand. They leave me nothing."

Slattery nodded. "They're greedy, all right. Land hungry, beef hungry. They steal what they can't grab any other way."

"*Sí*," the man said. "You understand that. But you do not understand the other." The man was cracking now, misery coating the dark seamed face. Slattery stared at the face. Lopez was very dark, his hair thick and black. There might have been the blood of Spanish kings in Lopez, but there was other blood too.

Slattery said, "I understand the other, too."

Lopez smiled sadly. "No," he said. "You can not. You are American. You are big and strong. You fire the gun. You read, you write. You know much things. You do not understand."

The man was a half-breed. Pueblo blood, Spanish blood, probably the blood of a drunken American trapper or two.

Slattery said, "I won't tell anybody. It doesn't matter to me. You must stop bleeding the sheepers, that's all. You understand?"

Lopez nodded. The girl stared at him, in disbelief. "What is in the trunks?" she asked.

They went down through the trapdoor, the old man leading the way with a torch. He kicked the trunks. They rattled with an empty hollow noise.

"Nothing," he said. The girl moaned.

Slattery pointed to a dim corner where cobwebs threw gossamer over a rusting trunk. "That one?"

Lopez looked wildly up at the trapdoor, saw it was open, knew it was no escape. He went to the trunk and brushed away the web. He pulled on the lid. It creaked open.

The trunk bulged with money.

They sat on the floor, over the trapdoor. Slattery said, "Return it."

The man sobbed, his head down, shaking back and forth. "How can I? I have told so many stories. They believed me. What can I tell them?"

"The truth," Slattery said. But what was the truth? That the man needed something to bolster him over the long shameful years? That he was trying to be something he wasn't? Who would understand? Nobody.

The girl said stiffly, eyes dry, "I will take the money back. I will say Lopez has decided we can not win. The law is too strong. That Lopez say we must take our grievance to the governor, and, if necessary, beyond."

"What good will that do?" Lopez said. "They will not listen."

"Perhaps," the girl said. "But we must tell them anyway."

Lopez said, "It takes them so long to do anything, to act on a grievance." He was irritable now, a man denuded. "Nothing comes of it."

The girl leaned forward. "But still we must try. Someday—"

Slattery took a crumpled bandanna from his pocket. He untied it, poured the coins and few bills into his hand.

"Here," he said to the girl. "When you take back the money, take this too."

"But why?" she asked, troubled, wondering.

"No reason," Slattery said. "I ain't got any use for it. What time is it?"

Lopez said, "Nearly Angelus time, I think. Nearly six." He stared through the mica window. Shadow blotted the sun.

Slattery said, "Listen. I don't have much time, so listen. This is how it started …"

He was broke, in a bar, in a cowtown in Texas. It was hot, dry like this, and the dust was like sand in the throat. He'd prodded some cows for a man and then the man had welshed on the payroll, leaving Slattery and twenty other cowhands flat and deserted in a sun-bleached corner of hell. The men had grumbled and sworn and one of them said, "I'd like to kill that son of a bitch," and Slattery said, he'd like to kill him, too. Another man said, let's look him up, let's track the thieving bastard down and let's kill him, and they all talked like that, getting more angry and more hot, scrounging drinks from a sympathetic bartender and getting more drunk. Then the talk tailed off and Slattery staggered outside. A man was coming through the batwing doors—it didn't really matter who he was, Slattery had always said, always tried to say— and Slattery banged into him and the man into Slattery, and the man put out a hand and said, "Watch yourself." Slattery stared at the man's hand and then he said, thickly, "You dirty son of a bitch, I'm going to kill you," and he went diving for his gun, the man's hand stiff and pointed at him, pointing at Slattery, holding him there like a butterfly pinned to a corkboard. Slattery had the gun, finally, and he brushed the man's hand away, the pointing finger like an accusation, and he fired his gun in the man's face.

Men poured out of the saloon and stood in a small ring

around the two, Slattery with a foolish frightened grin on his sloppy face, the smoking gun in his limp fingers and the other man on the ground, still, the pointed finger collapsed on his chest.

Somebody said, finally, "Oh, hell, he's only a nigger," and the crowd of men broke up and went their ways. Slattery staggered off, to the future. But the future was a trapdoor, leading to hell.

..."You see?" he said He told them the rest, that he was a Negro, ashamed of it, living a lie.

They nodded, white-faced.

Then they turned, because they heard the horses, and Slattery walked to the door. He looked out and saw Fallon, and behind him, Martha Fallon. He said hoarsely, "Fallon, in here, man."

Fallon stopped and swung his horse down the littered path, stared into the door that led to a black room. Martha Fallon put a hand on his arm and said, "Don't, Dad," and Fallon remembered that he once thought he'd go down to Fort Heck and try to talk to those men. Well, now he had one of them right here, ready to be talked to. He said, "Coming, Slattery," and got off his horse and walked into the house.

Slattery watched him come on and he said to himself, this is the job, but it was a lie too, just as the words *white man, white man*, had been a lie every time he had killed. Fallon wasn't a job, he was a man, and they all were men, good, bad and indifferent, vicious and good-natured. Men, all of them, black or white, black and white men. He had tried to convince himself, all these long narrow years, that he'd killed because his father was a white man, and his father had enslaved him, and he was Negro. But that was his father, a man worth hating, maybe, but nothing else. He hadn't killed his father, he hadn't killed the white man who had dominated his life for fourteen years and filled him with hate.

When he killed, he killed a Negro, and it was clear now what he'd been trying to kill, never succeeding. He'd been trying to kill off himself, trying to deny what he'd been. It wasn't fair he was what he was, it wasn't right that a man be called a Negro and that the word mean slave, the word mean debasement, the word mean cringing obeisance to white men and authority. It wasn't fair, but that didn't mean a man took up arms in a personal vendetta. It was easy to hide behind that vendetta, but it was a lie, and Slattery knew it.

He also knew that he knew it too late.

His hand leaped toward his holster as Fallon entered the room, and the girl Dolores screamed and Lopez shrank into a dark corner of the dim room. Fallon stood straight, waiting for the bullet.

Slattery drew the gun, spun it quickly and pushed it at Fallon. He felt violently sick.

"Here," he said. "Is that what you want? My gun?"

Fallon took the revolver. He said gravely, "Don't you want it?"

"No," Slattery said.

"Don't you need it?"

"No."

"What are you going to do?"

"Do?"

"Go. Where are you going to go?"

"No place," Slattery said.

Fallon frowned. "You're free to go wherever you want, you know. Why don't you go out to California? Start fresh out there. They don't have to know what you've been."

"They don't," Slattery said. "But I know."

Fallon started to say something and then he stopped. He knew he wasn't going to get anywhere with the big man whose skin was the color of pale sand, the color of softly polished wood, darker than his own, lighter than the Mexican's who cringed in the corner. Fallon didn't know what this place was, but he knew it meant something to Slattery. The man seemed to belong here.

Slattery looked past Fallon, past the open door, past Martha Fallon, so blonde and lovely she made his heart ache. He saw Martha Fallon's horse. He said to the girl, "Take your horse and ride away from here."

Fallon said, "Why?"

Slattery said, "Just do as I say. You'll see soon enough. God, what time is it?"

Fallon looked at his watch. "A minute to six," he said.

"Go on," Slattery said to Martha Fallon. "Get the hell out of here. Take your horse and get the hell out."

Fallon turned and said, "Go on, Martha," and the girl turned and mounted her horse and led it back toward town. Slattery watched her, hungrily, knowing more went with her than just the horse.

The first sound of the Angelus reached him. He slammed the door shut and strode into the tiny *jacal*. The girl Dolores sank to her knees. Lopez sat in his corner, head bowed. Slattery and Fallon stared at each other, and then Slattery went to the window and looked at Chisholm's grass where he had seen the gray mare, knowing whose horse it was.

Slattery counted the tolling peals that cleft the quiet sky. He said, aloud, at the end, "Nine." The girl Dolores murmured, eyes closed, "The Word was made Flesh," and she crossed herself.

Slattery said, "Wait here, all of you. You'll be able to see it from the window." They moved to the window, and Fallon said, "Where are you going, Slattery?"

"Out there," he said, pointing to Chisholm's grass.

Fallon said, "But you wanted to see me, about Chisholm and the ranchers who lost their cows. What is it?"

Slattery stared dumbly at the governor. He said, "I can't

tell you."

"What is it, man?"

Slattery shook his head.

"You know those men who are opposed to cattle amnesty," Fallon said, "those Jackson ranchers. You know Frick and the rest, don't you?"

It was a last chance. He could tell Fallon about Frick. Frick's handwriting had dated the check. He could tell Fallon how they'd hired Slattery to kill the governor but that wouldn't be fair because Chisholm had tried to do the same thing. He laughed, a short horrible twisted sound, like pain. When Chisholm said he wanted Fallon dead, Slattery had thought that ended it, that he couldn't kill Fallon because of the horror and irony of it.

Another lie.

He hadn't been able to kill Fallon from the start, and he knew it.

He'd ached for his freedom, for his pardon and with five thousand dollars and amnesty, he thought he was going to have it. It was the new life, the fresh start Fallon had talked about.

But Frick came along. Frick said, "Fallon," Fallon was the target. The man giving the pardon was the victim. Slattery had started out to do the job, but all along he must have known it was impossible. He'd waited until daylight before he started, just so The Kid could get on his back. He moved slowly, to the Mexican sheep town, just so The Kid would be able to track him. He wandered and talked and tried to find some place where he belonged (like in hell, he thought grimly), trying to make up for all those years of being alone and a loner. Lone Wolf Slattery. Never again. Now he'd revealed himself, to others, and to himself. A yearning man. Black didn't matter. White didn't matter. What was inside did matter.

He'd been groping, here in the capital, knowing there wasn't much time, knowing he couldn't make much of it up, or any, really, but trying. He had to know some companionship even that of a tight-lipped bartender or a soft-lipped white woman or a half-breed crook (who really was terribly honest) or a dark broodingly beautiful girl who believed in the incarnation—The Word is the Flesh—and who thought The Kid was a god.

Fallon said, "What about Frick? What's his game?"

There was the proof, Slattery thought suddenly. The proof that he hadn't planned on killing Fallon at all. He had got the check from Frick before Chisholm also had asked him to kill Fallon. The check was the proof, that he never intended to kill Fallon. He had got the check early, so he could show it to Fallon. All he had to do was hand it to Fallon. He shook his head, half in self-pity. Who the hell was he, Slattery thought, to point a finger at any man? Only honest men can go crying to the law. And that was funny too. He laughed the pain-noise. He said, "Don't sign the amnesty on cattle."

Fallon said, "I won't. I never intended to."

"That's good." Good? Frick would kill Fallon now, get somebody else to kill him, now that Slattery had failed. Yet Slattery couldn't say a word. None of it—them—mattered. They were all pawns. Fallon knew it. They were symbols. Fallon was an honest man, always, always would be. If they killed him, they'd kill him, but not his spirit. The Word was made Flesh. They'd bury Fallon, maybe, but Fallon meant law. Fallon meant decency and order. There'd always be chaos in order, there'd always be the jungle in law. But there'd always be more Fallons. The Fricks could keep cutting them down, they'd grow twice as strong, thrice as many.

Slattery said, "Just wait here. That's all."

Each man did what he could. Slattery had been stripped down to another man. Now that other man would do what he could.

The Kid heard the rider. He ripped a last piece of grass and he ripped it again. He looked up and saw Slattery, on a bay horse, riding slowly. The Kid studied the blade of grass, eyes intent on the slender slice of plucked-up life, now dead, in his hands. His nails very carefully took the length of grass at its very tip, and the tear began to run down toward the bottom. The Kid's hands began to shake a little, but then he took a deep breath and he steadied himself. He tore it swiftly, the full length. He had never done it before, this third time. He held the two slender halves and stared at them, the giggle rising full in his throat. Then he blew them, and he saw how the wind carried them to the northwest. He frowned for a moment, remembering the kerosene-soaked grass.

He got to his feet and reached to his shirt pocket for a match. He scratched it aflame against the chewed edge of his thumbnail and he tossed it behind him. Instantly the flame roared up.

It would be a big one, The Kid thought, a hell of a fire. They'd come from miles around to see this one.

He said, "Hello, Wolf, get off your horse." He watched Slattery's eyes, knowing something was different about the man.

Slattery got down from the bay. He patted the animal and said, "Beat it." The horse moved a dozen strides away and stopped, looking back at the fire that licked the grass, and where it licked, consumed. Slattery saw the fire, and knew that The Kid had given him the last answer. The Kid had been worthwhile, in his way. Chisholm was being reduced to charred ruin. The blaze was halfway to the canyon wall. He heard a muttered lowing and he knew the cattle were pinched between the flame and the canyon cliffs. It wasn't going to matter whose cows they had been. They weren't going to be anybody's.

He said to The Kid, "That's a big load off my chest, Kid."

The Kid said, "Yeah? What the hell does that mean?"

"You wouldn't understand," Slattery said.

The Kid kept his eyes on Slattery, studying the man's face, because the big man was different. The Kid couldn't figure it. He wiped his right hand across his trouser leg.

Slattery said, "Nervous, Kid?"

"Hell, no," The Kid said. "Why should I be nervous?"

"Just scared, that it?"

Slattery saw the yellow flame leap in The Kid's eyes. He'd touched him. He'd have to touch him some more. Nobody had ever really faced The Kid. That had been The Kid's trouble all along. The Kid had thought just because a man stood in front of him with a gun that he was being faced. Now he was finding out different.

Slattery said, "You're really a punk, you know that, Kid?"

The giggle snapped in The Kid's throat. It turned to a snarl.

"Yeah?" he said. "I ain't one of them bottles, back in McCall's saloon."

Slattery smiled, but his eyes never left The Kid's. Their eyes were locked. They saw nothing else. The two men stood twelve feet apart. Slattery said, "Hell, you're not even one of those bottles. You're less. You're nothing." He started to walk toward The Kid, waiting for the flame to erupt again, knowing that it would be soon, it had to be. The Kid wouldn't take this torture much longer.

They were five feet apart and The Kid wiped his hand again, but the sweat kept forming.

Slattery moved another stride, cutting the distance in half. He said, "You're yellow, you're a two-bit punk, you don't know what it means to be a man. You're a coward." Slattery leaned forward and with his open right hand very slowly swung it in a long lazy arc against The Kid's cheek. Slattery watched the white finger marks form; then they filled in with blood.

The yellow flame washed The Kid's eyes. It streaked his face deeper than the imprint of Slattery's hand. He said, in a choked voice that was more an animal's than a man's, "Reach, reach, you bastard reach." Slattery watched the twitching fingers.

He said, "Don't be silly, Kid, I don't even have a gun on me."

The scream was long and horrible, a coyote's moan, a hyena's laugh, a man torn apart.

Slattery turned slowly, as deliberately as he was able—the final insult—knowing he'd stepped into the trapdoor, finally, knowing he'd found his true end.

Five bullets thudded into his back.

Slattery heard the horsebeats fade, knew The Kid had gone. Then he heard other steps, and finally the girl Dolores's words:

"The Kid, he shot him in the back!"

Fallon said quietly, "And Slattery never even had a gun."

Slattery wondered if he was smiling, he felt like smiling. The Kid wasn't going to live forever, after all.

17

When the rains came, an hour later, and men broke onto Chisholm's spread to fight the tiny grass fires that still sputtered, Fallon left Slattery's body.

He worked his way carefully toward Chisholm's ranch house.

It was too late, of course.

The man had apparently stationed himself at the edge of the graze where the grass ran out and the cliffs began, and where he'd been seen by one of Chisholm's riders—holding out his arms, trying to stop twenty thousand stampeding cows.

But on they came, the fire behind them, and over the cliffs they tumbled. Chisholm's body was trampled into the ground he'd stolen.

Fallon went back to the plaza. He went to his office. It was late, but some of the men had been waiting for hours.

The governor opened the door and called, "Next?"

THE END

Arnold Hano was born in New York in 1922. His first job was as a copy boy at the *New York Daily News* in 1941. The next year he enlisted in the Army and served in the Pacific until 1946. After the war, Hano became managing editor at Bantam, then editor-in-chief of Lion Books, where he worked to develop authors like Jim Thompson and  David Goodis. He has taught writing at the University of Southern California, Pitzer College, and the University of California, Irvine. He has also enjoyed a career as a freelance novelist and sportswriter, authoring many books on baseball, including the classic, *A Day in the Bleachers*. In 1955, he moved with his wife Bonnie and their family to Laguna Beach, California, where they live today. And now in his 90s, he still writes a monthly column for an environmental organization.

Black Gat Books

Black Gat Books is a new line of mass market paperbacks introduced in 2015 by Stark House Press. New titles appear every three months, featuring the best in crime fiction reprints. Each book is sized to 4.25" x 7", just like they used to be. Collect them all!

1 Haven for the Damned by Harry Whittington
978-1-933586-75-5 $9.99

2 Eddie's World by Charlie Stella
978-1-933586-76-2 $9.99

3 Stranger at Home by Leigh Brackett writing as George Sanders
978-1-933586-78-6 $9.99

4 The Persian Cat by John Flagg
978-1933586-90-8 $9.99

5 Only the Wicked by Gary Phillips
978-1-933586-93-9 $9.99

6 Felony Tank by Malcolm Braly
978-1-933586-91-5 $9.99

7 The Girl on the Bestseller List by Vin Packer
978-1-933586-98-4 $9.99

8 She Got What She Wanted by Orrie Hitt
978-1-944520-04-5 $9.99

9 The Woman on the Roof by Helen Nielsen
978-1-944520-13-7 $9.99

10 Angel's Flight by Lou Cameron
978-1-944520-18-2 $9.99

11 The Affair of Lady Westcott's Lost Ruby / The Case of the Unseen Assassin by Gary Lovisi
978-1-944520-22-9 $9.99

Stark House Press

1315 H Street, Eureka, CA 95501 707-498-3135
griffinskye3@sbcglobal.net www.starkhousepress.com

Available from your local bookstore or direct from the publisher.